FRANCINE MANDEVILLE

Midnight In Paris

ZEBRA BOOKS
KENSINGTON PUBLISHING CORP.

*This book is dedicated to
Marc F. and Michael C.
from whom I am finally
learning to understand men.*

ZEBRA BOOKS

are published by

Kensington Publishing Corp.
475 Park Avenue South
New York, NY 10016

Copyright © 1992 by Francine Mandeville

All rights reserved. No part of this book may be reproduced in any form or by any means without the prior written consent of the Publisher, excepting brief quotes used in reviews.

Zebra, the Z logo, Lucky in Love, and the Lucky in Love cover design are trademarks of Kensington Publishing Corp.

If you purchased this book without a cover you should be aware that this book is stolen property. It was reported as "unsold and destroyed" to the Publisher and neither the Author nor the Publisher has received any payment for this "stripped book."

First Printing: November, 1992

Printed in the United States of America

Chapter One

There was a damn good reason Parisians began deserting their beautiful city in droves every year as July edged into August.

Heat.

Heat radiating in waves off the centuries-old stone of Gothic churches and curling off the pavement of narrow pedestrian passageways and wide tree-lined boulevards. Heat trapped and held by the finely wrought masonry of stately civic buildings and reflected off the translucent green water of the Seine River winding its way through the heart of the city.

Oppressive, suffocating, energy-sapping heat that had to be at least eighty percent humidity.

Kendra Martin stepped onto the escalator behind her charges, bracing herself to leave the air-conditioned comfort of the subterranean marble admittance hall. A few moments later, the escalator emerged into the glare and hothouse atmosphere locked within the controversial glass pyramid entrance to the Louvre museum.

The twelve teenagers with Kendra, ranging in age from thirteen to fifteen, were students at a private all-girls academy in her hometown of Carmel, California. The children of wealthy, and in some cases, famous parents, she had fondly dubbed them "the daughters of privilege."

Seven days into her scheduled ten-day tour of France with them had given Kendra a glimpse into a world of ease and luxury which she had always known existed but never seen at such close range. A world she had certainly never experienced personally. Nor was she likely to do so, she mused with a wry little smile, except through magazines, movies, and her own very fertile imagination.

Kendra was the oldest of four children in a close-knit, solidly middle-class family. She had grown up on a decent street where her parents owned a nice but modest home. Her charges lived in exclusive neighborhoods on estates with swimming pools, tennis courts, and wrought iron privacy gates. She had shared household chores with her sister, while her two brothers took turns mowing the front lawn on Saturday morning. Her charges were accustomed to housekeepers and weekly gardeners. She and her sister, with rare exceptions, still bought most of their clothes on sale at the local mid-sized department store, not on monthly excursions to the best specialty shops in San Francisco.

Kendra, along with her sister and brothers, had all been raised expecting to work their way through college, and she was very proud of her business degree from California State University in Sacramento. Her charges had been in expensive private schools from their first day of kindergarten and took for granted that they would attend equally expensive private universities when the time came.

Kendra's childhood vacations were a series of two-week jaunts where the entire family piled into the station wagon and took off for destinations like the Grand Canyon, Disneyland and Yosemite National Park. The "daughters of privilege" jetted over to France for a ten-day tour of museums, cathedrals, chateaux, and monuments. They stayed in luxury hotels, traveled on land by first-class Eurail passes, and bought clothes, gifts, and souvenirs whose cost came close to what Kendra earned in a month.

The twelve girls on her tour had an unself-conscious sophistication that only money and early exposure to the luxuries of life could accomplish in girls so young. Kendra couldn't say she envied them exactly, but she had found it both interesting and enjoyable to travel through France like a "daughter of privilege" herself the past few days.

"So, what next?" Kendra glanced around her group. "Culture, cathedrals, shopping?"

"Food!" came the answering chorus.

"Great idea. Those little *baguette* and Camembert sandwiches we ate at noon in the museum cafeteria weren't exactly my idea of a filling meal." Kendra checked the plain gold watch she'd received from her parents for her college graduation five years previously, shaking her head. "It's still too early for a restaurant dinner. We need something like a *brasserie,* or *salon de thé,* or . . . I know, Au Pied de Cochon—"

"No way. I'm not eating in any restaurant called 'pig's feet'!" said Mary Lee Taylor firmly. Intelligent, sensible, and friendly, she was a natural leader among the girls on tour. Kendra had quickly come to depend upon her, not least for her smattering of French, which was the equal of Kendra's own.

"But Au Pied de Cochon's practically an institution, a landmark," explained Kendra. "They're open twenty-four hours a day, and they're famous for other things besides pig's feet, like French onion soup—"

"And big old trays of cold slimy oysters and sea snails, and all kinds of other horrible ocean stuff that you have to eat raw." Lisa Perretti rolled her eyes to the sympathetic gagging noises of the other girls. "My older sister told me all about it. She ate there on her trip to Paris two years ago."

"They make delicious *profiteroles*—crispy little cream puffs filled with vanilla ice cream and smothered with warm chocolate sauce for dessert," tempted Kendra.

"We want real food," said Lily Warren. The youngest girl on the ten-day tour Kendra was leading through France, Lily, at thirteen, was an "early bloomer." She had the heart, mind, and soul of a young girl, but the figure of a twenty-year-old beauty queen. Her sultry brunet good looks would be downright dangerous in the not-too-distant future. Kendra had endured more than a few tense moments helping the girl ward off unwanted attention from men old enough to know better than to flirt with a girl so young.

Kendra spared a momentary sympathy for her

boss, Bob Warren. He was going to have his hands full seeing Lily safely through to maturity.

"Yeah, no offense or anything, Kendra," said Amy Burke, the daughter of a prominent attorney. "But I'm just starving for something normal without any *interesting* ingredients . . ."

"Or any gloppy sauces."

"Or any kind of weird animal organ, no matter what kind of delicacy it's supposed to be!" Tiffany Lewis, whose mother owned a ritzy boutique known for lacy, romantic lingerie with astronomical price tags, had turned out to have a very squeamish appetite.

Kendra laughed, a deep, husky sound that caused a pair of Frenchmen engaged in conversation nearby to turn their heads her way and smile appreciatively, identical gleams of speculative interest brightening their eyes.

"Okay, okay, you win. Where would you like to eat?"

"Anyplace we can get a hamburger," said Julie Gray.

"And fries," added her twin sister, Jeannie.

Kendra suppressed a grin at the irony of Julie and Jeannie, whose parents owned three world-class, world-renowned restaurants wanting to eat something as pedestrian as a hamburger and fries in Paris. She could hardly wait to share the tale with them.

"There's supposed to be a McDonald's on the Champs-Élysées," offered Heather Lawrence, the daughter of Teddy Lawrence, the songwriter.

"Nope," said Kendra. "If you want hamburgers

and fries, fine, but we're eating them at a French fast-food joint. The place I'm thinking of is also on the Champs-Élysées so we can walk there—"

"Not another death march!" several girls protested.

"—either through the Tuileries gardens, then on past the Place de la Concorde—"

"Please, no more monuments until we get some food!"

"—or via the Rue de Rivoli, if you want to stock up on more souvenirs along the way."

"Give it up, you guys," said Mary Lee. "Kendra's bound and determined that we get the most out of this trip, and that means seeing every site on her list. Let's just start walking." She set a brisk pace across the courtyard and into the Tuileries.

Tall leafy chestnut trees cast dappled shadows on the graveled pathways, giving the illusion of respite from the heat. Straight ahead, the Obelisk rose like a spire in the Place de la Concorde. Further off in the distance, the Arc de Triomphe was silhouetted against the hazy sky, shimmering in the rays of late afternoon sun like a mirage. To the left of the Arc, Kendra sought and found the Eiffel Tower, the universal symbol of Paris.

All around her were the sights and sounds and smells of Paris—the distinctive two-note police sirens, the strong diesel fumes, the streams of tourists clutching cameras and gaping at historic monuments, the continual parade of slim, chic Frenchwomen, their silk scarves fluttering in the slight breeze made by their passage, the occasional whiff of some intoxicating perfume, the sharp, sometimes fetid tang rising from the Seine less than a hundred yards away.

And everywhere, constantly, the liquid spill of rapid-fire French conversation.

Kendra took a deep breath, unable to suppress the thrill of pure excitement racing through her veins. She was in Paris, and she was reveling in the experience.

As a travel agent, she had taken a fair number of trips in the last five years, though much fewer in the last three since she had been promoted assistant manager at the Carmel branch of Bob Warren's Let's Go Travel agency. But in all her rovings, no other destination had come to embody for Kendra the adventure, the glamour, the undiluted romance of travel the way Paris did. She had dreamed of visiting Paris her entire life, now she was enjoying her second trip here in the space of four short years.

Kendra didn't even bother to try suppressing the smile of satisfaction she felt sweeping over her face. Her life was firmly on track. She had worked hard to put it there. And she fully intended to enjoy any rewards that came along as a result.

This trip to Paris was one such reward, despite the endless hours planning and coordinating the details of a perfect tour for twelve teenaged girls. True, she was on assignment and not on vacation, but that fact didn't diminish the pleasure of being in Paris one iota. Even the myriad problems and aggravations of chaperoning the girls twenty-four hours a day seemed easier to handle in such glorious surroundings.

She had coped with everything from lost luggage

to lost passports, mild stomach upsets to a full-blown allergic reaction when Kary Lyons had unknowingly eaten seafood bisque containing shrimp. Kendra had defused the short-tempered bickering caused by exhaustion, dried the tears of homesickness, and comforted the distress of culture shock. She'd been patient, firm, cajoling, protective, instructive, and indulgent as each situation warranted.

She couldn't honestly say her performance on this tour had been perfect, there were too many things she ought to have done better. Like talking Lisa Perretti *out* of buying more than a single three-hundred-dollar Hermès silk scarf, or talking Tiffany Lewis *into* trying frog legs provençale, something she'd clearly been dying to taste despite the merciless teasing and protests of the other girls. And she had yet to convince her group that a *bateau mouche* ride on the Seine at sunset was not unspeakably corny but in fact a good way to see Paris from a new and interesting perspective.

Kendra squared her shoulders proudly. No, she hadn't done a perfect job, but she had done a good job, she admitted silently and without false modesty, a very good job, of making their first trip to France both fun and educational.

If Bob Warren harbored any lingering doubts about her competence to manage the Monterey branch office of Let's Go Travel, the successful completion of this current assignment ought unequivocally to convince him that she fully deserved the promotion she hoped to receive upon her return.

"I'll have an answer for you when you get back."

That was all her boss had been willing to promise, though he'd seemed very receptive when she'd made her formal pitch for the position she knew would soon be available. Three more days, and she would be home. Three more days, and she would have her answer.

An answer she was almost positive would be "yes."

Kendra's smile widened. Yes, indeed, her life was very firmly on track. She slowed her pace to a halt as the Tuileries Gardens ended in a flight of stairs leading down to the Place de la Concorde. Her smile twisted with mischief.

"Anybody know what happened down there, in the Place de la Concorde?" Kendra's tone was innocent as her slim fingers pushed back a heavy handful of honey-blond hair curling damply around her face.

Grumbles and groans were her only answer.

"During the French Revolution, the guillotine was set up here." Kendra's arm made an expansive sweep in front of her, the gesture taking in the great circular plaza now jammed with the beginnings of rush-hour traffic. "Louis XVI, Marie Antoinette, and over a thousand other people lost their heads in this exact spot."

Expressions of interest began to appear on the girls' faces.

"Crowds gathered to watch and cheer, blood flowed freely as heads rolled, and talk about a stench—"

"Kendra!"

"Oh, gross!"

Kendra grinned. "Shall we get extra ketchup with those fries, girls?"

There was a moment of silence, then an outburst of raucous laughter as the girls followed Kendra across the Place de la Concorde and onto the Champs-Élysées, dodging cars with youthful exuberance and catlike agility.

Jackson Randall bit into a surprisingly respectable version of an American cheeseburger and took a long pull on a watery, not-so-successful rendition of a chocolate milk shake, enjoying the view.

From his corner booth on the second floor of Freetime—an enterprising French businessman's triumphant response to McDonald's bid for fast-food supremacy in Paris—Jack had a perfect vantage point from which to regard the panorama of the Champs-Élysées stretched out below in all its spectacle and diversity.

Fast-walking, fast-talking businessmen rushing to appointments in thousand-dollar suits weaved their way among youth packs sporting ghetto blasters and spiked gloves. Immaculately groomed society sophisticates gestured languidly at richly filled display windows as they stepped carefully around hard-eyed gangs in black leather preening beside enormous gleaming motorcycles parked right on the sidewalk. North African immigrants in native costume rubbed elbows with nervously excited tourists already lining up for the dinner show at the Lido.

That wasn't the view Jack was enjoying.

His eyes were glued to the procession making its way to a nearby cluster of empty tables clutching heavily-laden trays of food in eager hands. They were a good-looking bunch of young girls, he thought, bright-eyed, smiling, and brimming with health and vitality. Probably German or Dutch, he guessed. But it was the woman with them, their teacher or whoever, who had captured Jack's undivided attention.

She was as good-looking a woman as he'd seen since arriving in Paris three months ago — and Paris was a banquet of beautiful women.

His superiors had called his new duty at the U.S. Embassy a "reward" posting for recent valor. Personally, Jack didn't consider his actions all that valorous. As for Paris, well, once he'd taken in the major tourist attractions, Paris was just another posting, except that the food was better than in most places.

Jackson Randall was a thirty-five-year-old career marine and proud of it. Lofty concepts like valor didn't really matter to him. Commitment did. A marine's commitment, his own commitment, to be "Semper Fidelis" to the corps, and to the men who served under and with him. For Jack, the motto "Always Faithful" meant putting his whole self on the line — heart, mind, body, and soul — whenever, however required without counting the cost in personal terms.

Still, he was willing to bet that if his superiors even suspected how flat-out scared he'd been on that desert raid he'd led to rescue a downed pilot, he would probably be guarding latrines in that same desert outpost right now.

He only had eight years before he could retire with a full pension and benefits, but there'd been some pretty tense moments on his last tour in the Middle East. More than once, he'd wondered if he would live to use as a civilian the engineering degree he'd earned in the corps.

He counted himself damn lucky to be watching a beautiful woman eating a hamburger in Paris, France.

The woman was younger than he was. Middle to late twenties, Jack surmised. Her hair was dark blond, and she wore it long, tied back at the base of her neck with some kind of lacy scarf thing, though a number of curling strands had escaped to frame her face. Jack was partial to long hair. He purely hated the current fashion of short hair for women — especially when they chopped it off so near their scalps they looked like raw recruits.

He wasn't close enough to tell what color her eyes were, but the rest of her features made up a lovely, sweet face. He liked the clean sweep of her cheekbones, the small forward thrust of her chin, and the fact that she didn't wear a lot of makeup like most of the women in Paris did. Just some delicate pink lipstick on a soft-looking mouth that seemed to be always smiling and didn't really need cosmetics to draw attention to its sensuous curves.

And he'd noticed right off that while she wasn't much above average height, she had the kind of long, athletic legs a cruder man than himself would fantasize locked around his waist in the throes of passion. He preferred to think of those strong, slender legs flashing in exuberant dance to wild music.

She was a wholesome, winsome beauty, he thought, smiling with the pleasure of just watching her. There was a sudden drop in the restaurant's noise level. Jack's smile widened as he caught snatches of animated conversation from the woman's table and realized that she was American. Not that the fact would do him any good. She was clearly a tourist, and that meant she was only in Paris for a short time.

If there was one thing Jackson Randall had learned from seventeen years as a marine it was that fly-by-night encounters didn't lead anywhere he wanted to go at this point in his life. A corollary but equally important notion was that long-distance relationships were mostly doomed from the get go.

Oh sure, a marriage could withstand the occasional separation of a temporary tour of duty, and a good marriage could even survive the unavoidable longer tours that entailed separations of a year or more. Such things were an accepted, expected part of a military career. But a man was crazy if he let himself be drawn into a relationship he knew from the outset was destined to be long-distance.

Which didn't mean he wasn't almighty tempted to walk over and introduce himself to the woman sitting nearby. Just that he knew better, and that knowledge made him content to admire from a distance his all-American beauty with her shining, honey-colored hair, her clear, pretty skin and her girl-next-door smile.

Until he heard her laugh.

No girl who'd ever lived next door to him had

laughed the way this woman did. This woman's laugh was a low, throaty, entirely sensual ripple of sound that affected him like a long, red-tipped fingernail drawn slowly and provocatively down his naked chest from his throat to his groin.

Kendra wasn't sure just what made her realize that the choking sounds coming from nearby were potentially life-threatening.

One minute she was debating with Lisa and Tracy Weber the relative merits of two different streets as possible venues for a window-shopping excursion on their way back to the hotel. The next, there was a lull in the general restaurant din and the sounds of distress caught her attention.

The noises were coming from a small boy of five or six at the table across from her. His mother was trying to make him drink some milk from a paper cup. His father was slapping him on the back. Neither action was having much effect in stopping the boy's coughing and gagging.

"Kendra!" Tracy Weber's tone was impatient. "What do you think?"

Kendra returned her attention to the girls seated around her, but she couldn't help glancing back uneasily at the table across the way.

"Sorry, Tracy. Ask me again. What do I think about what?"

"About doing both Avenue Montaigne and Rue du Faubourg Saint-Honoré. Look." She pushed a street map toward Kendra, pointing out a route with her finger. "If we walk down Avenue Montaigne this way, we end up at a Métro stop that will take us right to—"

"Don't be stupid, Tracy," interrupted Mary Lee derisively. "By the time we see all the shops on Avenue Montaigne it'll be way late."

The little boy was obviously in distress, noted Kendra, trying to keep track of the conversation swirling around her.

"So what?"

"So, I don't want to take the Métro that late at night," said Mary Lee.

"I don't want to take the Métro again, at all." Heidi Clayton wrinkled her nose with distaste. "It smells, and there are too many weirdos down there. Why don't we take a taxi?"

"Well, I think the Métro sounds exciting," countered Lisa.

"Besides, getting enough taxis for all of us is a huge hassle," added Tiffany Lewis.

Kendra ventured another glance at the little boy's table. His complexion had turned pasty and a fine sheen of perspiration filmed across his forehead. She didn't like the looks of this. Not at all.

"We think the Métro sounds too dangerous, and doing both streets tonight sounds like too much walking."

"We're going to do Saint-Honoré because when we get to the end of the street, we're practically at the entrance to our hotel."

The Gray twins spoke firmly and in unison, their entire demeanor conveying the impression that the issue was no longer open for discussion.

"Who died and left you two in charge?" challenged Lisa. "It's Kendra's decision. What about it, Kendra? Can we do both streets?"

The boy's cheeks reddened; in fact, his whole face was turning scarlet. Ignoring Lisa's question, Kendra rose from her seat so quickly the chair turned over and covered the distance to the little boy in three purposeful strides. Pushing his father aside, she grasped the boy's face firmly in her left hand, forcing his jaw down.

She was peripherally aware of the boy's father running toward the stairs shouting for help in French, but she didn't dare take the time to apologize for her abrupt intervention. Hooking the index and middle finger of her right hand, Kendra swept the boy's mouth, hoping to dislodge whatever was stuck in his throat.

Nothing. Damn!

The boy's mother dropped her tight hold on her child's arm and began inching fearfully away. Kendra swore silently, wishing she spoke more French so she could reassure the woman that she knew what she was doing, and that she meant the boy no harm.

The boy's eyes were panicky, beginning to bulge, and his thin little body was trembling.

"Be calm," she told him, hoping he understood her French. "I'm going to help you breathe now."

She stepped rapidly behind the child. Then hugging his back to her front, she performed the Heimlich maneuver in one smooth, effortless motion, remembering to use her fingers as recommended for small children, instead of both fists as she would have done for an adult.

A walnut-sized chunk of barely chewed hamburger spewed out onto the table, and after a couple of stuttering coughs, the boy began to breathe. Then he turned his head, raised huge watery blue eyes to hers and began to sob as though his heart were breaking.

Kendra looked around for his mother, but the woman was nowhere to be seen. She'd probably gone after the father. The two of them were probably calling the police this very minute to come and arrest the crazy American woman who had attacked their child, she told herself.

The boy was still sobbing noisily, so she pulled him up into her arms, rocking him, crooning to him, smoothing his lank, matted hair with her hand. His narrow shoulders heaved with the force of his tears, and the back of his grubby t-shirt was damp with sweat. He smelled like he hadn't had a bath in a week, but his skinny little arms were clasped around her neck in a death grip, and Kendra didn't have the heart to dislodge them.

The girls clustered anxiously around her, unsure of what to do. Heather Lawrence shoved a chair under Kendra, and she sat down gratefully. Despite his thinness and his small size, the boy was an awkward bundle to hold standing up.

"Tell me how I can help."

The voice was unfamiliar to Kendra. Not only that, the voice was male, pleasantly deep, polite, and most importantly at this moment, the voice was speaking English . . . with a slight midwestern twang.

Kendra looked up. The first thing she noticed was his face, a calm, mature, trust-inspiring face. A seasoned face, plainly stamped with years of experience meeting and conquering far worse situations than the one at hand. A face that promised a man on whom a woman could depend.

A face Kendra found entirely too handsome to meet in a circumstance like the one she now found herself.

And then she noticed the uniform—dark khaki trousers with knife-edge creases and a lighter khaki shirt pressed to perfection.

"Thank God, the cavalry." Her tone conveyed a world of relief and appreciation that she wouldn't have to deal with the aftermath of the barely averted disaster alone. Now that the little boy was breathing again, Kendra felt shaky and drained, and not a little uneasy about what to do next.

"No, ma'am." The soldier grinned rakishly. "You're in luck. The Marines."

Chapter Two

"I'm Captain Jackson Randall. Now, tell me how I can help."

The man was born to command, thought Kendra, from his crisp military haircut to the toes of his spit-shined shoes. Even relaxed, he had a shoulders back, feet apart stance that only just missed being aggressive.

And he was big.

Not just tall, though he had to top six feet by a respectable three inches. Not just broad, though he had the wide shoulders and deep chest of a man not merely fit, but naturally athletic — the kind of physique that raised more than a shred of envy in most men and more than a flicker of interest in most women.

But big in the sense that he seemed to dominate the space around him. Probably the people, too, suspected Kendra with amusement. Growing up the oldest in a large, boisterous family hadn't allowed her personality to develop along particularly submissive or retiring lines. As a result, bold, forceful people didn't intimidate her.

Rather, she found herself attracted to them.

A whimper made her refocus her thoughts on the more pressing matter of the boy on her lap. She stroked his back reassuringly. "Could you go downstairs and find this boy's parents and let them know he's okay?"

Captain Randall shook his head. "I only speak about twelve words of French. And I couldn't identify the boy's parents in any case. My attention was . . . otherwise engaged."

The warmth of his regard was unmistakable. Under less awkward, more appropriate circumstances, Kendra would have been tempted to explore the spark of interest, the enticing sense of promise that seemed to spring from nowhere to resonate between them.

"I speak enough French to talk to the little boy's parents," offered Mary Lee.

"And I definitely remember what they looked like," said Heidi Clayton. "The father was short and skinny, with kind of greasy gray-brown hair. And he was wearing—"

"Okay, Heidi. I believe you." Kendra held up one hand to stop the river of information. If there was one thing the "daughters of privilege" possessed it was an eye for sartorial detail. "You and Mary Lee go with Captain Randall. The rest of us will wait here."

She considered the still distraught boy nestled into the space between her shoulder and her neck. In careful, quiet French she asked his name.

After a long pause, he responded, his voice a barely audible whisper. "Rémy."

"The rest of us will wait here with Rémy." Kendra glanced up. "Thank you, Captain Randall."

"No problem, ma'am."

"I'm Kendra Martin. Please," she said. "Call me Kendra."

"With pleasure. With very great pleasure, Kendra." He drew out the syllables of her name like a slow caress, then pivoted on his heel and strode toward the stairs, Mary Lee and Heidi in close pursuit.

The other girls huddled together close to Kendra. They were subdued, watchful, talking quietly while they gave Rémy gentle pats with tender hands. Little by little, he grew calm, the loud sobs diminishing to occasional soft hiccups and sniffs.

Amazingly, except for a few curious glances, some low mutterings accompanied by discreet gestures in her direction, and one or two off-hand queries in French if everything was okay, the other restaurant patrons had gone back to their meals as though nothing especially untoward had happened.

"Kendra, we couldn't find them." Heidi sounded surprised when she returned a short time later, only steps ahead of Jackson Randall and Mary Lee. "I even looked in the women's rest room. Rémy's mom wasn't there."

"She wasn't anywhere," added Mary Lee. "I went outside and around the back just to make sure. The manager didn't notice her, and neither did anyone else."

"That doesn't make any sense." Kendra refused to

believe that a woman would simply leave her choking child to the uncertain mercies of a stranger. Especially not a woman who had watched Kendra's actions as though she feared for her son's life.

"No luck finding the father, either, I'm afraid," added Jackson Randall. "Not even with Heidi's incredibly detailed description. And before you ask, yes, they made me search the men's room. The guy isn't in the restaurant, and neither is his wife. Nor are they anywhere in the immediate vicinity. I don't know what to make of this."

"Something isn't right here," said Kendra, biting her upper lip, trying to puzzle out the peculiar facts. "Do you think we should call . . ." She looked up in consternation. "I don't even know who to call. The police? Child welfare? Who?"

"What about the rest of Rémy's family?" suggested Amber Carlisle.

"Of course, Amber. You're exactly right." Kendra gave the girl a warm smile of approval. "Why didn't I think of that?"

She whispered some nonsense syllables in Rémy's ear, tickling him with her breath, trying to make him look at her, trying to make him smile. He pulled away from her fractionally, his arms still locked around her neck. The face he turned up to hers was old beyond its years, his expression blank, unreadable. Only his eyes gave any indication of what he might be feeling.

And in his eyes Kendra read a sadness so deep, so heavy, so terrible, she almost feared to question him. No child should have eyes like that, thought Kendra. No child should bear such a burden of sadness. No child.

"Rémy," she asked him in French. "Can you tell me your last name?" Kendra made her voice as gentle as she knew how, but the boy didn't respond. After a few moments, it became clear to her that he wasn't going to. "Can you tell me your mother's name, or your father's name?"

No answer.

"Will you tell me your grandparents' names? Or the name of your favorite aunt?"

Still no answer. Just those knowing eyes gazing at her gravely. Kendra saw more than sadness in those eyes, she saw caution, even fear. Again, she wondered what kind of life this little boy had led.

"Where do you live, Rémy?"

No response.

"Do you live here, in Paris?"

Silence.

Kendra thought for a few moments, then tried a new tack. "Do you have pets, Rémy? A puppy, or a kitten, or maybe some goldfish?"

A flicker of interest flared in his eyes, then died out.

"Aha," said Kendra. "I thought so. You look exactly like the kind of boy who has a pet . . . elephant."

"No. Not an elephant!" The words burst out as though he was unable to contain them. "I have a pony named Prix de Caen!"

"Oh, a pony. And does Prix de Caen live with you?"

"Of course not. He lives in . . . the stables . . .

at. . . ." His explanation slowed, then halted completely.

"Where does your pony live, Rémy? Where are the stables?" prompted Kendra.

Yet again, the infuriating refusal to respond. Damn! Why wouldn't he tell her?

"Maybe he has some kind of identification in his pockets. Or something else that will help us find out who he is." Jack made a slow, careful move toward Rémy.

The boy let out a shriek that nearly split Kendra's eardrums and caused heads to swivel disapprovingly in their direction from several sections of the restaurant. Kendra clasped the boy close to her body in a comforting hug, murmuring a mixture of French and English endearments. He began to tremble, and once again, he began to cry.

"This is just exasperating," she said to Jack in an undertone. "I'm at a complete loss. What in the world should we do now?"

"I guess the only thing we *can* do at this point is call the police. I hate to turn over a kid that small and that distraught, but as long as you stay with him, I guess we can straighten this mess out eventually with some help from the authorities."

"Captain Randall—"

"Jack," he corrected. "My friends call me Jack."

"Jack," she acquiesced, liking the strength, the simplicity of the abbreviated version of his name. It suited him.

Then, impatient with herself for dwelling on something so irrelevant under the circumstances, she made her voice deliberately crisp and businesslike, gesturing to the group around her. "I'm a travel agent on tour with these girls. I'm solely responsible for them. I can't drag them down to some police station and keep them there while we spend hours 'straightening out this mess.' "

Jack fell silent. Kendra watched him, seeing the swift workings of his brain in the myriad expressions crossing his face—a narrowing of eyes, a pursing of lips, a clenching of jaw. A hard, square, handsome mass of jaw, she couldn't help noting, with a shadow of late-afternoon beard beginning to grow.

After a minute or so, he exhaled sharply and pushed back from the table. Kendra felt a surge of anticipation. She hoped he had come up with a sensible solution . . . because she was drawing nothing but blanks.

"Okay. Here's the plan. You and the girls keep Rémy calm. I'm going to call the embassy—that's where I'm posted. Usually matters between U.S. citizens and foreign nationals are handled by the U.S. Consulate, but I don't know anyone over there. Strictly speaking, I shouldn't involve embassy staff, but my commanding officer is a decent, understanding guy with a houseful of his own kids. I'm sure he'll help us out. Sit tight while I make the call."

Jack's long stride covered half the distance to the public telephone in the corner, then he turned back, retracing a few steps. "Shoot me your passport. My C.O. will need some information for his report."

Kendra managed to disengage one arm from around Rémy, dug in her purse, and tossed her passport at Jack. He snatched it out of the air with a deft backhand grab and a quick wink. Then he reached into his shirt pocket, pulled out one of the telephone debit cards that had almost completely replaced the *jetons* formerly used for making calls from public booths, and began to place his call.

"Colonel Morgan, please. Captain Randall calling."

"Morgan here."

"It's Randall, sir. I have a situation I'm not quite sure how to handle."

"That's a first. What's your location?"

"Freetime. It's a hamburger joint on the Champs-Élysées a couple of blocks from the embassy."

"I know the place. Spit out the particulars."

With a minimum of words and fuss, Jack began to explain. He hadn't spoken more than six sentences before the colonel interrupted.

"Say again, Randall."

"The boy looks to be about five or six, light brown hair, thin, can't or won't give his last name, or his address—"

"No, that bit about the pony."

"The pony, sir?"

"Yes, dammit, the *pony!*" The colonel's tone had gone from brisk but tolerant to downright impatient.

Jack hastened to obey the order. "The boy has a pony named, bear with me on the pronunciation here, sir, named Prix de Caen."

"And what was the woman's name again?"

"Kendra Martin," said Jack.

"Is there any way you can get access to her passport?"

"I have it in my hand, sir."

"Good work. Give me the passport number and her most recent date of entry into France."

Jack complied, then flipped through the pages of Kendra's passport, noting her age and shamelessly committing to memory her hometown address and telephone number. "Is there a problem, sir?"

"Randall, this is very important. Are you absolutely certain that this woman, Kendra Martin, had no contact with the boy prior to the choking incident? She didn't come in with the boy and his parents? It didn't look like she was meeting them at Freetime? That she had some kind of connection to them?"

"Sir, she was a complete stranger, but it's my opinion that her quick action saved the kid's life. That's her only connection to him."

"Okay, Randall. Hold for a minute."

Jack didn't understand the flap about the pony, or the colonel's persistent questions about Kendra, but a sense of unease began crawling up his spine.

"Captain Randall?"

The deep, cultured tones were unfamiliar, but Jack comprehended instantly the power in the man's voice. "Yes, sir."

"This is Ambassador Whittington. I'm passing you to my aide, Jon Craig. Listen carefully, then do exactly as he says."

"Yes, sir," said Jack, increasingly mystified.

"This is Jon Craig, captain. Let me brief you on the situation we believe you've stumbled into."

A full five minutes later Jon Craig finished imparting his explosive information. Jack didn't immediately respond. He couldn't. He simply turned to look from Kendra to the boy and back, then silently mouthed an obscenity he didn't dare utter aloud to the ambassador's aide.

"What are my orders, sir?"

"Get the boy and the woman to the embassy immediately. The couple you saw with the boy may be lying in wait nearby. They could be armed, or have accomplices."

"I don't believe that's a cause for concern, sir. The man and woman took off as soon as the boy began choking. I've searched the immediate surrounding area, and there's not a trace of them or of any accomplices."

"We still don't want any reporters or other media representatives to catch wind of these developments quite yet. Be out front in ten minutes. We're sending a car from the embassy."

"Sir, that's not going to work. The woman is a travel agent. She's got twelve teenage girls with her. We'll need more than one car."

"You want me to send four or five embassy cars screaming up to an entrance on the Champs-Élysées? Then wait while twelve teenage girls mill around deciding who rides with whom? No way." Jon Craig's tone was emphatic. "We can't risk attracting that kind of attention."

"Sir, you don't understand. The woman won't leave the girls—"

"Then leave the woman and her tour group there, and hustle the boy downstairs."

"There's another complication. The boy won't leave the woman, in fact he gets hysterical if—"

"And I am hereby ordering you not to leave that boy's side. His safety and anonymity are paramount. We want you to get him to the embassy as quickly and unobtrusively as possible."

"Understood, sir." Jack impatiently shifted his balance from one foot to the other. "But what about Kendra Martin and the girls."

"Hell, Randall, I don't know. You can hardly march a young woman, twelve teenage girls, a uniformed Marine and an intermittently hysterical little boy all the way down the Champs-Élysées to the U.S. Embassy like some kind of parade."

Jack smiled, the pieces of a plan beginning to fall into place. "Actually, sir, I think hiding in plain sight is just about the best way to handle things."

"I'm not sure I like the sound of that, Randall."

"You will, sir. Round up four young marines named Hopwell, O'Reilly, Harris, and Beck. They should just be getting off duty. Tell them to change into exercise gear, cut through that little grassy park in front of the embassy and start jogging up the Champs-Élysées." Though Jack's expression had relaxed, his entire body tightened as adrenaline began pumping through his veins, readying him for action while he explained the rest of his plan.

"Done," said the ambassador's aide. "Anything else?"

"Yeah. Tell them I said to jog fast."

Kendra felt a sinking sensation in her stomach as Jack came toward her, his bearing erect, his expression no longer aghast as it had been seconds before, but set now in firm, purposeful lines.

"Jack, what is it? What did your boss at the embassy say?"

"I want you to get up from the table and follow me downstairs with Rémy and the girls."

"Why?"

"Just do as I say." He moved around behind her, pulling out her chair.

"You're scaring me. What's going on?"

"Be casual. We've finished our burgers, now we're leaving. No big deal. And smile, Kendra. Smile like you mean it."

"Are you crazy? I'm not moving an inch, and neither are Rémy and the girls until you give me a satisfactory explanation for all this, this—"

"Subterfuge," said Jack, leaning over her shoulder to whisper in her ear. "And that's exactly what you're going to do. Now, move."

He was so close Kendra could smell the last faint remnants of the aftershave he'd used that morning. A toned-down, no-nonsense fragrance with a clean, citrusy tang she found far more appealing than the heavy, almost cloying colognes she'd noticed that Frenchmen favored. She inhaled appreciatively, unconsciously inclining her head toward his—until she felt the sting of a single sharp bite on her earlobe.

A decidedly unfriendly bite.

"Kendra, honey, move your tail. And I mean *now!*"

"Captain Randall, I don't recall joining the Marines. And I have no intention of taking orders from a perfect stranger without an excellent reason. Now—"

"Perfect, huh?"

She ignored his remark. "Are you going to explain, or shall we sit here sparring for a while longer?"

"Trust me. There's no time for questions, or lengthy explanations right now. We have to get Rémy and the girls out of here."

"Are they in danger?" Alarm sharpened her tone and stiffened her spine.

"Please, just . . . trust me. Can you do that?"

Kendra shifted Rémy on her lap, twisting around in her chair to face Jack. Once more she was struck by the strength of character, the integrity stamped on every lean plane and hard angle of his face. She reminded herself of her initial impression—that Jack was a man upon whom a woman could depend. She thought about her responsibilities to the twelve girls clustered around her, her duty to keep them safe, well, and happy until she returned them to their parents.

"Kendra, we really don't have much time. Please . . . come with me."

The intensity, the earnestness in his low voice were hard for Kendra to resist. She felt the tension, the pull of two equally strong forces within herself. The calm, rational, businesslike side of her personality was demanding explanations . . . while every female instinct she possessed was screaming at her to get up and follow Jack. She took a deep breath and made a huge leap of faith, praying she was doing the right thing.

"Okay, girls, gather up your purses and postcards and souvenirs." She smiled at Jack, smiled like she meant it. "We're going with Captain Randall."

"Where are we going?" asked Mary Lee, her tone practical and matter-of-fact, but not unduly concerned.

"For a little stroll down the Champs-Élysées," responded Jack. "How would you like to meet some buddies of mine? Nice guys, kind of athletic, not too much older than you girls."

Kendra's admiration for Jack's motivational ability grew by leaps and bounds as she watched the girls begin subtle preening motions, murmurs of interest supplanting the natural curiosity that would otherwise have demanded more involved explanations.

The same kind of explanations Kendra intended to wrest from him before too many more minutes had passed.

"Oh, very good. *Athletes* not *too* much older than the girls?"

"What can I say? I have two younger sisters who were once teenagers. I have a little insight when it comes to women."

Kendra raised one feathery eyebrow a quarter of an inch. She'd be willing to bet a healthy sum that not all of Jack's insight had come from his sisters . . . and that the vast majority of his probably substantial knowledge related to adult women, not girls.

His organization and command skills were first-rate, too, she admitted silently. In short order, and without much commotion, she found herself walking down the Champs-Élysées, Rémy clinging tightly to her hand, but finally willing to permit more than a few inches to separate her from him. The girls walked in front of her, eagerly scanning the block ahead for the first sight of Jack's "buddies."

Jack himself seemed to be everywhere at once. Kendra felt his large warm hand in the small of her back, a moment later he was four feet ahead of her, teasing Amber Carlisle and Kary Lyons. His tall, broad frame moved back and forth among the group with coordinated ease. He was constantly aware and keenly, though inconspicuously, observant. She doubted there was a single person within a fifty-foot radius of their group that Jack hadn't weighed and measured as a potential threat.

She felt the grip of tension ease slightly . . . until four good-looking, extremely *young* men wearing shorts and sport shoes jogged up to Jack, greeting him like a long-lost brother.

"Great," said Jack. "The reinforcements."

"Please, tell me you're kidding." Kendra eyed the new arrivals with dismay. The oldest couldn't have been more than nineteen, and every fit single one of them possessed the kind of muscular, well-developed torso that turned their simple olive drab T-shirts into body-molding provocations.

"Nope. Uncle Sam's best," said Jack, issuing a few terse orders.

The girls divided effortlessly into four groups of three, each accompanied by a lean, handsome marine. Kendra's nerves began to jangle as the groups took off in four different directions. Consumed with doubts about the wisdom of her actions, she was suddenly sure of only one thing.

Agreeing to Jack's plan was going to cost her promotion. Hell, it would probably cost her job.

"This is crazy. Idiotic." Kendra panicked. "I've just turned twelve teenage girls loose on the streets of Paris with four teenage boys—"

"You've just entrusted four *marines* with the responsibility of escorting twelve young *ladies* safely to their *hotel rooms*—"

"Hotel rooms," she repeated, horrified. "Oh, my God!"

"Where said marines will make certain that said young ladies stay in—"

"High on my list of worries, I assure you—"

"And everyone else, themselves included, stays out until we arrive."

"I'd rather entrust those boys with the defense of my country," she muttered under her breath.

Jack laughed, pulling her tightly against his chest in a squeeze Kendra was sure he meant to be comforting, but which failed miserably in its intended effect. He was too vital, too male, altogether too much of everything Kendra found attractive in a man for a hug that close to be merely comforting.

"Come on. The sooner we reach the embassy, the sooner you can get back to your girls."

They had walked about a block when Jack turned to her and said, "So . . . how are you enjoying Paris?"

"Nice try, Jack, but you have a lot of explaining to do. Start talking."

He chuckled, then rested his hand briefly on Rémy's head. The boy flinched, but remained silent. "This little guy is almost certainly Rémy Bourquel, the grandson of Jean-Michel Bourquel—"

Kendra gasped. "The industrialist? The one who's been on a first-name basis with every U.S. president since Truman?"

Jack nodded. "The old man is a real mover and shaker in Europe generally, but especially in his native France. Eleven days ago, little Rémy Bourquel disappeared from the family's seaside villa in Normandy, where he was spending his summer holiday. Twelve hours later, a ransom demand was received from the purported kidnapers. A quiet but intensive search has been under way for the boy since his disappearance, but according to the higher-ups at the embassy this is the first real break in the case."

"Apart from the name Rémy and the physical description, both of which could be coincidence, what makes the embassy so certain this is the same boy?"

"At the time of his disappearance, Rémy Bourquel was riding his pony along a deserted stretch of heavily forested coastline and became separated from the stableman accompanying him. The pony's name is Prix de Caen—out of Prix de l'Arc, the horse that two years ago won France's version of the Kentucky Derby."

Kendra felt the blood drain from her face. She couldn't speak, sympathy for the horrific experience Rémy had undergone clogging her throat. She simply squeezed the little boy's sticky hand, letting Jack guide them across a busy street and into a small grassy park shaded by huge leafy trees.

Just ahead on the left, she was grateful to see at last the massive white edifice of the U.S. Embassy. A smartly uniformed marine guard stood at attention beside a sentry box located behind iron gates twelve feet high. As Kendra, Jack, and Rémy approached, the gates opened swiftly and silently.

Four marines, fully armed with state-of-the-art automatic weapons, rushed to the gates to escort the small party inside.

Chapter Three

A four-member reception team was waiting for them in the cool marble foyer of the main embassy building.

Jack saluted an older marine whose left breast was emblazoned with an impressive array of ribbons and medals. Kendra's glance skimmed over the others — a man wearing a white lab coat and a younger, rotund man carrying a briefcase. A slim silver-haired man stood slightly apart — exuding elegance, authority, and power from every well-bred pore.

The full impact of the situation struck Kendra when the slim silver-haired man came toward her with a measured step, his hand outstretched.

"Ms. Martin?"

Kendra nodded, her mouth suddenly dry. Her own contact with important personages had so far been limited to brief glimpses of incognito movie stars week-ending in Carmel. She was wholly unfamiliar with the protocol required in diplomatic circles. Yet here she was, about to meet a man who could only be the United States ambassador to France.

"I'm Ambassador Whittington."

"It's an honor to meet you, sir." Kendra shook his hand, horribly self-conscious of her casual attire.

Her tan twill walking shorts, rose pink cotton-knit top, and flat leather shoes were clean, comfortable, and perfectly appropriate for sight-seeing on a hot summer day. They were hardly the clothes she would have chosen to wear when meeting a U.S. ambassador in his official capacity. Even so, she squared her shoulders, too proud to let her discomfiture show. "Thank you for your help."

"Any thanks due are owed entirely to you, Ms. Martin. You saved a boy's life and returned him to his family . . . scoring a number of diplomatic points for your government in the process." Ambassador Whittington turned to the younger man on his left. "Let me introduce my aide, Jon Craig. I've asked him to help you with the one or two small formalities necessary to wrap up this incident."

Jon Craig was short and pudgy with the kind of innocent baby face most people wouldn't take seriously. Kendra read shrewdness, ambition, and intelligence in the dark eyes staring at her intently. After a brief acknowledgment, he squatted down and spoke to Rémy in liquid, idiomatic French, his tone gentle, friendly, and honestly kind.

"Ms. Martin," he said, looking up at her a few moments later. "Ambassador Whittington would like your complete statement for the official record."

"Of course," said Kendra, relieved and happy to

see Rémy relax under Jon Craig's skillful attentions.

"Thanks. Now, I've promised Rémy a toilet and a snack in that order. Afterward, Dr. Wardell is going to give Rémy a medical once-over so we can reassure his parents about his physical condition once they arrive."

The white-coated man stepped forward to take charge of Rémy. His hand tightened on Kendra's, but after several earnest assurances from Jon Craig and a solid hug from Kendra, he released his grip and went with the doctor.

"Let's get right on that statement, Ms. Martin. Rémy's parents and grandfather will be here shortly, and they've asked to meet and thank you—"

"Oh, that's not necessary," protested Kendra. "I'm just glad I happened to be there."

"Ms. Martin," interrupted Ambassador Whittington, giving Kendra a warm, approving smile. "I can see that you're the kind of young woman who would be uncomfortable with a great show of thanks or praise for your courageous actions, but as a personal favor, won't you please meet the Bourquel family? You would certainly ease the rigors of my job by agreeing."

"Put that way, ambassador, I don't see how I can refuse."

"Splendid."

There was no time for a private word with Jack. No time for a personal goodbye, however awkward such a farewell would have been in front of witnesses. Before Kendra had a chance to do more than meet his gaze and smile once softly, she found herself flanked by the ambassador and Jon Craig, be-

43

ing guided up a carved marble stairway of impressive proportions. She let her steps lag as they approached the first landing, unable to resist turning her head for a last glimpse of Jack's face.

She was disappointed to discover that the foyer was empty.

Kendra's eyes were a rich warm brown—the color of good whiskey, mused Jack, following Colonel Morgan down a long red-carpeted hallway to the office where he would make his own report.

He felt dazed from the impact of her smile as though from a blow to his head. He wanted to hold the moment in the forefront of his mind forever. She'd sought him out with those soft brown eyes, and she'd smiled at him as though he was the only person in the room. Then she'd floated up those stairs with the grace of a queen and a walk like—well, suffice it to say that her walk was purely female.

Even Colonel Morgan's eyes had lingered a moment or two on the flex and release of Kendra's slim, firmly muscled calves and the sway of her smooth hips and taut backside as she climbed the stairs. And the colonel was a man well-known for his devotion to, his utter infatuation with his wife of twenty-five years.

Jack was equally impressed by Kendra's poise. By God, did he admire her poise. Not an hour after the harrowing experience of saving Rémy's life and learning of his kidnaping, she'd stood exchanging pleasantries with the ambassador and his aide. Jack knew from his surreptitious examination of her passport that she was only twenty-seven years old. Yet, she had exhibited the grace and control of a forty-five-year-old aristocrat at a diplomatic tea.

"Still coming, Randall?" Heavy irony infused Colonel Morgan's voice.

"Right behind you, sir."

Jack frowned. He hadn't even had a chance to say goodbye. Though goodbye was the last thing he wanted to say to Kendra. He grabbed the back of his neck, absently massaging the knotted muscles there. He knew better. He really knew better than to pursue his interest in a tourist he'd encountered by chance. But something about the woman drew him. Hell, he admitted silently, a whole lot of things about the woman drew him. But what to do about that fact?

What to do?

Kendra read over the typed pages of her statement, amazed at how quickly and easily the job had been accomplished.

Seated on a comfortable sofa in Jon Craig's office, she had simply recounted her experiences from the time she had walked into Freetime with the girls until the moment she had entered the embassy grounds. A stenographer had quietly transcribed every word on her machine, including Jon Craig's intermittent questions and requests for clarification, or further detail.

Satisfied with the typed version, Kendra signed her name beneath a declaration under penalty of perjury that her statement was both voluntary and true, then handed the sheets of paper back to Jon Craig.

"Thank you, Ms. Martin." He placed her statement in a plain buff-colored file, locked the file in his desk drawer, and buzzed his secretary. "Are the Bourquels here yet? Good. Let Ambassador Whittington know we're at his disposal."

A few moments later, he ushered Kendra into the ambassador's office. She noted the U.S. flag, the official portraits of the presidents of the United States and France, and occupying pride of place above the ambassador's massive mahogany desk, the great seal of the United States.

A sense of awe enveloped Kendra as the sheer immensity of power represented by those symbols hit her. She felt way out of her league in such surroundings, despite Ambassador Whittington's welcoming smile as he stepped forward to introduce the trio of adults standing with him. Rémy was nowhere in sight.

"Messieurs Bourquel Madame Bourquel, I present Kendra Martin. Ms. Martin, I present Rémy's grandfather, Jean-Michel Bourquel, and his parents, Laurent and Nadine Bourquel."

Kendra had immediately recognized Jean-Michel Bourquel from photographs she'd seen over the years in newspapers and magazines. A summerweight wool suit, though handsomely cut and obviously custom-made, could not disguise his stocky build, massive bull-like shoulders, and thick neck. Iron-gray brush-cut hair emphasized his square head. He possessed a purposeful stance, an erect posture and a penetrating gaze that belied his eighty years, as did the intense vitality he emanated even at rest.

Kendra found him an altogether daunting old man.

Laurent and Nadine Bourquel were daunting, too, but in an entirely different way.

The raw power Jean-Michel radiated had been transposed in Rémy's parents into an aura of wealth, prestige, and sophistication. They were impeccably groomed, expensively dressed, and in Nadine's case, exquisitely made up.

More than ten years separated Laurent, who was clearly past forty, and Nadine, who was perhaps thirty. The age difference wasn't especially disconcerting to Kendra. She knew that European men frequently married much younger women. What unnerved her was the couple's utter control. Nothing in their faces or their demeanor gave the slightest hint of the ordeal they'd just been through.

Kendra knew that she could never have exhibited the restraint, the self-possession of the younger Bourquels had she found herself in similar circumstances. She would have been an emotional wreck from beginning to end, and she wouldn't have been able to hide that fact.

"Mademoiselle Martin, you have my family's gratitude for your brave actions in saving my grandson's life and thus facilitating his return to us." Jean-Michel gently grasped Kendra's hand, raised it to his lips, and kissed the air just above the skin of her fingers.

The old-fashioned courtly gesture surprised Kendra given what she had read of Jean-Michel's reputation for ruthlessness and craft in both his business dealings and his behind-the-scenes political maneuverings.

"I'm pleased to have been of help, Mr. Bourquel, but it really was just a matter of being in the right place at the right time."

"And having the courage to intervene on behalf of a total stranger." Laurent Bourquel's English bore the merest trace of an upper-class British accent. He was taller than Jean-Michel and built along leaner lines, but the purposeful stance and penetrating gaze were identical.

"Rémy is a darling little boy, Mr. Bourquel. I'm glad I was able to help him."

"After your inestimable service to my family, you must call me Laurent. Please." Laurent pressed Kendra's hand warmly between both of his.

"And I am Nadine." Nadine Bourquel leaned over in a subtle drift of some delicious French perfume. She rested a perfectly manicured hand lightly on Kendra's left shoulder and brushed a formal kiss on each cheek. "I cannot begin to express my thanks, Kendra. Rémy is my only child. This experience has been terrible, but now, thanks to you, it is over."

"I'm just happy everything turned out so well," said Kendra, increasingly uncomfortable with their continued expressions of gratitude, however reservedly expressed.

"Ms. Martin, on behalf of my family, I would like to give you a small token of our deep appreciation," said Jean-Michel.

"That's not necessary, Mr. Bourquel. Rémy's safety and well-being are reward enough."

"No, they are not." Jean-Michel's tone brooked no refusal. He held out a flat white box tied with narrow black-and-white ribbons imprinted with the distinctive interlaced letters of a famous couturier.

Ambassador Whittington cleared his throat discreetly. Kendra glanced over at him, catching an emphatic though barely perceptible nod.

"Please, Ms. Martin." With an insistent flourish, Jean-Michel extended the box closer to Kendra.

Kendra had no choice but to take it from his hands. She untied the ribbons and lifted from the inside tissue an extraordinarily beautiful black handbag complemented by what looked to be karat gold clasps and trim. She was unable to prevent the sigh of appreciation which escaped her lips. A handbag like this, she thought, was the kind of perfect accessory a woman could carry on any occasion throughout her entire life.

Reverently, she stroked the supple, masterfully worked leather. "I don't know what to say, except thank you. I have never seen a more gorgeous handbag."

"Open it," ordered Jean-Michel.

Mystified, Kendra unfastened the simple clasp, half afraid of what she might discover inside. Reaching into the bag, she withdrew a check made out in her name . . . *a check for two million francs!* She gasped. At the current exchange rate, even a quick, rough estimate of the U.S. equivalent was somewhere in the neighborhood of three hundred and fifty thousand dollars.

"I mean no disrespect, Mr. Bourquel." Kendra's glance swept Laurent and Nadine, including them in her words to Jean-Michel. "But I simply cannot accept, cannot *possibly* accept a sum of money this size. Of any size," she amended hastily.

"You can, and you will, Ms. Martin." Jean-Michel was adamant. "We offered this exact sum merely for *information* leading to Rémy's safe return. You not only returned him bodily to us, you saved his life in the process. We can do no less than give you this reward. You can do no less than accept it."

Kendra felt like squirming with discomfort at her quandary. She was uneasy about the size of the check Jean-Michel was pressing on her. Even more significant was her instant, visceral distaste for the notion of profiting financially from saving Rémy's life.

Yet, how did one gracefully, *diplomatically* refuse a man of Jean-Michel's influence? Particularly with the U.S. ambassador to France looking on?

"Perhaps you could reconsider, Ms. Martin?"

Kendra discerned a steely resolve beneath Ambassador Whittington's mild suggestion. Before she could respond, Jean-Michel spoke again, his words softer, thoughtful.

"We have become a small family, we Bourquels. Many of my generation were killed in the Second World War. Later, we lost others in the colonial conflicts. I myself lost a son, his wife, and their baby in Indochina, and later, a daughter and her husband in Algeria. Rémy is our future, our guarantee of continuity. You must let us show our gratitude."

"I understand your feelings, Monsieur Bourquel. And on that basis I will be delighted to carry this beautiful handbag. But the check," she said, shaking her head. "I can't accept the check. Especially not such an enormous sum."

Jean-Michel impatiently waved his hand in a dismissive gesture. "The sum, after all, is not important. It is merely a token, an outward sign of the gratitude we carry within." The smile he gave Kendra was sincere, but expressed more than a hint of innuendo. "I'm afraid I must insist that you accept the check as written. I simply cannot let you leave France without it."

Kendra opened her mouth to speak, but found no words. She clamped her lips shut and simply stared at the old man, racking her brain for a solution to the dilemma. Jean-Michel Bourquel had wielded tremendous power his entire adult life. She had absolutely no doubt that, however kindly, however charmingly he spoke, he meant literally every word he said about not letting her leave France without that reward.

Glancing surreptitiously at Ambassador Whittington, Kendra saw that his gaze was fixed intently upon her, and his patrician jaw was clenched. She could almost hear his perfect teeth gnashing as the silence spun out, strained and heavy. Clearly, international diplomacy, if nothing else, required that she accept the Bourquel's two-million-franc reward.

"Very well, Monsieur Bourquel. I accept." Reluctantly, Kendra replaced the check inside the black handbag, then snapped the clasp with a resounding click.

"I know Kendra greatly appreciates your wonderful gesture, Monsieur Bourquel, though, of course, she hadn't the faintest notion it was your grandson she was rescuing this afternoon." Ambassador Whittington rested his hand on Kendra's shoulder, his smile beaming approval. "She's the kind of citizen the U.S. is most proud to claim."

"Speaking of Rémy, is there any chance that I might see him before I go?" asked Kendra, sidling away from the ambassador. She was beginning to find the intricate dance of diplomatic words and gestures suffocating. "I'd like to say goodbye to him."

"But of course," said Laurent. "His nanny should be nearly finished helping him bathe and change his clothes."

"Ambassador Whittington kindly offered his private facilities," explained Nadine. She wrinkled her nose. "Rémy looked and smelled like a street urchin, poor darling."

"He suffered a horrible experience for a five-year-old boy," added Jean-Michel. "For anyone, really. Still, he has the resilience of youth and the Bourquel strength. He'll recover and forget quickly."

Kendra wanted to plead for huge measures of love, patience, and understanding to be added to Jean-Michel's prescription for normalizing Rémy's life. Some judicious spoiling and plenty of snuggling would also go a long way toward making the boy feel secure and happy again, she thought. But she bit down hard on her back teeth to keep from saying so aloud. Jean-Michel, Laurent, and Nadine were Rémy's family, after all. Surely, they would shower him with love and understanding once they had him safely ensconced back home.

A discreet knock announced Rémy's arrival, a uniformed nanny at his side. The transformation in his appearance was nothing short of miraculous. His hair was neatly combed, and his pale face was scrubbed to a shine. He wore a starched white shirt and white short pants with a navy blue linen blazer. White knee socks clung to his thin legs, and navy blue strap-on sandals to his feet.

Only his huge blue eyes tinged with sadness were the same.

Rémy walked up to his mother and kissed her on both cheeks before shaking hands with his father and grandfather. Kendra watched in amazement. No five-year-old child of her acquaintance was that reserved, that controlled, that grave. No parents or grandparents, either, for that matter.

The Bourquels spoke quietly with Rémy for a moment. Kendra's sense of unreality grew. The whole scene was so, so . . . *polite,* so formal, she could hardly believe she was watching a family reunion after traumatic circumstances. She simply had to be experiencing one of those weird, inexplicable culture gaps she'd warned the girls on her tour to be wary of judging negatively.

Still, she couldn't help thinking that if Remy had been her son, she'd be squeezing him tightly and covering him with kisses. She'd only known the boy a couple of hours, and she was fighting the urge to do just that this very moment. And no uniformed nanny would have bathed him, either. The privilege of bathing and examining every square inch of his precious little body to reassure herself of his physical well-being would have been a jealously guarded one.

"You must thank Mademoiselle Martin, Rémy," said Nadine.

"No more thanks are necessary. Really." Kendra bent down on one knee in front of Rémy, embarrassed by her limited French in the face of the Bourquels' perfect English. "I'm so sorry for everything that has happened to you the past few days, Rémy. I wish I could have met you a different way, but I want you to know that I think you're very brave."

"Brave?" Rémy hung his head. "No, Mademoiselle Martin, I cried very much at first. Then they hit me, and I was too afraid to cry."

Nadine gasped, but didn't say a word.

Kendra swallowed hard, trying to contain a violent upsurge of rage as images of abuse flooded her mind. She took a few deep, calming breaths. "Then I think you're not only brave, but smart."

"Smart?" Rémy sounded doubtful.

"Sure, by being quiet and patient you did exactly the right thing to protect yourself until someone could help you get away from those stupid people. That was very smart." Kendra held out her arms. "Do you think I could have a hug before we say goodbye, Rémy?"

The boy launched himself into her arms, hugging her tightly around the neck. "Thank you for saving me, Mademoiselle Martin."

"Believe me, Rémy, it was my pleasure. You're a

terrific kid, and I'm very proud to have met you." Kendra blinked rapidly several times, hoping to prevent the tears gathering in her eyes from spilling over. She rubbed his back, kissed him warmly on his cheek, and whispered in his ear. "Try hard to forget all the bad stuff, Rémy. Ride your pony, play with your friends, and just have a good rest of the summer, *d'accord?* All right?"

"Okay."

"Rémy, you're crushing Mademoiselle Martin," reproved the nanny. "Shake hands properly."

Kendra ignored the woman, cupping the boy's thin little face between both of her palms for a long moment, memorizing him. Then she stood, and let the nanny lead him from the room.

"Thank you for your kindness," said Nadine. "My son seems quite taken with you."

"The feeling is entirely mutual."

"I know that you must be anxious to return to your hotel," continued Nadine. "Ambassador Whittington has explained that you are chaperoning a group of young girls on a tour through France. But, please, before you go, my husband and I have an invitation for you."

"An invitation?"

"When your tour is completed, and the girls have returned home, we would love for you to spend a few weeks at our place in Normandy."

"Normandy." Surely, the woman wasn't serious, thought Kendra.

"We have a little seaside villa near Deauville," added Laurent.

"A villa." Kendra felt her palms begin to perspire

as she looked back and forth between Nadine and Laurent, noting their sincere, earnest expressions. Good lord, they *were* serious. She was being invited to go on vacation with one of the world's wealthiest families. The realization stunned her.

"And I can promise that even greater security measures will be in effect from now on, so you needn't fear for your safety. Really, I believe you would find it quite delightful. We have our own stretch of beach, the staff is very good, and the weather is generally most agreeable during the month of August."

"I'm sure I would find your villa . . . impeccable, Laurent." Kendra managed to stifle the nearly uncontrollable urge to laugh bubbling just beneath her surface composure.

Spend a few weeks at the family's seaside villa in Deauville? She could count on one hand the personal friends who could afford five days in a modest vacation condo once a year. And they didn't rent those condos in places like *Deauville*. Images of glittering casinos, elegant balls, *bellé époque* mansions, gentlemanly horse races, and the cream of high society frolicking in the sea unrolled behind her eyelids like scenes from some glamorous movie.

The yawning chasm between the Bourquels' lifestyle and her own was becoming more evident, more *real* to her, by the second.

Sure, she understood that the rich and famous were different. Her tour with the "daughters of privilege" had let her see first-hand the kind of comfort and luxury that affluence afforded. But people who routinely spent the entire month of August vacationing at a family villa in Deauville were more than affluent.

They were completely beyond her ken.

Knowing intellectually that there existed people so wealthy their children risked being kidnaped for ransom was one thing. Meeting them face-to-face was quite another.

Reading magazine articles about people who were important in the international scheme of things was a far cry from watching a U.S. ambassador do everything but jump through hoops to please them.

Wealthy industrialists who handed out two-million-franc rewards with the same aplomb they handed out designer original handbags were as foreign to Kendra as the food she had been eating, the sites she had been visiting, and the French she had been speaking for the past week.

"Can we take your silence for assent, Kendra?"

Laurent's question startled Kendra out of her musings.

"I'm afraid not." She held up her hand to stop the protestations she could see forming on Nadine's lips. "I took my vacation earlier in the summer with my family. Once I've escorted the girls home to California, I'll be back to my regular schedule at work."

"Perhaps your superior could be persuaded to give you a few more weeks of holiday," suggested Nadine.

Kendra thought of the promotion almost certainly awaiting her and shook her head. "Your invitation is very gracious, and I would love to see Normandy. But circumstances at work make this an inappropriate moment for me to ask for additional time off. I need to return home to my family, my job, my . . . life."

"We can certainly understand the demands of family and work," said Laurent, retrieving a silver card case from the inner breast pocket of his suit jacket. He proffered a square white card somewhat larger than a standard American business card. "But just in case you change your mind, please, take our private telephone numbers. You need only call to tell us the date and time of your arrival, and we'll arrange to have our driver meet you at de Gaulle."

"That's very kind, Laurent." Kendra slipped the white card inside her new handbag, more to keep as a souvenir than with any real intention of ever using the private telephone numbers printed across the front.

A round of polite handshakes and even more polite expressions of farewell followed. Then Kendra was escorted out of Ambassador Whittington's office by Jon Craig. She felt almost weak with relief. However interesting and different, her one encounter with the dignified rituals and elaborate courtesies of the diplomatic world was enough to last her a lifetime, she vowed.

"You did a great job in there, Ms. Martin," complimented Jon Craig, as they descended the massive carved marble stairway. "Even your initial reluctance to accept the Bourquels' check played well."

Kendra's eyes narrowed. "The desire to make a good impression was hardly the reason for my reluctance, Mr. Craig."

"No, no, of course not," he hastily assured her. "It's just that Jean-Michel Bourquel carries major clout, and the ambassador was a bit concerned that, well, that—"

"That a rank amateur might do or say something undiplomatic?"

"Exactly."

"Please remind the ambassador that American mothers still teach their children good manners," she said tartly. "And in this rank amateur's opinion, plain old-fashioned good manners result in appropriate behavior in any situation. Even diplomatic encounters."

Jon Craig shot her a sideways glance out of the corner of his eye. "Maybe you could just drop him a little note and tell him so yourself?"

Kendra chuckled. "No problem."

"Ambassador Whittington arranged for a staff car and driver to take you back to your hotel," he said as they reached the last step.

Kendra didn't respond. In fact, she didn't even hear him. Her whole attention was engaged by the sight of Jackson Randall in civilian clothing. One hard shoulder leaned against a marble pillar, and his arms were crossed over the wide expanse of his chest.

He was waiting. Clearly, patiently, unmistakably waiting.

Kendra felt a rush of exhilaration sweep through her body as she realized from the smile spreading over his face that he was waiting for her.

Chapter Four

"Everything go okay?" Jack pushed off from the pillar with a languid grace.

"Fine, just fine." The breathless, husky quality of her voice surprised Kendra, as did her pounding heartbeat. She had been sorry when circumstances denied her the chance to say goodbye to Jack and thank him for his help. But to feel such swift, sharp joy at seeing him again, well, that was something she hadn't expected and simply couldn't explain.

"Of course, if you've made other arrangements . . ." Jon Craig's speculative gaze moved between Kendra and Jack. "Ms. Martin?"

Kendra tried to control the flush she felt rising in her cheeks when she realized that he was waiting for a response. She'd been so intent on Jackson Randall, she hadn't even heard the question.

"I beg your pardon, Mr. Craig?"

"The staff car? To take you back to your hotel?" he prompted. "The car the ambassador ordered?"

"I'll see Ms. Martin safely to her hotel." Jack moved forward to slip one hand smoothly into position just above Kendra's elbow.

She felt his fingers curve around the delicate bare skin of her inner arm scant inches from her breast. A sinuous warmth stole through her body when he touched her. She suppressed a sudden urge to move closer to him, thinking that safe was the last word she would apply to Jackson Randall's effect upon her.

"Fine." Jon Craig turned to Kendra. "Well, then, Ms. Martin, goodbye and—"

"Please," groaned Kendra. "No more thank-yous."

"Actually, I was just going to suggest that you and Captain Randall avail yourselves of the staff car. Take a little evening tour of Paris before returning to your hotel. The car is equipped with a fully stocked bar, and you'll find that the ambassador keeps a nice brand of champagne chilled and ready." His eyes twinkled as he shook Kendra's hand. "If anyone deserves a small celebration after today's events, Ms. Martin, it is you."

"I really shouldn't. The girls are—"

"Perfectly capable of getting along without you for another hour," said Jack. "Especially with my guys keeping an eye on them."

"There is a phone in the car. You could call the girls and let them know your whereabouts," suggested the ambassador's aide.

"Great idea," said Jack. "Thanks, Craig."

"Enjoy." He waved once as he disappeared through a wide door on the right.

"Ready to leave?" asked Jack.

"More than ready," said Kendra with feeling.

"All that rarified air upstairs get to you?"

"I don't know about rarified, but there was certainly plenty of *hot* air."

Jack laughed. The deep, relaxed sound telling Kendra that he laughed often and easily.

"You'll have to tell me all about it." He gave Kendra's arm a gentle squeeze, then ushered her out of the embassy.

Hazy purple streaks were beginning to encroach upon the rose-gold sky, and a soft evening breeze muted the last rush-hour traffic noises. Kendra took a slow, deep breath, feeling the tension and stress of the last few hours begin to melt away and the magic of Paris begin to envelop her once more.

A long black limousine was waiting for them. U.S. flags flew from the front fenders, and a uniformed driver stood at attention beside an open door offering a tantalizing glimpse of the luxurious interior.

Jack whistled appreciatively.

Kendra took one look at the plush gray carpeting, deep leather seats, and high-gloss burlwood bar and felt her resolve weaken. The subtle gleam of chrome and a peak of high-tech plastic promised an array of state-of-the-art gadgetry that begged for examination at closer range.

"Well?" asked Jack.

"This *is* probably the only chance I'll ever have to ride in an ambassador's limousine."

"Staff car," teased Jack, urging her toward the

open door with a subtle movement of his hand on her arm. "You should see what they call a limousine around here."

"I suppose the girls wouldn't mind waiting just a *little* bit longer."

Jack chuckled. "How many more excuses do you need to dream up before you jump into that comfortable nest of a back seat?"

"Five or six ought to be enough."

"Wrong." Jack acknowledged the driver with a nod, ducked his head, and climbed into the limousine. Then he held up a familiar-looking blue document, waving it delicately between his thumb and forefinger. "I still have your passport, and I'm not giving it back until you get in here, share a glass of the ambassador's champagne, and tell me stories about Paris only a tour guide would know."

"That's blackmail."

"Persuasion. Just ask my sisters. The technique works perfectly on both of them." He sprawled back against the leather upholstery with a sigh of pleasure and patted the empty space next to him.

"You're forgetting one thing, Jack." Kendra eased into the limousine, leaving a careful space between them.

"Nope. I don't think so."

"Sure you are." She leaned forward and plucked her passport from his fingers. He had nice hands, she noted, strong-looking, with broad palms, long blunt-tipped fingers, and well-tended nails. A woman would enjoy having those hands shape her pleasure, she thought. A delicious shiver raced down her spine. A second shiver followed as she remembered his profession.

He was a marine, and those bare hands were also lethal weapons if he needed them to be.

"What am I forgetting?" asked Jack.

"You didn't say 'nyaa, nyaa, nyaa-nyaa, nyaa' in that particularly obnoxious way only brothers can manage."

"You sound like you speak from experience."

"Plenty. I have two brothers."

"Older than you are?"

"Younger . . . which was my only advantage when they hit a stage at about eleven or twelve years old where even my mother wanted to lock them in the closet until they reached maturity."

"And, of course, you never goaded them into any of the behavior you found so aggravating."

"We-ell, maybe once or twice. But any serious incitement came from my baby sister. I swear that from the time Kimmie was born, she knew exactly how to drive both Kyle and Kent straight up the wall. She could have them hollering and foaming at the mouth in about ten seconds flat. She still can."

Kendra's expression softened as she remembered the boisterous fun of her childhood, and the pleasure of the solid, loving relationships that existed today among the members of her family.

"Kendra, Kyle, Kent, and Kimmie?" Jack's carefully polite tone was at odds with the naughty glint in his eyes and the even naughtier expression spreading over his face. "And I suppose your parents are Kevin and Kathy?"

"Careful, that's the family honor you're treading on."

"Kurt and Kelly?"

"Better men have suffered for lesser insults." Despite her stern warning, Kendra was unable to prevent a wide grin from forming on her mouth.

"Kirby and Karen?"

"Kirk and Kristen," she capitulated in exasperation. "And we always thought it was neat to have names that started with the same letter. We thought our parents were brilliant to have thought of doing such a thing. Naturally, they did nothing to discourage our belief in their genius."

"Your family sounds nice, close."

"We are. Close, that is. As for nice, well, we have our moments."

"Such as?"

"You don't really want to hear all my family stories."

"I want to know everything about you, Kendra."

She was saved from responding when the privacy window opened with a low shushing sound, and the driver looked back. "I know your ultimate destination is the Inter-Continental Hotel, Ms. Martin, but is there a particular route you would like me to follow?"

"The longest route possible," murmured Jack in an undertone clearly meant for Kendra's ears alone.

She thought for a moment, innate caution at war with a budding excitement. He wanted to prolong the ride. He wanted to be alone with her. "Could you drive up the Champs-Élysées toward the Arc de Triomphe, then circle around L'Étoile once or twice?"

"Certainly. And after that?"

Kendra hesitated, unwilling to take undue advantage of the ambassador's generosity. On the other hand, Jon Craig had been the one to suggest an evening tour of Paris, and the temptation of doing so in Jack's company was a strong added incentive.

What harm could there be in a simple drive?

Yes, the man exercised a powerful allure she would have had to be dead to ignore, but surely the circumstances of their acquaintance neutralized the danger of that attraction. They were destined to remain friendly strangers. There was neither the time nor the opportunity for them to become anything else. She was too sensible, too responsible, too controlled to forget that fact, no matter how seductive a web Jackson Randall spun.

And no matter how much he was aided by the romantic, sensual ambiance of Paris at twilight.

"After that, head down the Quai d'Orsay and follow the Seine all the way to Notre Dame," continued Kendra in a more confident tone.

"You'll see a fair number of sights," confirmed the driver. "Shall I drive through the Latin Quarter as well? Or maybe go up to Montmartre? There's a splendid view of the city from the steps of Sacré Coeur."

"The view from Sacré Coeur sounds wonderful," she acknowledged with regret. "But I really don't have the time."

"I'll have you back at the Inter-Continental in an hour," he promised, handing her a laminated instruction sheet written in several languages. "This will explain how to use the bar and access the telephone or other amenities you might desire. Enjoy the ride."

The driver turned and started the ignition. As the engine purred to life, the privacy window closed with the same low shushing sound as before. The limousine slid out of the embassy gates and onto the streets of Paris.

Kendra felt suddenly shy at finding herself alone with Jack. She gripped the flat white box containing her new black handbag as though clinging to a lifeline. The limousine interior, which had only moments before appeared enormous, seemed to have shrunk to a space she could only describe as intimate.

The quiet was profound. She could hear Jack's deep rhythmic breathing above the soft hum of the limousine's powerful engine. The faint citrus tang of his after-shave mingled with the rich scent of the leather upholstery. And the tinted windows, while affording a perfect view of the colorful Parisian street scenes unfolding before them, also provided a sense of complete privacy, of isolation from the outside world.

She was intensely aware of Jack. Aware of the breadth of his hard shoulders filling out a lightweight cotton-knit sweater and the way the sweater's ivory color complimented his deep tan. Aware of his muscled torso narrowing to a tight waist and lean hips. Aware of the length and strength of his legs outlined by his charcoal denim jeans. Jeans that fit snugly because he was a big man at the peak of his physical power and fitness.

Aware, most of all, of the steady, still way he watched her, as though absorbing her every thought and emotion, and willing her to understand his.

Kendra backed down from the heat blazing to life in his sea green eyes. She looked away, pretending a keen interest in the view from her side of the limousine. There was too much feeling, too much honesty in his eyes. She might acknowledge in some hidden corner of her soul the intense attraction pulling at her. But she didn't dare allow herself to respond to, let alone encourage, a man she had met only hours before. A man about whom she knew virtually nothing . . . and was very probably seeing for the last time.

She was a sensible, practical, prudent woman.

Wasn't she?

"Relax." Jack finally broke the heavy silence. "If you clutch that box any tighter, your fingers are going to puncture the cardboard. What have you got in there, anyway? Government secrets?"

"No. The Bourquels insisted that I accept a reward." She opened the box and showed him the black handbag.

"Very classy. But I'm surprised."

"I was, too. I didn't expect a reward." She grimaced. "You can't imagine how awkward I felt accepting this, but Jean-Michel was adamant."

Jack shook his head. "That's not what I meant. People like Bourquel usually write checks as rewards."

Kendra blushed. "He did that, too."

"Why are you embarrassed? Rémy would still be kidnaped and in danger if not for you. Most people wouldn't have been so ready to involve themselves. I have a lot of respect for the kind of guts and caring you displayed today. You should simply enjoy the purse, and treat yourself to some nice little extravagance with the check."

"I suppose you're right," she murmured, warmed by his praise, but mortified to divulge the size of the check she'd been obliged to accept.

She hadn't even begun to consider the 'nice little extravagances' she could now afford. In fact, she hadn't dared to think at all about the ramifications of having three hundred and fifty thousand dollars. Just carrying around a check worth that much money made her nervous. She could scarcely imagine such a sum in her savings account, let alone in her purse.

No, she didn't intend to think about the ramifications of her windfall until later. Much, much later . . . when she could indulge in a nice little fit of hysteria all by herself. Right now, she wanted to think about the incredible luxury of seeing Paris by limousine.

So she wouldn't have to think about the disturbing effect Jackson Randall had on all her senses. Her good sense in particular.

"Look." Kendra pointed to the Arc de Triomphe, rising majestically from a high point on the Champs-Élysées.

The last rays of the setting sun painted the sky with a final burst of glowing colors. Pink and mauve, lemon and turquoise swirled together, creating a dramatic backdrop for the Arc's imperial dimensions and magnificent sculptures. The limousine slipped into the chaos of traffic racing in a circle around the monument.

The driver executed a fast, expertly maneuvered turn onto one of the twelve streets radiating out from the Arc like a star. Kendra braced herself against the seat with one forearm to keep her balance. Ahead, in the distance, the Eiffel Tower pierced the slowly darkening sky.

"This guy drives like an old man." Jack made a disgusted noise as several cars cut in front of the limousine. "He should have poured on the speed making that turn. And he should have pulled more sharply to the right."

"Are you crazy? Any faster on that turn and I would have been in your lap!"

A slow, lazy grin spread over Jack's face, softening the hard angle of his jaw. "Exactly."

That grin could make a woman forget all sense of time, place and propriety, mused Kendra, unnerved by her own immediately pleased response to his outrageous boldness. The man was just plain dangerous to a woman's peace of mind.

"I'd . . . I'd better call the girls."

"You do that," he said, a knowing light in his eyes.

Following the instructions on the laminated sheet, Kendra found herself talking to Mary Lee Taylor midway through the first ring.

"Kendra, are you okay? Is Rémy okay? What's going on? When are you coming back?"

The girl's excited tone and anxious questions reverberated loudly in Kendra's eardrums. She held the phone away from her ear a fraction of an inch, smiling indulgently.

"I'm fine, Mary Lee, and so is Rémy. He'd been kidnapped—"

"Kidnapped? That poor little kid!"

"He's had a frightening ordeal. But he's on his way home with his parents and grandfather now." Kendra touched Jack lightly on the arm to get his attention, pointing out the brilliant golden dome and large grassy esplanade that marked Les Invalides. "It's quite a story. I'll tell you everything when I get back to the hotel."

"When will that be?"

"No more than an hour," she promised the girl, feeling the corded muscles of Jack's upper arm bunch reflexively beneath her fingers. He was solid, and he was strong, with the kind of hard muscles that came from a lifetime of vigorous use, not a series of vanity workouts in a gym.

Jack slid closer to peer out the window on her side of the limousine, one hand braced against the burlwood bar, the other pressed knuckles down into the soft leather seat near her knee.

"Isn't Napoleon buried in Les Invalides?" He bent his head and whispered the question against her ear as she continued speaking.

Kendra nodded, trying desperately to maintain the thread of her conversation with Mary Lee. Jack's question was innocuous enough, but Jack's lips brushing her ear, his warm breath fanning the strands of hair on her temple, the husky vibrato of his voice all caused a riot of impure thoughts to crowd her mind. The knowledge that his strong hand could span the distance to her bare leg simply by uncurling his fingers made her pulse race.

"How are you girls doing?"

"Fine. We were just worried about you."

"Don't worry, sweetie. I'm fine." *Fine?* She sounded like she was strangling. She felt like she was strangling. If Jack didn't quit breathing in her ear, whispering questions and comments about the monuments along their route, she wouldn't have to worry about her conversation with Mary Lee. She would simply suffocate from the heady waves of excitement clogging her throat and lungs and be done with it. The French government could bury her in Les Invalides along with Napoleon.

"You sound weird, Kendra."

"Must be the cellular phone in the limousine—"

"Limousine! What—"

"Later, Mary Lee."

"Okay . . . umm, Kendra?"

"Yes." She could almost hear the girl's brain working. "Is Captain Randall still with you?"

"Ye-es." Kendra answered warily, hearing whispers and giggles in the background.

"Well, don't feel like you have to rush back or anything. Take your time. Everything's cool here. We're waiting for you in the suite, and the guys are out in the hall making sure no one bothers us."

"Good."

"So if you want to, like . . . go out, or . . . something. Well, that would be okay," she finished hastily.

Great, thought Kendra. Just what she needed. Twelve teenage matchmakers spinning romantic fantasies about her and Jack.

"No, thank you, Mary Lee."

"Are you sure?" "Positive," she said firmly.

"Okay. 'Bye."

"I assume from what I overheard that everything is quiet back at the hotel," said Jack.

Kendra simply nodded, embarrassed to tell him about the apparently unconditional imprimatur he'd just received from the "daughters of privilege." She watched the Palais Bourbon, seat of the French National Assembly, and the Musée d'Orsay, a renovated iron and glass railway station housing a luminous collection of French Impressionist paintings, flash by the limousine windows. The Louvre was rising in dignified splendor on the opposite bank off the Seine, and the lights were coming on in all the little cafés and bars that lined their route. They were nearly to Notre Dame and still her breathing was erratic and her senses were on full alert.

"Good, then let's tackle this bar." He bent forward, elbows propped on his knees, to inspect the formidable array of buttons displayed on the polished burlwood console in front of them. He pushed one button experimentally, and the lush strains of a classical symphony swirled around them.

"Nice sound system."

"Very nice," agreed Kendra, trying to ignore the vulnerable expanse of smooth warm skin exposed between Jack's shirt collar and his hairline. He had a fine neck, she noted, admiring the way the taut column rose from his wide muscled shoulders with a powerful yet elegant grace.

He pushed another button and a small refrigerated drawer divided into several compartments slid open. "Caviar and all the condiments, plus some kind of cocktail crackers. I'm glad to know my tax dollars are being well and tastefully spent. What next?"

"According to the instruction sheet, the red button on the left is supposed to unlock the brackets holding the liquor bottles and glasses in place."

"That does it all right." Jack glanced up, his grin turning rakish, almost taunting. "So, Kendra . . . what's your pleasure?"

Something in his voice, some brash, confident, unabashedly masculine quality challenged her femininity on a primal level. Challenged her in a way she'd never before experienced. A rising tension throbbed between them like an unspoken dare.

"What are you offering?"

"Champagne, Armagnac, vintage wine . . . something else?"

She settled back against the buttery soft upholstery, trying to contain the reckless, provocative mood he evoked in her. "Any other options?"

"Scotch, vodka, French mineral water, raspberry or pear *eau de vie, crème de menthe*. Shall I go on?"

"There's more?"

"There's probably more than you could handle."

"You'd be surprised at how much I could handle."

He gave her an assessing look. "You're right, I would be surprised."

"Then, to prove my capacity, I'll have . . . champagne."

He exhaled sharply. "For a young woman, you live dangerously."

"Because I'm about to drink a glass of champagne?"

Jack didn't respond. Instead, he peeled the dark green foil off the top of the champagne bottle and removed the wire entwined beneath. He gripped the bottle securely between his knees. His gaze met Kendra's, holding her attention captive by the sheer unyielding force of his will.

"Careful," he said softly. "Popping corks can be dangerous."

A perverse inner devil made her disregard the layers of warning, the double meaning she discerned beneath his words. "Don't worry. I'm willing to bet that the windows are bullet-proof."

"The trick is to exert enough . . . control, at just the right . . . juncture." As he spoke, he twisted the cork smoothly out of the bottle in one easy motion. The delicate fragrance of good champagne seeped into the air with a small pop and a slight fizz. "Of course, experience helps."

"You've opened a lot of champagne bottles?" Kendra swallowed hard, her mouth going dry at the string of seductive images Jack's words evoked. She found it entirely too easy to imagine the kind of control he undoubtedly possessed in bed. And the kind of experience.

The man packed a physical and emotional wallop that could devastate a far more experienced woman than herself. Even on a scant few hours' acquaintance, she knew with instinctive certainty that a relationship with Jack would be deep, all consuming, and enticingly, dangerously intimate. And though she had far fewer relationships to her credit than most women her age, she knew that it would be intensely satisfying, as well.

"I'm thirty-five years old. Let's just say I've had my share of 'bubbly.' "

"I'll bet," she murmured, accepting a thin crystal flute from him and raising it to her lips. His hand shot out and gripped her wrist, forcing the glass away from her mouth.

"We haven't made a toast yet."

"Oh, by all means. We *must* have a toast."

"Kendra, do you have any idea how much this

champagne costs?"

"Um, no, Jack. I can't say as I do. I recognize the name on the label, but unlike you," she said sweetly, "I'm only twenty-seven—nowhere near the connoisseur you evidently are."

"Then trust me when I say that the champagne in this bottle is as worthy of a toast as any champagne you or I will ever see in our lifetimes."

"Should we drink, or genuflect?"

"We should toast."

She raised her glass and said lightly, "Cheers."

"Some poor monk spent his life in a cave to develop champagne, and that's all the better you can do?" Jack shook his head. "How about we drink to good fortune?"

Kendra squirmed in her seat. Somehow the idea of toasting two million francs bordered on the obscene, even if Jack didn't know the size of the check in her new handbag.

"I guess that's as good a toast as any." She raised the glass to her lips once more.

"Excuse me, but I'm not done yet."

"Excuse *me*, I hadn't realized marines could be so long-winded. I thought you guys were all supposed to be men of action."

"We are. But sometimes the best form of action is slow, careful, and deliberate." Jack's gaze roamed the contours of Kendra's face, lingering for a long moment on her mouth. Then he cleared his throat and with a serious demeanor, spoke again.

Chapter Five

"To good fortune," toasted Jack. "Rémy's, because your intervention saved his life and returned him to his family. Mine, because I've had the opportunity to meet you. Yours—"

"Because I get a quiet hour away from the girls?" Kendra interrupted in a rush, afraid of what he might say. Afraid of the emotion she read in his eyes, afraid of the increasingly strong physical magnetism sizzling between them like live wires.

Just plain afraid of the way this man made her feel.

"Because I'm a fighting man, not a Romeo," he said. "You'd be irresistible temptation to a man with romance on his mind."

"Fighting men don't appreciate romance?" She made her question light and whimsical in an attempt to cool the sweet heat flowing between them.

"Fighting men are interested in more basic instincts."

78

"Survival." She nodded sagely, deliberately misunderstanding.

"That's one of them. Other instincts make me want things I have no business wanting from a pretty tourist." He rotated his glass slowly between his fingers, watching the bubbles rise to the surface. "Does that shock you?"

"A little," she admitted.

"Don't worry. I'm good at resisting temptation. And it's been a long time since I found sport . . . loving the least bit satisfying."

Kendra sucked in her breath. "You're blunt."

He shrugged. "Like I said, I'm no Romeo."

She raised her champagne flute in silent salute. Jack touched his glass lightly to hers. The clear ringing tones of crystal clinking against crystal hung in the air.

Kendra watched him tilt back his head and drink, her attention riveted by the strong column of his throat as he swallowed. He licked a small residue of champagne from his upper lip with his tongue, and a strange unsolicited excitement built in her.

She wanted to jump out of the car, run away, do anything to stop the onslaught of sensual feelings besieging her. And she wanted equally as much to lean over and lick the moisture from his lips herself, feel with the tip of her own tongue the steady pulse beating in the warm hollow at the base of his neck.

Appalled at the direction of her thoughts, she took a quick draft from her own glass, sputtering a little as it went down the wrong way.

Jack groaned. "Don't do this to me, Kendra."

"Do what?" she managed to gasp between coughs.

"Make me take you in my arms strictly to perform one of those lifesaving maneuvers you laid on Rémy this afternoon."

Kendra laughed, relieved at the chance to recover both her breath and her equilibrium . . . agitated by the thought of being held in Jack's arms.

He removed the tin of caviar from its chilled compartment, scrutinizing the label. "Some beluga with your champagne?"

She made a gagging noise. "If you open that tin, I'm pushing you into the street. I've lived in a coastal village all my life—"

He gave a derisive hoot. "Village?"

"And I *still* get sick to my stomach at low tide. Believe me, I have no desire to sample canned fish eggs of any sort."

"Village, yeah right. I read an article in a recent golf magazine that described Carmel as the 'Monaco of California.' "

Golf? Kendra swallowed a giggle. This big, rugged marine played golf? Rugby, rock-climbing, kick-boxing, bungee-jumping, even tractor pulls, she could believe. But the thought of Jack Randall striding around the links wearing plaid knickers, a sherbet-colored cardigan, and two-toned oxfords with fringed tassles was nothing short of hilarious.

"Carmel may be the 'Monaco of California' to

tourists and golfing fanatics, but it's still just home to me," she informed him. "And for the record, I think you were extremely nosy to snoop through my passport extracting personal information while waiting for your boss to confirm that I wasn't an ax murderer on the lam."

"We've already established that I'm bold, honey." His expression was unrepentant as he flipped the tin of caviar back into its slot.

"No beluga for you, either?"

"I'm an Oklahoma boy. Except for the occasional tuna sandwich, I'm not big on fish. I'm more partial to beef."

Boy? Hah. Kendra took a small sip of champagne. She'd never seen so much *man* in her whole life. She chanced a surreptitious glance at Jack from under her lashes.

He was tucking a clean cocktail napkin imprinted with ambassadorial insignia into the back pocket of his jeans. The action pulled the denim fabric even more snugly across his powerful thighs.

"You collect napkins?" she teased; trying not to stare. Looking led to wanting. And wanting led to trouble.

He colored. "My mom would get a kick out of hearing her son rode around Paris in the ambassador's limo. I'll send her the napkin next time I write. Now, tell me, do you travel to Paris often?"

"I've only been to Paris once before, about three years ago. And this is the first time I've escorted a tour with a stop here."

"I thought travel agents were constantly on the go seeing the world in first-class luxury at cut-rate prices."

"There are some nice perks," she acknowledged. "But the job sounds a lot more glamorous and exotic than it really is. I actually spend most of my time poring over maps, brochures, and airline schedules, or on the phone trying to confirm a reservation of one kind or another."

"No wonder you sound as familiar with Paris as a taxi driver. I've been here three months, and I still spend half my time lost."

"I put in a lot of overtime planning every aspect of this trip. I made a special point of learning my way around," explained Kendra. "At least on paper."

"Any special reason for all the extra work, apart from the obvious one of wanting to do a good job?"

"Self-defense. Chaperoning teenage girls through France is no mean feat. I thought superior knowledge would help even the odds."

"They seem like nice girls, but with twelve of them, I can see where you'd want every possible advantage on your side."

"Especially since my boss's only daughter is part of the tour." Kendra gave him a rueful smile. "Not only that, but since becoming assistant manager of my branch office, I don't escort many tours anymore. I wanted to remind my boss that I had sharp road skills, as well as administrative ability."

"Sounds like you're planning to ask for a raise."

"Actually, it's a promotion I'm after. I'd love to manage the Monterey office of Let's Go Travel. The current manager is going to retire in September."

What was it about Jack that made her feel comfortable telling him the personal details of her life as though they'd been friends for years, she wondered bemusedly?

"My boss has promised me a decision when I get home," she added.

"Better take good care of his daughter between now and then," advised Jack with a quick grin. "How much longer will you be in France?"

"Paris is our last stop. We'll be here tomorrow and Friday. We leave Saturday afternoon."

"Will you have dinner with me at least once before you go?"

"No, but I'll leave you my phrase book which has a huge section on ordering in a restaurant."

"Your vocabulary isn't the reason I want to have dinner with you."

"Even if I wanted to—"

"Do you?" His expression hardened.

Kendra watched, mesmerized as the face of a warrior emerged from the lean planes and handsome angles of his face. The unusual misty green color of his eyes glittered with a stormy light. His lips narrowed to a hard, unyielding line. The thrust of his jaw became aggressive. His whole expression was set, demanding, relentless.

There was more, much more, to Jackson Randall than met the eye, she realized. Despite his easy-going manner, this was not a man to play with.

He was lean, fit, and implacable, the perfect embodiment of a twentieth century warrior.

She suspected that his passions ran deep and hot. His woman would never go hungry for sensual pleasure. And his military training aside, he would be a dangerous man in a fight. Kendra's breath caught in her throat as all that raw power and intensity was focused on her.

"Answer me."

"What I want is beside the point. I *can't* have dinner with you—"

"Are you engaged, or involved?"

"How do you know I'm not married?"

He grabbed her left hand in both of his, rubbing his thumb over her ring finger. "You strike me as the kind of woman who wouldn't take off her wedding ring even to wash her hands."

"No, I wouldn't," she agreed, amazed at his insight. "And I'm not engaged, or involved, either, but that's beside the point."

"That's exactly the point. You're free. I'm free. There's nothing stopping us from seeing each other."

"Jack, I don't have time for a date. And I'm not at all sure it would be appropriate for me to accept one, given my responsibilities to the girls."

"Do you have to spend every waking minute with them?"

"Once I return to the hotel, yes."

"You're being unreasonable—"

"I'm being practical. Two-and-a-half days is barely long enough to cram in all the sight-seeing I have planned."

"Skip something."

"I can't. This isn't a vacation for me. Making sure these girls get the most out of their trip is my job!"

He was silent for a moment. Then, he said grudgingly, "So, tell me about this jam-packed itinerary of yours."

"I've scheduled one of what the girls call my 'death marches' tomorrow. We start early with a walking tour of the Latin Quarter, go on to the Cluny Museum to see the unicorn tapestries and the Roman baths, then grab a quick bite of lunch."

"Is that when you call for ambulances to resuscitate those poor kids?"

"No," said Kendra, laughing. "That's when we catch the Métro to the Île de la Cité to see Notre Dame and Sainte-Chapelle. The stained glass windows are best seen with the late afternoon sun streaming through. Afterward—"

"There's more?"

"Just dinner and bedtime. I have a day trip to Versailles planned for Friday."

"Sounds exhausting. I hope you're planning to let the girls sleep in on Saturday morning."

"Not a chance. The girls can sleep all they want on the plane home. In fact, I hope they do." Kendra shuddered delicately, remembering the near pandemonium of the trip over.

Jack shook his head. "If you could only manage to sound mean, fierce, and merciless, you'd have real potential as a marine drill instructor."

Kendra watched the remaining blocks to her hotel slide rapidly by with a sense of regret. She hadn't realized how much she'd missed adult company while on tour with the girls. Jack's quick intelligence and lively, teasing humor made her wish she had another forty-five minutes to spend getting to know him. The sexual electricity charging the air between them made her wish she could somehow manage to carve out the time to have dinner with him.

Both wishes were suppressed with ruthless self-control.

She could spend the remainder of her time in Paris getting to know Jackson Randall, and it wouldn't matter in the least. She could let her initial attraction develop into a real liking for the man. Hell, she could fall head over heels in love with him, and the essential stumbling block around which her deepest regret focused would remain.

She and Jackson Randall lived separate lives on opposite sides of the world. However much she might wish otherwise, the immense unexpected affinity pulsing between them from the moment they'd met would simply have to remain unexplored.

The limousine pulled up in front of her hotel. A wave of muggy heat surged into the backseat as the driver opened Kendra's door and stood a discreet distance away.

"I guess this is goodbye." She turned awkwardly to Jack, unsure of what to say, reluctant to leave now that the moment for doing so had arrived.

"It doesn't have to be goodbye," he said with quiet intensity.

Common sense warred with uncommon attraction . . . and won.

"I've enjoyed meeting you, Jack. I can't thank you enough for your help today. I wish . . . I wish we'd met under different circumstances." Impulsively, she leaned forward and brushed his hard cheekbone with her lips. His skin was warm, the stubble of his afternoon beard prickly. She inhaled one last fragrant breath of his citrusy after-shave, then slid across the seat toward the door.

"Kendra . . ."

Jack reached for her hand, but she slipped her fingers from his grasp without comment, afraid to meet his gaze, afraid of the undisguised interest she knew would be written plainly across his face. Hurriedly, she thanked the driver and entered the hotel.

She didn't give a single backward glance. She simply didn't dare.

Kendra gave a sigh of relief as she closed the door on the last of her charges. She curled up in a Louis-something chair upholstered in blue satin damask and let her gaze roam the elegantly appointed sitting room of her suite.

It was a pretty room, cozy, and inviting despite the formal decor. Watered silk in a pale buttery yellow covered the walls. The high ceiling with its delicate crown molding created an airy framework for the furnishings within. A dainty escritoire set along one wall was a perfect place to write postcards, while the artfully arranged sofas and chairs, all reproduction period pieces, had proved surprisingly comfortable.

There was a mini-bar replenished twice daily with soft drinks, liquor, and cocktail snacks. A high-resolution television was hidden within a converted armoire. An extravagant floral arrangement of pink rubrum lilies, white tuberoses, deep purple irises, and trailing ivy graced a marble-topped bombe chest, scenting the night air with a heady perfume.

Voile sheers fluttered beneath blue and gold brocade drapes hung from the tall windows overlooking the Rue de Rivoli several floors below and the Tuileries gardens across the street. Kendra had opened the windows earlier, not so much for the fresh air as to drink in the sounds and smells of Paris after dark. Now she took a deep breath and willed herself to relax.

The girls had been unremitting in their questions, refusing to leave until they'd grilled her about every last detail of her activities from the moment they'd left her until the moment she'd returned. For the most part, Kendra had complied.

She'd explained in detail about Rémy's kidnaping and recounted her meeting with the ambassador and Rémy's family. She'd shown them her new handbag and the reward check, watching the awe spread across their faces as they translated the francs into dollars. She'd described the limousine tour of Paris right down to the champagne and cellular telephone. The only details she hadn't shared were the specifics of her encounter with Jackson Randall.

Her attraction to him was a private matter. She hadn't entirely come to grips with her feelings in the depths of her own mind. She certainly didn't feel like discussing her unruly emotions with twelve rabidly curious teenaged girls—no matter how probing their questions and comments on the subject. Unfortunately, details about her and Jackson Randall were what the "daughters of privilege" wanted most to hear. And they hadn't been shy in their attempts to ferret out information.

She grinned suddenly, considering Jack's probable response if he'd heard himself described as "sort of a hunk for an old guy." He was definitely a hunk for a guy any age.

Kendra shifted her position in the chair, one foot bobbing up and down in a jerky rhythm. She should probably be in bed, considering the extensive sightseeing on tomorrow's itinerary. But now that she had peace, quiet, and solitude, she was too keyed up, too restless to sleep.

She recognized that her flustered emotions were partly the result of the day's extraordinary events. But she was honest enough to admit that her anxious, edgy, unable-to-relax, state was primarily a lingering response to Jackson Randall.

The man had woven a spell of attraction around her that she couldn't seem to break. And worse, she wasn't sure she wanted to.

Kendra leaned forward to select a ripe plum from a huge basket of fresh fruit resting on the coffee table. She sank her teeth clear to the pit, enjoying the contrast between sweet, pulpy flesh and sharp, tangy skin. She'd been right to turn down Jack's invitation to dinner. If she felt this way after a simple drive, she didn't even want to think about the state of her nerves following a quiet, romantic meal.

Tossing the pit into a crystal ashtray, she licked plum juice from her fingers and picked out a handful of plump raspberries. She popped them into her mouth one after another like candies.

A glint of gold and the sheen of expensive leather caught her attention. The girls had left her new black handbag on the sofa. She dug Jean-Michel's check out of the inside zippered pocket, staring once more at the neat row of zeros, so many zeros. Maybe the money would seem real once it was converted into dollars.

Which posed another problem.

Where exactly did an American citizen without a French bank account go to cash a check this size? And just how did one go about doing so?

And that check was only the beginning.

She was absolutely loath to lug around three hundred and fifty thousand dollars in cash for the remainder of the trip. Worrying, about losing it.

Or having it stolen. Or even worse, that one of the girls would get hurt in some way because she was carrying around such an enormous sum of money. No, she would simply wait until she returned home to attend to the details of her reward.

Other questions spun in her head. Did she have to pay income tax on her reward? Had she really done the right thing by accepting the money in the first place?

Kendra shuddered. The entire situation was impossible.

Last week the fifty-dollar bill her parents had pressed on her at the airport with the admonition to "buy yourself something nice" had seemed like a fortune. She'd spent the money in her head a hundred times before deciding on a small bottle of her favorite fragrance, a rich scent of lilies, roses, and jasmine. She'd worn the fragrance as cologne on special occasions since college, but until her parents' generous gift, she'd never dreamed of buying the perfume. Even with the hefty discount and favorable exchange rate offered by the tax-free boutique on the Rue de Rivoli, the tiny crystal flacon had cost every penny of her parents' fifty dollars.

But she'd thoroughly enjoyed every second of the purchase.

Now, here she was with a check for two million francs in a designer original purse that had probably cost more than her car, and she was worrying herself silly. She should be giddy with joy. She should be planning a shopping spree. She should be pacifying her nerves with something lots more exotic than fresh fruit.

The buzz of the European-style telephone broke her train of thought.

"Hi."

"Jack." Kendra felt her heart lurch at the sound of his voice.

"I'm in the lobby. Come out with me."

"Are you crazy? It's midnight!"

"So what? This is Paris. They don't roll up the sidewalks at ten p.m. We'll go for a walk along the Seine, have coffee or a drink in some quaint left-bank cafe, and we'll talk."

She was tempted. Lord, was she tempted. What woman in her right mind wouldn't love a midnight stroll through one of the most romantic cities in the world? Especially with a man like Jackson Randall for an escort. His strength ensured her safety. Everything else about the man guaranteed her entertainment.

"I can't leave the girls here all by themselves."

"They're not babies, Kendra. Come down and join me for a nightcap in the lounge."

"I can't. One of the girls might wake up and need me for something. They'd be upset if I wasn't in my room."

"Okay, I'll come up and see you."

"That's not a good idea. I was just getting ready for bed. I've already put on my nightgown—"

"Not exactly a dissuading argument."

"Will you be serious?"

"I'm being completely serious. I start a twenty-four-hour shift tomorrow morning at six a.m., you're taking the girls to Versailles all day the next day, the day after that you're leaving. When am I supposed to see you again?"

"Maybe seeing each other again isn't such a good idea, Jack. I'm grateful for your help with Rémy this afternoon—"

"Screw grateful. I want—"

"And I really enjoyed the limousine ride with you, but—"

"Dammit, Kendra, will you give a guy a break?"

"It just seems so . . . so pointless, Jack."

"Kendra, I'm not suggesting an orgy of perverted sex. I just want a chance to talk to you."

"I don't know." She could feel herself weakening.

"Aren't the girls all fast asleep in their own rooms?"

"Yes," she admitted.

"Then, where's the harm in letting me come up for a sedate nightcap and some simple conversation?"

Kendra didn't immediately respond.

"Quit stalling. We *need* to talk." He paused. "Unless, I've misunderstood . . . unless, I'm way off base. If you really don't *want* to see me, just say so. I'll hang up. You won't hear from me again."

Kendra sensed both pride and vulnerability in his brusquely clipped syllables.

"So, what's it going to be?" he asked stiffly. "Shall I come up, yes or no?"

"I . . . want to see you. Room 714."

"I'll be there in five minutes."

Kendra raced into the bedroom to change out of her nightgown and robe, not daring to question her actions, her motives, or her sanity in agreeing to see Jackson Randall once more.

Hastily, she donned clean underwear, a pair of linen slacks in a rich persimmon color, and a thin silk shirt in pale peach. With shaking fingers, she tore the wrapping off her new bottle of perfume and stroked some behind her ears and in the valley between her breasts. She had just finished running a brush through her hair and slipping her feet into her leather flats when she heard a peremptory knock. Swallowing nervously, she crossed to the sitting room and opened the door to admit Jack.

He filled the doorway.

Light from the outside corridor burnished his dark hair with bronze highlights. He was wearing the same clothes as before. The charcoal denim jeans still hugged his muscular thighs, and the ivory knit sweater still emphasized his deep tan. He'd shaved and reapplied the citrusy after-shave she had liked so much earlier, but that was the only change she could discern.

"Planning to keep me out in the hallway while we talk?" he asked in a husky voice.

She blushed and shook her head, opening the door wider and motioning him inside. "I was just wondering how you acquired that tan in Paris."

"I didn't. My last tour of duty was a one-year stint in a Middle Eastern desert."

She wrinkled her nose. "Sounds like fun."

"Oh, loads. I slept on a cot in the sand the last six months. An improvement over the first six, I should add, when we didn't even have cots. No booze, no women, no privacy. But plenty of sand, wind, heat, and enough sun to burn a tan seven layers deep. It'll probably take the rest of my life to wear off." He raked a hand over his short hair and flashed her a nervous smile. "Help me out here. I'm babbling like an awkward teenager on his first date."

"Please, let's not talk about teenagers," she said with feeling, closing the door behind him.

He laughed. Then he moved more fully into the room and looked around. "Fancy digs. Is this one of the perks you were talking about?"

She shrugged. "The girls' parents chose this hotel because of its location for sight-seeing, as well as for its safety. I'm just along for the ride."

"Don't knock it. This suite sure beats a cot in the desert. Besides, I have a feeling you earn whatever perks come your way."

Kendra walked over to the mini-bar. "Would you like something cold to drink? There must be twelve different kinds of beer in here."

"Is that what you're having?"

"Actually, I'm crazy about this particular brand of orange soda. We don't have it in the States." She held the bottle out, turning it so he could see the label. "I swear it tastes like freshly squeezed juice, only carbonated."

"Sure, I'll try some."

He came to stand beside her, close enough so that she could feel the warmth radiating from his skin. She held her breath as he reached for the bottle, anticipating the brush of his fingers where their hands would touch. Instead, he gripped the bottle around its base, leaving her oddly disappointed when he pulled it from her hand without touching her and moved slightly away.

"There's nuts and some chips if you feel like a snack," she offered.

"No."

She took a sip of her soda. "So, Jack, what exactly do you do in the Marines?"

"I fight."

"And when you're not fighting?"

"I teach other men to fight."

"I see."

"I doubt it. Most civilians 'see' the military in terms of patriotic hoopla, or get all hung up in philosophical discussions of war and peace." He tipped the bottle, draining half the soda in one deep swallow. "Look, I didn't come up here to discuss my military career."

"What *would* you like to discuss?"

"I think you have a damn good idea. Can we please stop dancing around each other and talk? Talk honestly?"

She nodded. "Okay."

"Sit down, you're making me nervous."

"I'm not the one prowling the room like a restless animal."

"Listen, I am not good at this. It's been too

damn long since I've been involved with a woman. Too damn long since I've been with a woman, period. Now, here we are alone, and there are things I want to tell you, want to ask you." He jammed his hands into the pockets of his jeans and continued pacing. "But you look beautiful, you smell great, and I know if I touch you, you'll feel as soft and as sweet as every hot dream I ever had in my life. All I can think about is how much I'd like to . . . hell, I *feel* like a goddamned restless animal."

Her eyes widened, and she took a step back, not in fear, but because his intensity was so powerful, so startling. Desire, stark and unashamed blazed in his eyes.

"Don't be afraid. Not of me. Not ever."

Her chin came up, and she faced him squarely. "I'm not afraid of you. I'm . . . surprised."

"How could you be surprised?" He stared at her. "What did you think was going on in that limousine? Hell, from the first minute I spoke to you in that fast food joint? You trusted me. I protected you. I would have protected you with my life, if necessary. We were strangers, yet at some basic gut level, we connected. I don't know what to do about that fact. And I don't like the feeling."

"There's nothing to do. Whatever 'connection' you think you felt was a function of potential danger and adrenaline."

"Don't play games with me, Kendra. We don't have time for games."

"What do you want from me?"

"For starters, I want you to admit that you feel the same sense of connection I do, that you're as interested as I am in seeing how deep it goes."

"And if I do? What then? We live five thousand miles apart, and I'm going home in two days. The things you're saying, Jack, it's too much, too fast and given our circumstances, it's all wrong."

"No, what's wrong is that I don't have the time and the opportunity to go slow with you. I want to ask you out for friendly lunches, proceed to museum outings and walks in the park, advance to intimate dinners. I want to take you dancing. I want to *savor* the experience of getting to know you, not rush through it like a starving dog falling on a meaty bone."

She spread her hands in a helpless gesture. "Maybe we can write, call each other occasionally. If you ever get to California—"

"I don't want a goddamn pen pal!"

Kendra set her jaw at a stubborn angle. "That's why we're going to wish each other well and say good night."

He set his soda bottle on an end table and closed the distance between them with sure smooth steps. "No, Kendra. I don't think so."

"No?" she whispered, her throat tight with emotion.

Jack didn't answer. He reached out his hand and threaded his fingers through her hair, cupping the nape of her neck in a gentle embrace. His hand was warm and strong, and the pleasurable friction of his thumb rubbing the sensitive skin behind her ear could all too easily become arousal.

Kendra closed her eyes and swayed toward him. His grip tightened, and she thought, she hoped, he was going to kiss her. Her mouth softened in readiness. Instead, he drew a ragged breath, released his grip, and let the strands of her hair slip slowly through his fingers.

"We're going to spend some time together in the next two days. I don't know how. I don't know when. But we're not just going to say goodbye and go our separate ways like—"

"Strangers?" she suggested, wryly.

"Kendra, I promise you this. Whatever else we may be when you get on that plane Saturday afternoon, we *won't* be strangers."

Chapter Six

A soft but persistent tapping brought Kendra fully awake in an instant. She squinted at her travel alarm, trying to make out the numerals in the pale gray pre-dawn light. Five o'clock. She groaned, tempted to ignore the continued knocking, roll over, and go back to sleep.

Instead, she tossed off the summer-weight blanket and grabbed her cotton batiste robe. She stumbled barefoot to the door, contemplating a number of dire consequences if one of the girls wasn't dying at the very least. Wrenching open the heavy door, she reminded herself to be patient.

"Good morning, beautiful."

"*Beautiful?* Jack, do you have any idea what time it is?" Even to her own ears, the sounds coming out of her mouth sounded a lot like impatient shrieks.

"You wake up a little cranky, huh? I'll make a note of that fact for future reference."

Kendra began closing the door in his face.

"Not so fast." He gripped the edge of the door

with one hand and pushed it back open with ease. "I'm actually here on official business."

"At five in the morning, you'd better be carrying a message from the president. An important message." Kendra stepped aside to let him enter the suite. She shivered in the early morning chill, her nipples puckering against the thin fabric of her nightgown and robe.

Jack handed her a crisply folded copy of the International Herald Tribune and a white paper cone emitting narrow ribbons of steam fragrant with the aroma of warm *brioches*. Her stomach rumbled with hunger and saliva pooled in her mouth. She loved *brioches,* preferring the yeasty butter-and-egg rolls even over the flaky *croissants* she'd been consuming by the dozen across France.

"Official business?" She raked her hand self-consciously through her hair. A tangled mess, she confirmed, realizing with dismay that she hadn't brushed her teeth or washed her face, either. Nothing like appearing her best to boost a woman's confidence.

"Check out page one, the article in the left-hand column." Jack settled himself comfortably in a wingback armchair, one ankle resting on his knee.

Kendra watched him, struck once more by his compelling presence. He was vital, physical, and wholly male. And he was handsome, so handsome, with his high cheekbones, square jaw, and sea-green eyes. He looked good in his uniform, too. The light khaki shirt hugged his wide shoulders like a lover, and the short sleeves displayed a tantalizing glimpse of hardened biceps and well-developed forearms. The flat khaki rectangle of his hat was tucked into a waistband that emphasized his tight belly and lean hips. And even at this ungodly hour, he was wide awake and smiling in a way that was dangerous to any woman with a pulse.

She set the paper and the *brioches* on the coffee table and knotted the sash of her robe more securely around her waist, aware of her own quickened heartbeat. Even more aware of the fact that beneath her robe and nightgown she was completely bare. "I'm going to order coffee from room service. Would you like some?"

He checked his watch, then shook his head. "I'll be gone before it arrives. I've got to be on duty at the embassy in a little while. I wouldn't say no to one of those little muffins, though."

Kendra chuckled. "They're called *brioches*, Jack."

"Whatever, just toss me one . . . make that two."

"Help yourself." Kendra handed him the paper cone, watching him demolish a couple of *brioches* in the time it took her to order her coffee. "I'll just be a minute changing."

She realized her error as soon as the words were out of her mouth.

Jack's gaze, which had been focused on her face, began a long, slow descent. He surveyed her figure with the expertise of a connoisseur, the tenderness of a lover, and a brazen familiarity that was uniquely his own.

Kendra knew that her ankle-length robe and nightgown were modest. No plunging neckline, no thigh-high slit, just softly flowing folds of pastel blue batiste that hinted at the curves of her body without overtly revealing them. Yet she felt Jack's scrutiny like an intimate caress against her naked skin. He looked at her in a way that made her feel both vulnerable and eager to learn the secret pleasures promised by his knowing smile.

A yielding warmth stole the rigid posture from her body. She felt a softening, a sweetness, a blossoming of emotion she was afraid to name, but couldn't deny. And when she noted the sudden clenching of his jaw, the small tic in the sharply cut plane beneath his cheekbone, she felt the first delicate tendrils of desire begin to unfurl in the pit of her stomach.

He wanted her. And he was making her want him. The sudden heat, the wetness between her thighs both stunned and embarrassed her.

"Don't bother changing. You look fine the way you are." The timbre of his voice was low and husky. "Just take a look at the paper, so I can be on my way before I do something . . . intemperate."

Self-consciously, Kendra seated herself in a corner of the sofa angled next to Jack's chair. She tucked her bare feet up under the folds of her robe and began reading aloud from the column Jack had indicated. Her voice was calm and steady, a slight waver the only hint of the sensual tumult

Jack had stirred in her.

" 'Industrialist's Grandson Rescued. . . .' " Kendra looked up, aghast. "Oh, my God, it's about Rémy."

"Keep reading."

> Kendra Martin, a California travel agent on holiday with a group of twelve American teenagers, played a major part in the rescue. Thanks to the detailed descriptions provided by Ms. Martin and her charges, the kidnappers were apprehended within fourteen hours of Rémy Bourquel's rescue. The Bourquel family is alleged to have rewarded Ms. Martin with the much-publicized reward of two million francs, previously offered for information leading to the boy's return.

Jack smiled. "Similar versions of the same story will appear today in all the major newspapers. I understand that when the reporter telephoned the embassy, Jon Craig took the call himself. He had an advance copy of the newspaper delivered to my quarters a little over an hour ago with instructions to make sure you received the good news."

"I had the feeling when we met that Jon Craig wasn't quite as innocuous as he appeared."

"Smart woman."

"Care to elaborate?"

"No."

Jack's briskly clipped denial and forbidding expression told Kendra everything she needed to know about Jon Craig.

"Well, tell him I send hugs of thanks the next time you see him."

"The *brioches* were *my* idea. Are you going to hug me, too?"

Masculine challenge shimmered in the air between them. Kendra allowed herself to dwell for exactly three seconds on his suggestion, a suggestion she found shockingly tempting. "I liked your subtlety right from the start, Jack."

"Give me half a chance, and I'll make sure you find a lot of things to like about me."

"Your modest and self-deprecating ways, perhaps?"

"My honesty. You may not always like what I say, but you'll know what I think and how I feel, and you'll always know where you stand. Starting right now." Rising from his seat, he closed the distance between them in one smooth step.

He gripped her shoulders between his strong hands, his face so close there was nowhere to look but into each other's eyes. "I'm interested. I've been interested since the moment we met. I'm interested enough to risk being late for duty, no minor infraction given my rank and my embassy posting. I'm interested despite the ridiculous circumstances of time and place in which we find ourselves. But, Kendra, I'm just going to ask you one more time. Will you have dinner with me? Will you give us a chance to get to know each other a little before you go home?"

"I can't leave the girls—"

He released her shoulders from his grasp, rotated briskly on his heel, and began moving toward the door.

Kendra reached for his sleeve and encountered warm, hard flesh instead. Her fingers curled around the knot of muscle tightening beneath his skin, his forward momentum pulling her to her feet.

"But . . . if you don't mind some company . . . if the girls came with us, I could see my way clear to accepting your invitation."

The muscles beneath her hand relaxed fractionally as he turned to face her. "Take twelve teenage girls out to dinner? No problem. Sounds like my idea of a dream date," he added in a dry tone.

"I don't expect you to buy dinner for the girls. Their expenses, including meals—"

Jack laid two fingers over her lips. "I'd buy dinner for a hundred girls if it meant you'd go out with me."

Her mouth tingled beneath his touch. A shiver of excitement raced down her spine, and her breath caught in her throat as his fingertips slid over her cheek and traced the outline of her ear. Delicately, his thumb stroked her jaw. She turned her face more fully into his hand, unable to still the small murmur that escaped her lips.

He inhaled sharply and closed his eyes. For a long moment, he stood perfectly still, tension emanating from his large body in almost palpable waves. Then he removed his hand and stepped away.

"I have to go. I'll call you later to arrange dinner," he said in a thick voice. "Don't even think about changing your mind."

A bellman arrived with Kendra's coffee as Jack was leaving, cutting off further opportunity for speech. With a brief smile and a half salute, Jack was gone.

The bellman placed the tray on a small round table near the tall windows overlooking the Tuileries gardens. He drew the heavy brocade drapes and opened the window a crack. Then he turned with a flourish and offered Kendra a spray of pink freesias along with the bill.

The faint sweet fragrance of the small blossoms mingled with the pungent aroma of strong coffee rising from a silver pot on the tray. She signed for the order, handed the man a ten-franc coin from a pile of loose change on the bombe chest, and wished him a good day.

Seven a.m. wake-up calls would rouse the girls, after which they were all supposed to meet downstairs in the hotel's café for breakfast at eight o'clock sharp. She had two whole hours to herself, thought Kendra. Almost enough time to calm her jangled nerves.

Jack's unannounced visit had unsettled her. She kept trying to hold him off, he kept overwhelming her defenses. A good firm "no" would have sent Jack away permanently, but when he had turned to leave, all she could think about was how much she wanted to see him again, learn a little more about him, spend just a little more time with him.

The smoldering chemistry between them disconcerted her. She'd known men before who had attracted her, men who had excited her physically. But never in her life had she met a man who exerted the elemental pull on her that Jackson Randall did.

With Jack, she sensed the promise of passion.

The kind of passion that was a fire in the heart, building, ripening, clawing for consummation on all levels — physical, emotional, spiritual. The kind of passion that won't be denied and won't be satisfied until the most profound wellsprings of emotion in a man and woman have been touched, plumbed and neither one is ever the same again.

The kind of passion she and Jack had no chance in the world of sharing.

He was too much man to be satisfied with an innocent flirtation. She'd never been the kind of woman to indulge in quickie affairs.

Kendra forced Jack from her mind through sheer effort of will and brought the remaining *brioches* to the table. Picking up the silver pot, she poured a stream of black coffee into a dainty china cup, added frothy steamed milk from a silver pitcher and a lump of sugar from a silver bowl. She leaned back in her chair to enjoy the sunrise.

Paris was beginning to awaken. The sun glinted off the gilded spikes topping the wrought iron fence enclosing the Tuileries gardens across the street. Delivery trucks and taxis rumbled and honked their way down the Rue de Rivoli just below. Several doors down from the hotel, tour buses were beginning to line up in front of the travel agency offering day tours. The gruff slang of street cleaners mixed with the occasional trill of birdsong. The rapidly warming air flowing in through the window guaranteed another hot, muggy day.

Kendra bit into a still-warm *brioche* and sipped at her *café au lait,* enjoying a moment of perfect peace and contentment. The day seemed filled with promise. She could hardly wait to begin exploring Paris with the girls.

She'd always experienced a vicarious thrill sending her clients to exotic locales with carefully prepared itineraries for each day of their trip. But nothing, absolutely nothing could compare to the sheer dizzying elation of knowing that she had a whole day to work her way through her very own itinerary of fabulous sights.

Nothing, that is, except the even more dizzying elation of knowing that she would see Jack again before she returned to California.

Stop thinking about Jack, she ordered herself sternly, double-checking the day's route on a detailed street map strategically highlighted in bright yellow.

She and the girls had spent most of yesterday indoors, touring museums, first viewing the Impressionist paintings in the Musée d'Orsay, then gorging on the wide-ranging collections in the Louvre. Today, they would attack the streets of Paris.

Too bad they didn't have more time. There was so much to see and do in Paris, she would spend a month if she could afford it.

The fragile china cup hit the saucer with a loud clatter as an astonishing realization struck her. Thanks to Jean-Michel Bourquel, she could afford to spend a *year* in Paris, if she so desired.

For a long moment, Kendra allowed herself to fantasize, letting her imagination run rampant. She would get a cute little apartment in some quaint neighborhood. She would take a class, maybe even at the Sorbonne, and learn to speak French as flawlessly as the Bourquels spoke English. And with a perfect accent, too.

She would tour every church, historic monument, and museum in the city and read every last word on the explanatory placards. She would sample every delicacy and leave no picturesque *rue, place,* or *marché* unexplored.

She would throw caution to the wind two handfuls at a time and delve the wild attraction between herself and Jack Randall. Taste the passion he offered, give the sense of connection he'd described a chance to develop into something more. All they needed was the luxury of time. And suddenly, Kendra was in a position to afford a few luxuries.

She . . . was an idiot.

Twelve sets of parents would be out for her blood if she didn't accompany their daughters home. Her own parents would kill her if she wasn't on the plane scheduled to land at Monterey

Peninsula Airport late Saturday night. Her boss would kill her if she wasn't at work Monday morning, rested and ready to take up her new duties as manager.

Kendra trained her thoughts along a more realistic route. She had a family, a career, a whole life waiting for her back home in Carmel. There was no way she could prolong her visit to Paris beyond the time already allotted. No matter how much she might want to stay . . . and no matter the reason, she was going home on Saturday.

Still, she thought, a slow, pleased smile curving her lips, she'd been right about one thing. With two million francs, she could now afford a number of luxuries.

First, she would buy her younger sister a whole ounce of that perfume she loved so much. The one Kimmie had received as a sample at a department store cosmetic counter and eked out a drop at a time for months.

Next, she was going to brave the terrifyingly chic *vendeuses* at the Hermès boutique on the Rue du Faubourg Saint-Honoré and buy her mother one of those beautiful scarves. She would stand before the long mahogany and glass display cabinets filled with hundreds of neatly folded, richly patterned *carrés* while a saleswoman snapped open each scarf with a flourish, piling up soft, luxurious drifts of silk twill for her perusal.

If she could dredge up a sufficiently haughty demeanor, she might even enjoy the experience.

As for her father, well, any man who ate liverwurst sandwiches for lunch three days a week was absolutely going to lose his mind over the tins of *paté de foie gras* she intended to bring home for him. Maybe she would surprise him with some French brandy, too. If she had any room in her carry-on bag, she would buy him a bottle at the airport duty-free shop.

And her brothers were going to get the surprise of their lives when they received, not the T-shirts she usually brought them from one of her trips, but a bottle of fine French wine. Each. Kendra grinned, imagining their reactions.

Kyle would taunt his college football buddies for weeks before sharing the wine with them. Then they'd probably drink it out of paper cups while munching popcorn and watching some risqué video.

Kent was such a romantic dreamer he would probably plan an idyllic evening with his girlfriend around his bottle of wine. Knowing the scope of her brother's imagination, Kendra was sure it would be a night the pretty coed wouldn't soon forget.

Thinking about her family created a fierce longing to see them, hear them, and she decided to splurge on a transatlantic telephone call. She glanced at the small china clock on the escritoire. Her father would still be at work, but her mother should be home.

She reached for the ivory and gold telephone resting on the console behind the sofa. Her mother was going to be so surprised when she learned everything that had happened in the last twenty-four hours.

Once more, an image of Jack flashed through her mind. She recalled the exquisite tenderness of his fingers touching the soft skin of her cheek.

Well, maybe her mother didn't need to learn quite everything, Kendra decided. She dialed the number with anxious fingers, suddenly consumed with a desire to hear her mother's sensible, loving tones.

"Mom? It's Kendra. Guess what?"

Wearily, Kendra paid the driver of the last taxi, hitched her canvas tote back onto her shoulder and blew a limp strand of hair off her forehead. She followed the line of girls straggling silently up the red-carpeted stairs. A perspiring, white-gloved doorman held open one of the heavy brass-framed glass doors leading into the cool hotel lobby. She smiled at him sympathetically, wondering how many doormen the management lost to heat stroke every summer.

Sight-seeing in August was hot, sweaty, exhausting work. Kendra had loved every moment of the day. More than once, she'd found herself thinking of Jack. The sights and sounds around her, something she would taste or smell would bring him vividly to mind.

She and the girls had set out immediately after breakfast, taking the Métro to the Left Bank. They'd roamed the tiny streets and noisy passageways of the Latin Quarter, happening onto a wildly colorful *marché* just off the Boulevard Saint-Germain.

Fresh figs, enormous red strawberries, greengage plums, and blood oranges had been piled high on rough tables beneath striped awnings. They'd watched countrywomen with meaty arms weighing out green beans, leeks, miniature carrots, and summer squash, as well as a number of oddly shaped fruits and vegetables none of them even recognized.

There were burlap sacks of coffee beans, wheels of pungent ripe cheese, fresh eels, and every kind of fresh fish imaginable.

Kendra had thought of Jack, enjoying a small private smile as she wondered what a man who hated seafood would say about sampling sea urchins.

Mary Lee had nearly caused an international incident by asking innocently in her schoolgirl French why there was no corn on the cob even though it was the height of summer. A sharp-tongued vendor had answered in thickly accented English, "In France we feed cobs to our cows. Buy some *légumes* or move on, I don't earn my bread answering questions!"

Kendra doubted the man would have raised his eyebrows, let alone his voice to Mary Lee if Jack had been with them, but before she could speak up to defend the girl, another vendor had intervened.

An old woman selling live poultry—squawking

chickens, ducks, guinea hens, even brilliantly plumed pheasant—had shouted a few insults at the first vendor and told him to shut up. Then she'd treated the girls to handfuls of roasted hazelnuts from the stall next to hers like some doting grandmother.

Farther on, the girls hadn't been able to resist buying tiny nosegays of white violets and sweet peas. They'd tasted sticky Moroccan pastries and taken pictures of each other in front of the various stalls.

After the bustle and color of the market, the girls had given short shrift to the Roman baths attached to the Cluny Museum, the former Parisian mansion of the wealthy and powerful Burgundian Abbots of Cluny. But they'd been fascinated by the extraordinary gold crowns and other jewelry in the treasury and by the Unicorn Tapestries, exclaiming at the lady's complete change of clothing in each of the six enormous panels. On their way out, the girls had thrown one-franc coins into the wishing well in the museum courtyard.

Kendra had thought of Jack, reaching superstitiously into her canvas tote for a whole handful of coins.

They'd walked a bit down the long stone corridors of the Sorbonne and ventured a peek inside a lecture hall before stopping at one of the numerous neighborhood *traiteurs* to buy food for a picnic lunch in the Luxembourg gardens.

After lunch, they had toured the great Gothic cathedral of Notre Dame. The girls had taken more pictures, bought more postcards, and been persuaded by Kendra to climb the two hundred twenty-five stairs of the north tower to view the gargoyles. As a reward, she'd treated them to ice-cream cones from a pushcart near the cathedral.

And wondered if Jack would appreciate the exotic flavors like passion fruit, cantaloupe, and black currant. Then she'd wondered if he even liked ice cream.

Sauntering leisurely, their energies flagging as the afternoon wore on, they'd traversed the Île de la Cité and arrived finally at the Palais de Justice. The medieval splendor of Sainte-Chapelle, a sight Kendra had missed on her first trip to France, was contained within the ensemble of buildings that comprised the seat of the French civil and judicial system.

Uniformed soldiers armed with assault rifles had stood sentry on either side of the portal gates set into a tall gilded railing. Inside the gates, she and the girls had been directed across the large courtyard to a turnstile and long corridor. One soldier had meticulously examined their purses by hand while another soldier slowly and thoroughly ran an electronic sensing device over their bodies before permitting them to enter a second, smaller courtyard surrounding the Sainte-Chapelle on two sides.

The security was tight, blunt, and unapologetic. The hard, uncompromising expressions on the faces of the soldiers had reminded Kendra of Jack. Like him, they were men not only comfortable with command, but excellent in the exercise of their authority.

She'd climbed a dark spiral stairway and stood in the upper chapel of Sainte-Chapelle. The medieval stained glass windows had blazed with jewel-toned light—emerald, ruby, gold, blue. Colors so pure, so brilliant, she'd experienced them not merely visually but emotionally and been swept with a sudden fierce longing to share the moment with Jack.

"Mademoiselle Martin? A moment please, Mademoiselle Martin."

Kendra started, her reverie broken. The concierge darted out from behind his desk and hurried toward her, carrying an armful of pink roses. She turned to Heidi, Amber, and Lisa. The three had lagged behind the other girls to peruse the windows of a famous jeweler who maintained a boutique in the hotel lobby.

"Meet the rest of us in my suite when you're done drooling over the diamonds," said Kendra.

The girls' expressions quickened when they noticed the flowers, but they simply nodded their assent, and went back to checking out an extravagant display of diamonds and pearls.

"Miss Martin, I am instructed by Captain Randall to place these flowers directly in your hands the moment you arrive."

"Thank you," said Kendra, accepting the bouquet.

"The captain has called every hour since *midi* to see if you have checked in for your messages," he confided with the air of a man who'd abetted many a romance.

Excitement curled and twisted in Kendra's stomach. Jack had called. Not just once, but several times. She bent her head to the soft petals and breathed in the delicate rose fragrance. She couldn't even remember the last time a man had sent her flowers. And so many. There had to be at least three dozen roses in the bouquet.

"These, too, are for you." The concierge handed her a stack of message slips.

"Thank you." Kendra scanned the slips briefly. They all said the same thing. *The Terrasse Fleurie for dinner. Eight p.m. Don't even think about changing your mind.* Her eyebrows rose. The hotel's garden atrium was a lovely and expensive place to dine. Without twelve teenage bodyguards, she was sure it would have been romantic, as well.

"Please, if you hurry, you will arrive in your suite before the captain's next call."

"Thank you," said Kendra. She walked quickly toward the elevators, her earlier fatigue miraculously gone. The concierge hurried after her.

"Mademoiselle!"

"Yes?"

"Unfortunately, the dining room is *very* busy tonight. At eight p.m., I am sorry, but we cannot seat your entire party together." An expression of mock regret passed over the concierge's face. "No, we are able to seat the young *mesdemoiselles* at three tables of four, but you and the captain, well, you must sit together . . . alone . . . at a small distance from the others. A table in the corner, very *intime*. The captain will be pleased, *non?*"

"I can't speak for the captain, monsieur," Kendra pulled a pink rosebud from her bouquet, snapped the stem, and tucked the flower into the man's lapel. "But I think you're wonderful!"

He accepted her accolade with a Gallic shrug.

Kendra pressed the elevator call button several times in impatient succession, her mind whirling. She had to shower, and do her hair. Maybe borrow some nail polish from one of the girls. She had to figure out what to wear. Not that she had a lot of choices. Her wardrobe for the trip hadn't been planned with dinner dates in mind. Maybe the sapphire blue shirtwaist, she mused. The color was good and the fabric was raw silk, even if the style was a little plain.

She had to explain to the girls that Captain Randall was taking them all out to dinner . . . and then she had to stand back and ward off the barrage of questions and comments that were sure to follow.

And she had to do it all by eight p.m. Kendra grinned.

No problem.

Chapter Seven

Jack stepped into the hotel at two minutes before eight. Kendra knew because she and the girls had arrived in the lobby only seconds before him. She was wearing the sapphire blue silk dress and a pair of low-heeled blue pumps. Rather than fight her hair in the heavy humidity, she'd simply left it down, letting it air-dry into a curling honey-colored mass around her shoulders.

The girls chattered behind her, but Kendra couldn't distinguish a single word. A throng of stylish women milled around her in the lobby, but she didn't notice a single outfit.

She was aware only of Jack, tall, handsome, and compelling as he strode confidently toward her. Swallowing the sudden knot of nerves and anticipation lodged in her throat, she stepped forward to meet him.

He wore a conservatively cut tan suit in summer-weight wool gabardine. With the pristine white dress shirt and the foulard silk tie he'd chosen, Jack could have been any well-dressed businessman arriving for dinner. Only his braced-shoulders posture and military haircut gave any hint that this wasn't a man who made his living behind a desk.

"Looks like everyone is here," he said to Kendra, smiling ruefully. He greeted each of the girls by name. "All fourteen of us."

"Jack, when you invited us out to dinner, I didn't expect you to choose a restaurant like the Terrasse Fleurie. We don't have to stay. This is Paris. We can get a great meal for a lot less than you'll pay here at any number of cafés and *brasseries*," said Kendra in an undertone.

"You're right, but I have to be back at the embassy, in uniform, in exactly two hours. I thought we'd have more time to enjoy our meal, and each other's company, if we didn't waste a lot of time driving back and forth to a restaurant." He flashed her a quick, honest smile that softened the hard planes of his face without diminishing its strength one iota. "Besides, I think I can get full on a glass of ice water."

"Oh, Jack—"

"Kendra, I'm teasing. I may not be in the same league as the Bourquels, or Ambassador Whittington, but one dinner won't break me. Not even dinner for fourteen at the Terrasse Fleurie." He tucked Kendra's hand into the warm crook of his arm, winked at the girls, and jerked his head toward the garden atrium located prominently in the center of the lobby. "Come on, everyone, let's go have a nice meal."

Kendra wasn't surprised to see the concierge waiting at the entrance to the Terrasse, beaming like an old friend as they approached. Nor was she surprised by the discreet flash of folded fifty-franc bills passing from Jack to the concierge as they shook hands firmly.

The girls were seated as the concierge had earlier described, at tables within sight of Kendra and Jack, but well out of earshot.

Jack stepped in front of the *maître d'* to hold Kendra's chair himself. He rested his hand on her shoulder for a moment, his fingers tangling in her hair.

"You look pretty," he said. "I like your hair down."

"Thank you." The casual contact made her heart race. She could feel the heat, the strength of his fingers through the thin fabric of her dress.

"The seating arrangements are a nice surprise." He waved at Mary Lee and Lily as he took his own seat.

"I think your hourly phone calls melted the concierge's romantic heart."

"That, or the prospect of a huge tip."

Kendra grimaced. "I'm really uncomfortable with the amount of money this is costing you."

"You don't like a guy to wine and dine you?"

"I'm not used to being wined and dined so extravagantly, but who wouldn't like this?" Kendra swept a small arc with her hand, indicating the crisp white tablecloths, the gleam of polished silver, the cut-glass bud vases with their curving sprays of miniature orchids, the pink candles casting a soft romantic glow.

The muted strains of a violin concerto issued from a hidden sound system. A dense profusion of flowering plants and leafy trees partially screened the tables from each other. Overhead, the glass roof had been opened. The evening air felt refreshing after the sweltering daytime temperatures. And though the sky stayed light until nearly ten at this time of year, Kendra spotted a few stars winking in the gathering dusk.

Jack caught the waiter's eye and nodded his head once briskly. A busboy brought over a silver wire basket of sliced *baguette,* a white and pink porcelain terrine filled with sweet butter, and a bottle of still mineral water. He opened the bottle and filled their glasses unobtrusively.

"I hope you don't mind," continued Jack. "But given the time constraints, I took the liberty of ordering a set meal in advance."

"As long as the waiter doesn't bring anything like sweetbreads or *rognons* within ten feet of our table, I'm sure I'll enjoy every bite. I haven't had a bad meal in Paris yet."

"No sweetbreads, and especially, no kidneys," Jack promised. "The chef's specialty is rabbit in a cognac cream sauce with *chanterelle* mushrooms. Tonight that's being served with an onion custard and two side vegetables — fresh spinach and honey-glazed carrots."

"Jack, that sounds absolutely delicious." A naughty twinkle lit her eyes. "If you ever get tired of being a marine, I think there's a whole new career waiting for you in a trendy restaurant. You recited that menu like a pro."

"Since you're from California, I'll defer to your experience of trendy restaurants."

"Actually, I don't eat out in restaurants much."

"Long time between boyfriends?"

She nodded, embarrassed to admit how long it had been since she'd had a steady man in her life. "That, too, but mostly, I like to cook."

"What's *your* specialty?" Jack leaned forward, his big hands resting palms down on the table.

"I have about a hundred recipes for fresh salmon."

"God! Say no more. The idea of eating fish a hundred times is making my stomach turn. What can you do with meat?"

Kendra chuckled. "I have a nice recipe for chicken breasts marinated in—"

"Chicken isn't meat," he said flatly.

"You'd really like this recipe, it has lots of—"

"Those nice little avocados you Californians are so fond of?"

"Don't be snotty," she retorted, laughing in spite of herself. "I haven't bought an avocado in weeks. Meat, huh? Let's see, I do a pretty good pot roast, and I've been known to broil a thick steak on occasion."

"Keep talking."

"I can fix barbecued spareribs slathered with a secret sauce my younger sister and I concocted about five years ago."

"What's so secret about the sauce?"

"We started with half a bottle of my father's best bourbon as a base and worked our way through his liquor cabinet from there."

Jack laughed, covering Kendra's hands with both of his. "Okay, you can cook for me sometime."

Kendra fell silent. She pulled her hands from beneath his and buttered a small piece of bread. The idea of cooking a meal for Jack exercised a heady appeal. Too bad she would never have the opportunity.

"I want you to know that I specifically asked to have our salads served before the main course." Jack sighed. "But I don't expect to see any lettuce until afterward."

"Don't take it personally, Jack." Kendra smiled, her momentary melancholy forgotten. "There's a certain order to a French meal—"

"Which was apparently written on stone tablets and handed to Moses with the same requirement of obedience as the commandments," he finished.

"I know. I keep asking for coffee *with* my dessert. They keep bringing it *after*." Kendra buttered another piece of bread and popped it in her mouth. Maybe she'd start buying unsalted butter when she got home. She just loved the taste of this stuff.

"I've also ordered some wine for us, a white burgundy," said Jack. "The girls can order soft drinks, or milk, whatever they want."

"They'll probably all order *citron pressé*. It's their new favorite beverage."

"Lemonade?"

"They like fussing with the little pitchers of water served on the side along with the sugared lemon slices," explained Kendra. "As for me, well, I'm not much of a drinker, but a glass of white wine sounds nice."

The busboy returned with a bucket on a footed stand. The *sommelier* was right behind him. He showed the label to Jack, then began the elaborate ritual of opening the bottle and offering him a taste.

"Kendra, about the only thing these people take more seriously than their food, is their wine." Jack took a swallow from a balloon glass and nodded. The *sommelier* poured wine into Kendra's glass, then filled Jack's. "You'd better act like drinking this burgundy is a religious experience, or this guy is liable to drag you off to the kitchen and invite the chef to feed you week-old scraps!"

Kendra took a sip, then smiled at the *sommelier*. "Delicious, thank you."

"*Je vous en prie, madame.*" The sommelier backed away.

"And thank *you,* Jack. For arranging dinner complicated by twelve teenagers, for the beautiful roses, for . . . everything."

"I only wish I had more than two hours to spend with you." He reached across the table and gently squeezed her fingers.

"Do you normally get a two-hour dinner break when you work a twenty-four-hour shift?" Her breath caught in her throat as Jack turned her hand over and began absently brushing his thumb back and forth across her palm.

He shook his head. "I skipped lunch . . . and I prayed things would stay quiet at the embassy so I wouldn't have to cancel out on dinner."

The waiter returned with their appetizers, a puff pastry shaped like a star and filled with slivers of quail breast in a light, buttery sauce.

Kendra took a small taste and closed her eyes, enjoying the sweet, subtle flavor as it slid over her tongue. "Mmm."

"Good?" asked Jack.

"Don't bother me, I'm having a religious experience."

"Experience quickly, we're about to have company."

Kendra opened her eyes in time to see the Gray twins arrive at their table. "Hi, enjoying your appetizer?"

"My dad would flip if he could taste the puff pastry—so light, so flaky, and not the least bit soggy beneath the *beurre blanc* sauce."

Kendra smothered a grin at Julie's knowledgeable tone.

Jeannie twisted the wine bottle around in the ice bucket so she could read the label. "Nice choice. Should be great with rabbit. I'd be interested to know if the wine seems a little dry for the cognac cream sauce, though."

"Their parents own a couple of restaurants in Carmel and Monterey," she explained to Jack, noting his stunned expression.

"Thanks for stopping by," said Kendra pointedly. The twins went back to their table.

"Nice try, Kendra," said Jack. "But here comes the second wave."

Tiffany and Amy approached, their faces filled with outrage. "Kendra, the lady at the table next to us has a *Pekingese* on her lap, and she's feeding him raw hamburger from his own plate!"

Jack and Kendra brought their napkins to their mouths at the same moment, their eyes meeting to exchange silent laughter.

"Some Parisian restaurants allow pets," she managed to gasp out.

"It's disgusting!"

"It's France, girls. The waiter is bringing your food now, so I think you'd better sit down. Tell the others no more visits until we all finish dinner, okay?"

Jack watched the girls go back to their table. His head was turned, exposing the smooth expanse of his neck. Funny, thought Kendra, until she'd met Jack, she'd never noticed how a short haircut could make a man's neck seem so . . . naked. So . . . inviting. She curled her fingers into her palm, stifling the urge to reach across the small table and trace the line of his shirt collar beneath his ear.

"Think we'll have any time to ourselves?"

"About what we've had so far. The girls will probably spend the rest of the meal thinking up little excuses to pop over and see what's going on. For some strange reason, they're fascinated by the idea of me . . . dating."

"I'm fascinated by the notion of dating you, myself."

"We've done this dance, Jack. I agreed to have dinner with you, and I'm enjoying the evening very much. But beyond that . . . Well, I'm still going home the day after tomorrow."

"Nothing a marine likes better than a good obstacle course," he said, smiling confidently.

The waiter arrived with their main course. Succulent morsels of crisply browned rabbit crowned a generous spill of cognac cream sauce the color of *café au lait*. A ring of sautéed *chanterelles* formed a dike around the sauce. A tiny rabbit cut from toasted bread was planted whimsically amid the mushrooms, fresh rosemary sprigs sprouting at his feet.

Kendra took a bite. "Wonderful. Very rich and slightly sweet. Of course, if you want the official critique, you'll have to call the Gray twins back over."

"Let's leave the girls alone . . . maybe they'll return the favor."

The rest of the meal passed quickly. Kendra consumed every bite with greedy delight and wished for perhaps three more morsels of rabbit . . . and about a gallon more cognac cream sauce. She enjoyed the lemon-thyme vinaigrette on the mixed field greens, and she taunted Jack into sampling a number of pungent goat cheeses during the cheese course. Before she realized the passage of time, the waiter was wheeling over a two-tiered dessert cart heavily laden with dozens of beautiful sweets.

Poached pears floated in dark wine. Tarts filled with red currants, blueberries, and sliced peaches glistened like jewels beneath an apricot glaze. Whole strawberries, fat and red, waited for a cloud of unsweetened whipped cream. A bowl of *crème anglaise* sat between a mound of fluffy meringue and a caramelized apple-pie. Bittersweet chocolate mousse filled the many layers of a light chocolate cake. Napoleons, rum babas, and *petits-fours* competed for space with éclairs and *charlottes*.

Kendra shook her head at Jack. "No way. I'd rather skip dessert entirely than be forced to choose only one from that . . . *embarrassment* of riches."

"Ah, Kendra, I do believe I'm beginning to know you." Jack's voice was silky and sly.

"How so?"

"You don't have to choose just *one*. I thought it might be fun for you and the girls to sample a few different desserts . . . so I ordered the assortment."

Kendra eyed the dessert cart, her interest rapidly engaged. "You're kidding, right?"

"Nope. My new buddy, the concierge, assured me that the *assortiment* something or other was being offered in many restaurants these days. So go ahead, dig in."

The waiter held two large tablespoons in his right hand and inclined his head toward Kendra. "Madame?"

"I sure hope the chef was warned," she said, happily pointing to various items on the cart. The waiter began preparing a dinner-sized plate with small servings of her choices. "Unless he tripled up on all his recipes, there's not going to be a thing left on this cart by the time the girls and I are through!"

The waiter arrived with small cups of espresso as Kendra was finishing the last bite of a chocolate éclair. She leaned back in her seat and smiled at Jack.

"That was an incredible treat," she said, taking a sip of coffee.

"Sure you wouldn't like another half dozen éclairs? Or perhaps three or four more of those apple-pies?"

"I couldn't possibly . . . but I think one more of those little chocolates would go nicely with my coffee."

Jack laughed. He motioned the waiter over and pointed to a hand-molded chocolate shaped like a heart. The waiter served the candy to Kendra on a tiny silver tray the size of a saucer.

"Perfect," she sighed, nibbling the edge.

Jack handed the waiter a credit card, then turned back to Kendra with a look of regret. "I wish we had hours more time tonight, but I have to change and head back to the embassy. I'm sorry."

"Don't be. The girls and I have to get up early tomorrow morning for our trip to Versailles. I wouldn't have been able to make it a late evening, anyway."

The waiter returned with the credit card slip. Jack spent a few seconds mentally adding the numbers, then scrawled his name across the bottom. He rose and came around to hold Kendra's chair. Mere inches separated them as she stood. Her eyes met his, and she was swept with a fierce desire to know him, to spend time with him, to have the chance to see where the attraction between them might lead.

"Thank you for dinner," she said softly.

"This still isn't goodbye, honey."

"No?"

"No." Jack brushed her cheek with his lips.

The contact was warm and sweet and tantalizing in its promise. The sensation lingered long into the night.

Kendra watched the "daughters of privilege" board the deluxe tour bus with a frown. Something was wrong. She drummed the backs of her fingers against the window on her right and frowned some more.

Five girls had boarded so far. Not one had spoken more than a few words to Kendra. Not one had met her eyes. Not one had taken the seat she'd patted next to her in invitation. Usually, there was a lot of jocular argument about who got to sit next to Kendra.

A few more girls filed by, taking seats behind her. They were all abnormally quiet, too. No question about it. There was definitely something wrong. Mary Lee and Heather got on the bus, giggling. They smiled at Kendra, sharing the seat across the aisle from her, but they didn't share their joke.

Kendra gnawed the inside of her jaw, beginning to worry in earnest. Maybe they were angry, or nursing hurt feelings about the way the seating arrangements had worked out at dinner last night? But that didn't make sense. The girls had been bubbling over with questions, speculation and conversation after they'd said good night to Jack in the lobby. They hadn't seemed upset when they'd thanked him for dinner, or later, when they'd all sat around the sitting room of her suite, talking before bed.

No, this weird behavior had another cause. And the only way to find out what was bothering them was to ask. She took a deep breath, trying to decide which girl to approach first. She rose to her feet . . . in time to see Jack swing his tall muscular frame aboard the bus. Her eyes rounded in surprise. Understanding dawned as she noted the wide grins spreading from girl to girl down the length of the bus.

"Good work, girls." Jack gave them a thumbs-up gesture.

"Jack, what are you doing here?" asked Kendra, watching him take the empty seat next to her. He looked lean and rugged . . . and exhausted. She remembered that he'd finished a twenty-four-hour shift a mere two hours before and felt a swift sympathy.

The bus driver sounded his horn, and the tour guide dashed out of the travel agency across the street to board the bus. The doors slid shut as the driver started the engine and maneuvered the bus smoothly into the morning commute.

"Looks like I'm going to Versailles," said Jack, leaning back in his seat and closing his eyes. "Wake me when we get there."

The trip to Versailles, only fifteen miles outside of Paris, took nearly an hour in the heavy traffic. By the time they arrived, Kendra had heard the complete story of how Jack and the girls had arranged for him to "crash" their day trip to Versailles. The girls had been gleeful and giggling as each one added details, or explained her part.

Jack had fallen into a deep slumber before the bus had traveled four blocks. He didn't awaken until the tour guide began his lecture as the bus pulled into the tiny city of Versailles right before they reached the magnificent chateau. And even then, Kendra had to wake him.

"Jack, we're here." She shook his shoulder as the girls began filing out the door. He didn't budge.

"Jack," she repeated, shaking him harder, and when he still didn't move, lightly tapping his face with her hand.

"You're supposed to wake me with a kiss," he muttered. "Not a beating."

"Clearly you're still asleep and dreaming if you think you're going to extort a kiss out of me with the Château de Versailles waiting to be explored. Up and at 'em, soldier!"

"You've got a real mean streak, woman," groaned Jack. He stretched in place, raising his arms high over his head and arching his back in a way that could only be described as sinuous. His T-shirt rode up, exposing a tantalizing strip of hard tanned belly lightly dusted with dark silky hair.

Kendra averted her gaze. She had enough trouble keeping her feelings for Jack in perspective without the added provocation of watching his rugged body move slowly through a full range of motion.

Lily peeked around the door to the bus. "The tour guide is getting antsy, you guys. He says three busloads of Italians are right behind us, and if we don't get started there's going to be a terrible bottleneck by the time we get to the State Apartments."

Jack glanced at Kendra, his eyebrows raised nearly to his hairline. He pointed out the window at the front façade of the massive sprawling brick and stone edifice. "A chateau that size crowded? Who is this guy trying to kid?"

"We're not going to see the whole chateau, Jack. Just the State Apartments and a little bit of the gardens. Maybe the Grand Trianon, the Petit Trianon and Marie Antoinette's Hamlet if the girls have the stamina." Kendra started down the aisle toward the door.

"A death march. I knew it." Jack slung the strap of a small automatic camera over his shoulder and caught up with her in two strides.

"May I remind you that crashing this party was *your* idea?" she asked, glancing back over her shoulder.

He tugged on her ponytail. "Why do you always wear your hair up like this, when it looks so beautiful down?"

Kendra was taken aback. She wasn't used to men offering such blunt unsolicited opinions about her appearance. Part of her wanted to retort that the way she wore her hair was none of his damn business. Part of her was so pleased by his compliment, by the heated regard shining in his eyes that she wished she had the nerve to reach up and pull the stretch lace ribbon from her hair while he watched. Instead, she simply shrugged.

"Too much trouble. My hair would be a tangled mess by the end of the day. And when I'm working I don't want to bother brushing it every five minutes." Kendra descended the stairs.

"I'll make you a deal."

"What?"

"You leave your hair down, and I'll brush it for you whenever you want."

The idea was tempting. Very, very tempting. "Don't be ridiculous. Come on, the tour guide *is* getting antsy."

"Scared?" he taunted, wrapping her ponytail around his fist to hold her in place.

"Terrified. The idea of you wielding a hairbrush defies imagination. Now let's go."

Jack released her. She expelled the air from her lungs, surprised to realize she'd been holding her breath. The two of them joined the throng of girls in the huge courtyard. The guide, a thin, nervous-looking young man, beckoned them to the bronze statue of the Sun King and the tour began.

By mid-afternoon, even Kendra's usually inexhaustible energy had waned. The King's Chamber and the Queen's Chamber, alone, had offered such a glittering array of splendors that Kendra was glad she'd had the foresight to arrange their own guided tour instead of trying to explain everything herself.

They'd visited the Hall of Mirrors, the white and gold chapel, the clock room, the throne room, the private office used by the king, and the opera house panelled entirely in wood painted to look like marble.

By the time the guide had led them outdoors to visit the extensive gardens, fountains and other buildings, Kendra had been on visual and cultural overload. She felt as though she'd seen enough gilded panelling, embroidered hangings, statues, paintings, chandeliers, marble, and gold to last a lifetime.

Their guide, despite his nervous manner, had turned out to have a calm, clear speaking voice. He knew an amazing number of interesting facts and anecdotes about the chateau, the Royal Family and French history, and he'd provided the girls with an excellent depiction of court life.

Even Jack had listened, spellbound. Quite a feat, she'd thought, considering he must be near toppling over with fatigue given the number of hours he'd gone without sleep.

Kendra smiled at Jack over the rim of her glass, listening to the girls discuss Versailles. The tour guide had given them an hour to continue roaming the gardens, or to have a cold drink before boarding the bus for the return trip to Paris. She'd led the group to a corner café only two blocks from the chateau. They'd taken seats on the patio at outdoor tables shaded by red and blue umbrellas.

She'd offered to treat Jack to a cold beer and a long baguette filled with paper-thin slices of pink ham and thick smears of creamy Camembert. Now, he was adding liberal swathes of Dijon mustard and crunching *cornichons,* tiny pickled gherkins, like a native.

"Feel better?" She took a sip of her favorite orange soda, watching a good third of the sandwich disappear in two quick bites.

"A couple more sandwiches and another beer, and I'll be ready to see the rest of the chateau."

"There *is* no more to see."

"Come *on,* we went through, what, twenty rooms? Thirty? There must be five *hundred* rooms we haven't seen, easy." He wolfed another third of his sandwich.

Kendra unobtrusively signaled the waiter to bring him another *baguette* sandwich and a second beer.

"But not all the rooms are open to the public, Captain Randall," explained Mary Lee, leafing through the pamphlet she'd bought in the gift shop.

He looked up, an expression of relief crossing his face. "You mean . . . we're done?"

Kendra laughed aloud. "All except for the ride

home."

The waiter arrived and placed the second sandwich and beer in front of Jack.

"Thank God!" Jack raised his glass of beer. "Here's to you, Kendra. I have to admit, I've been on training marches that were less grueling than the last five hours!"

She touched his glass with her bottle of orange soda. A certain wistfulness pervaded her spirit as she realized that the day was over. Her vacation flirtation was over. In a few minutes, everyone would board the bus and when they alighted in Paris, she would finally have to say goodbye to Jack permanently.

The idea depressed her more than she cared to admit.

Chapter Eight

"Make sure you have all your belongings, girls," admonished Kendra, depositing her next-to-last handful of francs in the tip tray cunningly provided by the bus driver. "And get your *détaxe* forms ready. We'll have to get them stamped and mailed before we check our luggage."

"Then can we go shopping in the duty-free stores? I want some of that perfume you bought for your sister."

"Amber, I swear all you think about is spending money," said Lisa.

Amber tossed her chin-length brown hair back from her face with an emphatic shake of her head and giggled. "That's not true at all . . . sometimes I think about boys."

The girls exited the airport bus in a laughing, chattering mass, bulging carry-ons and overstuffed purses banging awkwardly against their legs.

Jet engines roared overhead, making further conversation unintelligible. The thick smell of diesel fuel swirled in Kendra's nostrils as she counted heads and suitcases. Using hand motions, she shepherded her group into the noisy bustle of de Gaulle airport.

"There's the *détaxe* window." Kendra pointed to a long line of impatient humanity, anxiously fanning swathes of documents, checking watches, and grumbling. A bored customs official perused and stamped the forms necessary to receive the hefty sales tax discount available to tourists willing to undergo the arcane refund procedure.

"We'll be in line for *hours*," groaned Lily Warren. "With our luck, that customs guy will make us show him every single thing we bought."

"I hope not," Mary Lee said, her tone fervent. "I packed all my gifts and souvenirs at the bottom of my suitcase so nothing would break. It would take me forever to repack everything."

"The last thing that customs officer will do is the extra work involved in examining all your purchases," Kendra noted drily. "As long as he can see that you have your suitcases ready, he'll just stamp your form and send you on your way. Probably with a snotty comment about your contribution to the health of the French economy."

"Really?" Heidi Clayton looked doubting.

"Really," Kendra replied firmly. "Now, let's get in line."

The *détaxe* formalities accomplished as promised, passport control passed in record time, and their luggage checked through to the airport back home, Kendra and the girls found their way to the duty-free shops on the second floor. She watched the girls' eyes widen and their steps slow at the incredible array of goods visible through the plate glass windows enclosing each shop.

Lily, Amy, and Heidi came to a halt before a window filled with an extravagant display of chocolate. Bouquets of chocolate flowers — lilies, tulips, daffodils, and perfectly formed roses with petals so fine they seemed ready to tremble in a breeze — filled chocolate vases. Life-size chocolate kittens curled in a chocolate basket as if they were sleeping. Chocolate birds sang in chocolate cages, and chocolate truffles were piled into tall chocolate pyramids.

Kendra moved on with the other girls, breathing in the heavenly scent of freshly baked bread and pastries issuing from a bakery. She perused a display of crystal glasses and intricately cut decanters from the company that made barware for Napoleon. She lingered for a moment in front of a boutique displaying more Limoges porcelain than she'd ever dreamed existed. There were place settings, of course, but also soup tureens and other fantastic porcelain creations whose function at the table she could only guess.

The Gray twins ducked into a tiny *charcuterie* offering *boudin,* garlic sausage, and country paté. Whole Parma hams swung on cotton ropes, while pigs feet and organ meat of every description filled giant white trays in the refrigerated cases.

The girls hurried Kendra past a shop selling wheels of fresh cheese, the strong odors of Pont l'Évêque, Morbier, Livarot, and Roquefort making them wrinkle their noses. They dawdled in front of a tiny antique shop, admiring pieces of soft spidery lace, silver tea sets, old musical instruments, and antique jewelry. Kendra left them for a moment to purchase a bottle of brandy for her father.

The shop selling wine and spirits was busy, but quiet. Kendra threw herself on the mercy of the middle-aged *vendeur,* sure she would never be able to make a choice on her own, and emerged a few minutes later with only minor damage to her credit card.

The girls were waiting for her, excited to explore the other boutiques selling enough perfume, cosmetics, and high fashion to satisfy even Lisa Perretti and Amber Carlisle.

Kendra handed out tickets and boarding passes, making sure the girls all knew the location of their gate and reiterating their departure time. "You'll need to show these to the salesperson in order to buy anything. *Please,* don't forget them in one of the duty-free stores, and *please* don't be late."

"Aren't you coming shopping with us?" Mary Lee asked.

"Thanks, but I've already boosted French commerce sufficiently this trip." Kendra pointed to a small coffee bar nestled among the duty-free boutiques. "I'll be over there drinking coffee and thinking depressing thoughts about returning to the office grind on Monday."

The girls scattered like leaves in a breeze. Kendra claimed a seat at the front of the coffee bar in order to keep an eye on the girls' progress, then flagged down a waiter.

"*Café au lait* in the middle of the afternoon?" Jack's deep voice was incredulous as he slid into a seat at her table. "I was made to feel like such an incredible species of moron every time I ordered *café au lait* after ten a.m. that I finally gave up."

"I'm thick-skinned," said Kendra.

"No . . . your skin is soft. I know. I've touched you."

She flushed at the compliment, at the memory of his fingers stroking her face, her hand. "Well, anyway, I wanted *café au lait* so badly, I thought it was worth the risk of offending one last waiter by asking for some."

"That's sure not how it works for me." Jack slowly shook his head, casting a covetous glance at her cup. "I point to various items on the menu, the waiter brings me whatever he wants."

Kendra fiddled absently with the twin stainless steel pots containing strong coffee and steaming milk. "Jack, what are you doing here? You need a plane ticket and a boarding pass to enter this section of the airport."

"I'm your official Marine Corps escort, ma'am."

"Dressed like that?" She indicated his casual civilian clothing with a wave of her hand. "I don't think so."

Not that he didn't look unbelievably attractive. The man did more for a pair of button-fly jeans and a polo style T-shirt than a Madison Avenue whiz could dream up in his wildest, most provocative advertising campaign. The jeans flowed over his hips and thighs in a way that left no doubt about either his muscle tone or his personal endowments.

Kendra knew that both were impressive. She'd checked.

And while she was surprised to see a man as

bluntly masculine as Jack wearing a pastel pink polo shirt, she had to admit that the juxtaposition of soft color and hard male was downright striking. The way the knit arm bands clung to his tight biceps, the peek of tanned skin and dark silky chest hair weren't exactly rough on the eyes, either.

"Okay, I'm your unofficial escort. I called our pal, Jon Craig, and he pulled a few strings to get me admitted beyond passport control."

"I wish you hadn't done that, Jack. We said our goodbyes yesterday, after we got back from Versailles."

"A polite handshake? A round of thank-yous in the hotel lobby? Twelve teenage girls hanging on every word I said?" He drummed his fingers on the table. "I didn't want to leave things that way."

Kendra gave a resigned shrug. "What other way can there be?"

"Dammit, I don't know!" His hands slammed down on the tabletop with enough force to rattle the heavy ceramic cups in their saucers. "I just know I can't let you walk away from me as though things between us were over."

"It is over. I've got a plane to catch in a few minutes."

"Kendra, you're young, but you're not that young. At twenty-seven, you must have enough experience with men to know that these feelings between us are more than raging hormones."

"Is this a marriage proposal?" she quipped.

"Would you miss your flight if it was?" he shot back.

The intensity in Jack's eyes scared her. She didn't

know nearly enough about him, yet a part of her suddenly wished for things no sane woman would dare dream about with a stranger. The threads of her life, all the settled, practically taken-for-granted threads of her life, began to unravel every time they were together.

At some basic, gut level, she trusted him, trusted the honor and integrity that shone from him like a beacon. At an even more basic level she wanted him, wanted him in every way she knew how to want a man. She forced a deep, calming breath into her lungs, then slowly exhaled.

"Do us both a favor, Jack. Let it go. You said yourself that you didn't want a pen pal. I loved meeting you. Under different circumstances, I'd love . . . knowing you." Kendra heard the first boarding call for her flight and rose from the table, slinging her carry-on over her shoulder. "That's my plane. I have to go."

Jack rose, too, slipping the bag down her arm and up over his own shoulder with effortless ease. "Come on."

"I hate prolonged goodbyes, Jack."

"Too bad."

She reached for her bag, but he forestalled her. He covered her hand with his, twining their fingers together in a warm, firm grip that was as much caress as restraint. A lump of strong emotion rose in her throat, threatening to dissolve into tears.

He checked a nearby flight monitor, then said gruffly. "Let's go."

Kendra blinked rapidly several times as she followed. What difference did it really make if he walked her to the departure gate? In a few more minutes she'd be on her way home and everything would be over. Everything but the sense of regret, the sense of loss. The feeling that she was walking away from the one man who could mean the world to her.

By twos and threes the girls came out of the duty-free boutiques and fell into step around Kendra and Jack, making further meaningful conversation between them impossible. He refused to relinquish her hand as they walked, squeezing her fingers every few feet.

"Is everyone here?" asked Kendra when they reached the departure gate. She glanced around her. "Where are Kary and Tracy?"

"They're buying miniature guillotines for their little brothers in that toy shop across from the chocolate place." Mary Lee kept her eyes glued to Kendra's and Jack's joined hands as she spoke.

"I'll stay here and watch the carry-on luggage while one of you goes to get them. The rest of you take your passports and boarding passes to the counter for final check-in." She waited for the girls to scatter. Nobody moved.

"Mary Lee, will you *please* go tell Kary and Tracy to hurry?" asked Kendra, an edge to her voice. What were they all waiting for? Ten pairs of eyes flicked from Kendra to Jack and back again, then fixed on their still entwined fingers. Not one of the girls even blinked. *Oh hell,* she thought.

"They'll be here in a minute," Mary Lee calmly assured her.

The intercom announced their flight a second

time, calling passengers aboard in French, English, and Spanish. The sounds were garbled in the busy airport.

"Kary and Tracy may not have heard the announcement with all that static on the intercom," said Kendra.

"They know what time the plane leaves," said Heidi, her expression becoming increasingly interested the longer Jack held Kendra's hand.

"Fine, I'll go," said Kendra, exasperated. She had no intention of acting out some passionate farewell scene with Jack, but she wouldn't have minded a few minutes of relative privacy in which to say a final, dignified goodbye.

"I'll come with you," offered Jack smoothly.

"We'll all go," said Julie and Jeannie Gray in quick unison.

Jack chuckled. The amused, self-satisfied sound made Kendra want to smack him. *He* wasn't going to be trapped in a confined space for the next ten hours with the "daughters of privilege." The intense speculation written plainly across their faces told her that the girls had just made it their mission in life to discover what *exactly* was going on between herself and Jack Randall.

Kendra smothered a groan. She didn't know how she was going to stand the aggravation. Particularly, since she wasn't sure she could explain the feelings that existed between them even to herself. She tried to pull her hand away, but Jack simply tightened his grip and began exerting a slow, steady pressure, drawing her toward him.

"Hey, nobody has to go get Kary and Tracy. Here

they come." Heather waved excitedly. "Hurry up, you guys, the airline is boarding our flight *now!*"

"You girls go ahead and start finding your seats, said Kendra.

"That's okay, we'll wait for you," Tiffany responded.

"I wouldn't have chosen to do this in front of an audience," Jack's voice was low and intimate despite the avidly interested teenage girls clustered around him and Kendra. "In fact, if I had a brain in my head, I probably wouldn't do this at all."

"Please, Jack," begged Kendra. "Just say goodbye."

"That's exactly what I'm going to do . . . Marine style." He gave her hand a quick, sharp tug that jerked her up against his hard chest, imprinting the shape of his body the full length of hers. His arms slid around her waist, locking in the small of her back. Before she had a chance to protest, to draw so much as a single breath, he was kissing her.

His lips were warm and firm and knowledgeable as they moved over hers. He kissed her slowly, deliberately, enticing her response with tiny-incremental movements of his mouth. He turned his head gently from side to side, rubbing his lips back and forth over hers. He exhaled, and she breathed in his very essence.

All thought of the girls, of boarding the plane, fled her mind. All the good, sensible reasons against kissing Jack Randall were pushed aside. She knew only the sharp, shocking pleasure of his kiss. An explosion of pleasure. Pleasure that felt like fire in her veins, electrifying every nerve ending and melting all resistance.

"Put your arms around my neck and hold me tight," he whispered against her mouth. "I want to feel you closer . . . want to feel your breasts and your belly and your thighs closer."

The rough, husky sound of his voice excited her almost as much as his urgent command. Her hands slipped to his lean waist and up the center of his chest. Thick ridges of abdominal muscle clutched and hardened beneath her touch. His heartbeat thumped wildly against her palm, and his flat nipples peaked under her fingertips.

When her thumbs found the heated bare skin exposed by the open collar of his shirt, she stroked him, letting the dark silky strands of his chest hair twine around her thumbnail. He made an incoherent sound and closed his eyes, his forearms hardening at the base of her spine. "Hug me."

Kendra slipped her arms around his neck. Heat and desire pooled in her womb. Raw, aching desire that left her ready for a consummation that simply couldn't occur.

Never in her life had a man so aroused her with a kiss. Never in her life had a man kissed her with his whole body the way Jack was doing.

In the back of her brain, Kendra registered the final boarding call for her plane and the gasps of astonishment from the "daughters of privilege." She ignored them.

Jack lowered his head and kissed her again. The slow, deliberate enticement of his first kiss was gone, replaced by a relentless, driving passion that didn't so much ask for a response as demand one.

She gave it, parting her lips in silent invitation. Expecting the forceful assault of his tongue, she was surprised by his delicacy. He licked and nibbled and rimmed her lips. Then he angled his head and sealed their mouths together.

His tongue probed her mouth, sliding in and out with the full, deft, careful strokes of a man who knew how to please a woman. Kendra clung to Jack's wide shoulders, the tips of her fingers digging into his powerful muscles. She found herself gasping for breath, trembling with the force of her arousal. An arousal that was rapidly outgrowing her control.

"You're close, aren't you," murmured Jack against her ear. "I can feel you shaking in my arms."

Kendra blushed scarlet, embarrassed as much by his awareness as by the potent response he'd drawn from her.

"I need to get on that plane." The words felt like they were being torn from her heart. "Please, Jack."

"I'd love to please you, Kendra." He kissed her once more, kissed her hard and deeply. "Part of me wants to give you the release you need right here, right now. That's what a good marine does when he goes on tour and leaves his woman. He burns himself into his woman's soul. Burns away all possibility that she'll accept another man in his absence. Shall I do that? Shall I burn myself into your soul, Kendra?"

"I'm not your woman."

"You could be."

"This is crazy!" Kendra strained against the strong arms holding her. He eased his grip fractionally. She watched over his shoulder as the pilot and his flight crew marched briskly down the covered ramp leading to the plane. "Jack, I have to board!"

"We're not done with each other, Kendra. I'm going to write you. You're going to answer me. And one way or another we're going to chase down and resolve all this heat and lightning between us."

"I don't think so. You don't even have my address."

Jack smiled and tapped his temple with his index finger. "I memorized your address from your passport ten minutes after meeting you . . . and Lily Warren helped me out with your telephone number."

A uniformed flight attendant tapped Jack on the back. *"Pardon, monsieur,* the flight stewards are preparing to secure the plane as we speak. If your group wishes to take this flight you must board immediately."

"Don't fall in love with anybody before I see you again," said Jack, releasing Kendra from his powerful embrace and gently slipping her carry-on bag over her shoulder. He cupped her face between his hands for a long moment, then he kissed her once, softly, and walked away.

Kendra stared after him, rooted in place.

"Madame," said the flight attendant with impatience. "Does your group intend to board the plane?"

"Yes," she answered absently, still watching Jack's retreating form.

"You must run," the attendant instructed her. "I will call ahead and tell the head steward to hold the flight."

Run? She wasn't sure she had the strength in her rubbery legs to walk the short distance to the plane. "Come on, girls. We have to hurry."

Kendra turned away from the sight of Jack's broad back and long legs moving down the corridor with an easy grace. The "daughters of privilege" followed her, for once, speechless.

Chapter Nine

"Quick, somebody, help me before I drop Dad's brandy!" Kendra juggled a precarious armload of souvenirs, tucking her elbow to her waist in a desperate attempt to trap the heavy bottle of spirits under her arm.

"French brandy! What a luxury!" exclaimed her father, hurrying from his position on the living room sofa to relieve her of a few packages. He dropped a kiss on her forehead. "You shouldn't have spent so much money, but thank you, honey."

"That's not all, Dad. I have six tins of *paté de foie gras* for you in here, somewhere." She followed him into the living room where the rest of her family waited, depositing her gifts in a colorful pile on the coffee table.

Kimmie groaned. "Oh, God, *French* liverwurst! Kendra, how could you do that to me? You know I'm responsible for making Dad's lunch during summer vacation! I bet that stuff smells like cat food."

Kendra laughed, wrapping her younger sister in a tight hug. "You'll forgive me when you see what I brought you."

"Really? Which package is mine?" The younger girl's voice rose with excitement.

Kendra began rummaging around in the gaily wrapped pile of gifts.

"Stop that this instant and come give your mother a kiss," ordered Kristen, holding out her arms to Kendra. "*I* wanted to come to the airport last night to meet you—"

"But we managed to talk her out of it," said her brother, Kent.

"Yeah, we convinced her that career women didn't need their parents to pick them up from business trips!" added Kyle.

"You idiots," said Kendra, hugging the rest of her family in turn. "I wish you had come to the airport. I could have used some help with my luggage."

"I'm not surprised," commented her mother, arching one eyebrow as she watched Kendra root through the mound of presents. "You appear to have bought out Paris. Did you leave anything in the stores?"

"Perhaps one or two insignificant souvenirs," giggled Kendra, resuming her search for Kimmie's perfume. "Here."

"Ooh, I *love* this fragrance! And you bought me real perfume!" Kimmie ripped the clear cellophane off the padded red satin box and reached inside for the round crystal flacon. She twisted the stopper and dabbed perfume behind her ears, then offered the bottle to her mother. "Want to try some?"

Kristen dabbed a little perfume on her wrists, then held out her hand to her husband. "What do you think, Kirk?"

He sniffed, then kissed the inside skin of her wrist. "Irresistible . . . as always."

"So, what kind of T-shirts did you bring us this time?" asked Kent.

"No T-shirts this time." Kendra produced the two bottles of wine with a flourish.

"Oh, man, that's *great,* Kendra." Kyle lunged for his bottle.

She drew back a step, holding the bottle away from him with a teasing grin. "Promise me you won't drink this before you turn twenty-one."

"Two years? You bring me a bottle of French wine, and you want me to wait two years to drink it? Are you nuts?"

"I suppose Mom and Dad could be persuaded to hold onto the wine for you." Kendra pretended to consider.

"I really would have preferred that you not have brought him wine, Kendra," said her mother with a small frown. "But since you have, you might as well give it to him."

"Lighten up, Mom. He doesn't abuse alcohol. Neither of us do. One bottle of wine won't hurt him," said Kent, examining the label on his own bottle. "Thanks . . . I think. What exactly does this say, Kendra?"

"Bordeaux."

"That much even I can read," noted her brother

in disgust. "I mean all this other stuff, *prix* and *médaille,* and how about *premier cru?* What does all that mean?"

"That you'll like the taste." Kendra picked up the last gift on the coffee table, a square flat orange box tied with brown grosgrain ribbon. "Here, Mom, this is for you."

Kristen opened the box and pulled out a large square of silk twill with a hand-stitched rolled hem. Songbirds in every shade of blue from aquamarine to sapphire flew across an ivory background accented with tiny splashes of rose pink and bright gold. She looked up with a stunned expression. "Kendra, this is a Hermès scarf!"

"I know. Isn't it pretty?"

"It's beautiful, but Kendra, *a Hermès scarf?*"

Kendra's broad smile faltered. "Don't you like it? I know the more typical designs are horse motifs, saddles and reins, hunting dogs, things like that, but I thought you'd prefer this one, with little birds."

"Darling, the scarf is lovely, but where in the world am I supposed to wear it?"

"Anywhere, everywhere. Blue is your favorite color. You must have dozens of outfits you can wear with that scarf."

"Kendra, considering what you must have paid for this scarf, I should probably frame and hang it as art!"

"You don't like it," said Kendra, her voice flat, disheartened.

"I love you for thinking of me," said Kristen diplomatically. "But I don't think I'm nearly grand enough to wear this."

"Mom, quit being such a wet blanket. It's not like Kendra used her rent money or anything. She just got a huge reward for saving that kid's life. Let her buy you an expensive scarf if she wants to. She can afford it." Kimmie poked through the wrappings and ribbons littering the coffee table. "Where's mine? And where's Mom's perfume?"

"I didn't buy you a scarf, and I didn't buy Mom perfume."

"But you always bring me and Mom the same thing."

"Not this time, sorry."

"Gee, I really love that scarf," said Kimmie wistfully.

"I thought you'd like the perfume. You've been raving about that fragrance since you got the sample last Christmas," explained Kendra, a sense of failure rapidly taking hold. At least her brothers liked their wine. And her father had *seemed* excited to receive the bottle of brandy, even if he did think she'd spent too much money.

"The perfume is fine. I just thought that, considering your reward, you might have brought me something . . . well, I don't know . . . different."

Kendra watched her sister's pretty features twist in disappointment, suddenly sure that by "different," Kimmie really meant "more."

"Give us a break, Kimmie, you know Mom will let you borrow her scarf anytime you want to impress all your little girlfriends," said Kyle.

"There's a couple *you* don't think are so 'little,' " retorted Kimmie. "Beth and Anne got in a huge fight because you asked both of them out last weekend—one on Friday, one on Saturday."

"Why not? They both like me."

"You are *so* conceited. You think you're *such* a stud—"

"That's what the girls tell me."

"Shut up, you two. I want to hear more about Kendra's reward. Is it really two million dollars, like Dad said?" asked Kent, an envious undertone creeping into his voice.

"Man, I can't even imagine that much money," added Kyle. "You don't *ever* have to go back to work. You can quit your job—"

"I *love* my job." Kendra bounced a wadded-up ball of discarded wrapping paper off her brother's chest. "I'm up for promotion, remember? Besides, the reward was two million *francs,* not two million dollars. I'm hardly able to retire even if I wanted to, which I don't."

"I knew you must have misunderstood," said Kirk to his wife.

"Francs, dollars," dismissed Kristen. "At the time, I was excited to be talking to our daughter long-distance from *Paris.*"

"You can buy anything you want," continued Kyle.

"I'm sure your sister is going to save that money for her future," said Kirk.

"Exactly how much is two million francs in *real* money, Kendra?" asked Kimmie.

There was something avid about her expression that made Kendra mumble uncomfortably, "A couple of hundred thousand, I think."

"Oh, Kendra, your math is better than that," reproved her father, reaching for the Sunday paper on an end table. He turned to the business section. "At Friday's exchange rate, two million francs is worth, let me do some quick division . . . approximately three hundred and fifty-eight thousand dollars. Hmph . . . quite a lot of money for someone your age to handle. Don't let it go to your head."

"Three hundred and fifty-eight thousand dollars. Oh, my." Kristen sat back against the chintz-covered sofa, exhaling a long sigh.

"No shit!" exclaimed Kyle.

"Watch your mouth in front of your mother and sisters," warned Kirk, his brows drawing together forbiddingly.

"Too bad I wasn't there with you," said Kent, grinning. "Then you'd have had to split the money with me."

"She still can," said Kyle, a hopeful light brightening his eyes. "Put me down for about fifty, no, make that sixty thousand bucks. I can buy a Harley—"

"You're not buying a motorcycle no matter how much money your sister gives you." Kristen's tone was quelling. "You still have two years of college left. Longer if you plan on getting that MBA you've been talking about."

Kent's features tightened. "Sure wish it had been me. I'm still trying to figure out how to pay for graduate school."

Kristen smiled at Kendra. "If you're lucky, maybe your sister will loan you the money."

"Not if she ever wants to see it back," teased Kyle. "Kent's girlfriend is planning on a big wedding and lots of kids as soon he graduates next spring."

"Shut up!"

"That's enough, all of you. Your sister just got home. Give her a chance to relax and do some straight thinking about savings and investment plans before you jump all over her with requests." Kirk's tone made it clear that all discussion on the subject was over. "Now, your mother baked Kendra's favorite German chocolate cake to welcome her home. Let's go into the kitchen, and let her tell us about the rest of her trip."

Kendra shot her father a grateful glance, and began gathering up the discarded wrappings. A vague sense of unease lingered in her mind. She couldn't quite put her finger on what was bothering her, but it had something to do with her family's reaction to the news of her reward.

Amazingly, not one person had asked for any details about Rémy and his rescue, or even about Jack. Kendra remembered mentioning both of them to her mother when she'd called from Paris. True, she'd glossed over Jack's part in the drama, describing him only as a marine who had helped her. But ordinarily, the mere mention of a man would have alerted the family radar. Her parents would have gently probed for information. Her brothers and Kimmie would have been merciless in their teasing.

And while she certainly didn't see herself as any sort of heroine, she *had* saved a child's life. Surely, that was a lot more interesting than the reward she received as a result . . . wasn't it? Kendra knelt on the floor and retrieved the brown grosgrain ribbon from under the coffee table, twining it around one finger.

Maybe she was just being overly sensitive, but she'd sensed what she could only describe as a certain . . . jealousy of her good fortune. Her parents seemed a little put off by the reward. Her brothers and Kimmie had displayed a weird, grasping sort of . . . well, envy.

The feeling was uncomfortable and distancing. She felt a little like an outsider in her own family, a feeling as unfamiliar as it was discomfiting.

"Leave that, darling. I'll do it later. Come have a piece of cake, then go home for a nice long nap. I can tell from those enormous circles under your eyes that you didn't get nearly enough sleep on this tour."

The warmth and concern in her mother's voice brought a lump to Kendra's throat. Jet lag, she decided, that was the problem. She was exhausted and that was making her fanciful. The envy, the sense of distance that so bothered her were simply the result of fatigue and overwrought emotions brought on by the events of the last incredible few days.

An image of Jack Randall flashed through Kendra's mind, making her remember the two nights in Paris when she'd stayed up late talking to him. Another night had been cut short by his early morning visit. And her sleep, every night since they'd met, had been plagued with thoughts of his humor, his kindness, his extraordinary physical presence. No, she most definitely hadn't been getting enough rest.

"Mom," she said with feeling. "You don't know the half of it."

Kendra awoke on Monday morning surprisingly refreshed considering her difficulty in falling asleep the night before. Visions of Rémy's thin face and the grave expression in his blue eyes had churned in her mind until well past midnight. Images of Jack's lean handsome face and superbly conditioned body had kept her tossing and turning until her sheets were a tangled mess.

Remembering his searing kiss at the airport hadn't done much to create a somnolent mood, either.

With an exasperated sigh, she threw off the covers and bounded out of bed, refusing to be further distracted by renegade thoughts and memories. The sooner she forgot Jack, the better off, the *calmer* she would be. The man was thousands of miles away, and she was never going to see him again.

It was time to get on with real life.

Arriving punctually for work was a good way to start, she told herself sternly. She raced through her shower, spared a momentary regret that her breakfast of cornflakes and wheat toast wasn't *croissants* and *café au lait,* and turned up the volume on her television so she could catch the local news program while dressing.

Talking back to the relentlessly chipper co-anchors was a cherished Martin family tradition, but Kendra wasn't really in the mood to get off more than a couple of desultory zingers. There would be a million details to arrange if her promotion came through. Staffing needs to consider, sales strategies to plan, a long list of clients to inform about her new status . . . or not, she acknowledged with a sinking feeling in the pit of her stomach. Her heart beat faster, and her lungs constricted.

What if she didn't get the promotion?

She took a deep calming breath and hurriedly zipped the narrow skirt of her honey-colored silk suit. The only way to find out was to get to work. She slipped on her suit jacket, making a minuscule adjustment to the collar of her black and tan striped blouse as she passed the entryway mirror. Then grabbing her new black handbag for luck, she headed out the front door of her Carmel cottage for the ten-minute walk to the heart of town.

"Welcome home!" Lindy Hughes, the receptionist, came around from behind her desk to envelop Kendra in a warm hug. "Did you get them?"

"The raciest lace bra and most scandalous pair of panties in Paris for your trousseau," affirmed Kendra, returning her friend's affectionate squeeze. "You can pick them up at my place after work. Your groom is guaranteed to lose his mind *and* his control, when he sees them."

"Assuming I ever find a groom." Lindy clasped

her hands together in a prayerful stance and raised her eyes heavenward.

Tall, pretty, and vivacious, Lindy was wholeheartedly, unabashedly searching for a husband. Her friendly manner, spectacular figure, creamy skin, and cloud of dark hair had men lined up around the block wanting dates. But at twenty-nine, Lindy laughingly and with pride proclaimed herself the oldest living virgin in California and steadfastly refused all men she didn't consider "marriageable."

Moreover, she made clear on the first date to those few who conformed to her exacting standards that she intended to remain a virgin until her wedding night. Which, she ruefully acknowledged, pretty much eliminated most second dates.

"Your Prince Charming is out there, Lin," encouraged Kendra, depositing her handbag in her desk drawer. She leaned over and flipped on her computer. "I can almost hear the hoofbeats of his white charger now."

"What you hear is the limping of his lame nag."

Kendra laughed. "Has Bob come in yet?"

"No. He wanted to check our booths at the Convention Center in Monterey on his way in from Pebble Beach this morning. The Travel and Leisure show starts today, remember?"

"So that's where everyone is."

Lindy nodded. "You know Bob. He left skeleton crews at all the branches so he could make the biggest, splashiest presentation of any agency on the Monterey Peninsula. He's coming in to the office for your meeting. Afterward, the two of you are supposed to join the other Let's Go Travel agents at the Convention Center."

"I see." Kendra felt a thrill of anticipation. It sounded like Bob planned to announce her promotion at the trade show. "Listen, there's something I've been meaning to discuss with you, Lin. You know that I asked for the Monterey branch office when Joe McGhee retires in September."

The other woman's expression became guarded, but she didn't say anything.

"I'd like you to consider coming with me and training as an agent." Kendra's tone became confidential. "I have a good feeling about this job, Lin."

"Bob didn't tell you?"

"Has Joe changed his mind again about retiring? For crying out loud, the man is seventy-four years old. How much longer does he want to work?"

"Joe's gone, all right." A pained expression crossed Lindy's face. "I really hate being the one to break the news, Kendra."

"Good Lord, Joe didn't die, did he?"

"No . . ."

"Then, just say it, Lin."

"Bob already filled the position."

Kendra felt the blood drain from her face.

"That's not possible," she protested, shocked. "He promised me a decision on my application when I returned from France. Even Bob wouldn't just hire someone else behind my back while I was gone."

Lindy hunched her shoulders apologetically.

"Theo from the Salinas office got the job. Bob announced his promotion the day you left on tour with the girls."

"That conniving snake!" Kendra angrily paced the heavy-duty Berber carpeting in front of her desk. "He never had any intention of promoting me, let alone giving my application serious consideration."

"I'm sorry, Kendra." She spread her hands in a gesture of helplessness.

"Don't sound so miserable. *You* didn't promote Theo."

"Morning, girls. You two are looking sexy today."

"That's one, Bob." Kendra's ominous tone carried not the least hint of her normal good humor.

"Just kidding, *Ms*. Martin, *Ms*. Hughes." Bob Warren gave a hearty chuckle and let the bottom half of the Dutch door opening onto Ocean Avenue, Carmel's main pedestrian thoroughfare, swing shut with a bang. "Is the coffee ready yet, Lindy?"

"That's two, Bob," retorted Lindy.

Bob chuckled again. "Does that mean I shouldn't tell you to bring me coffee in my office while Kendra makes her formal report about the France tour?"

"No, Bob," said Kendra. "It means you should go ahead and tell Lindy to do exactly that . . . so she can file a grievance against you with the labor commissioner and retire on the punitive fine."

His expression hardened. "I'd excuse the two of you with a comment about the cycle of the moon and tides, but you'd probably jump all over me for that, too. So, I'll simply say the word 'insubordination' and let you draw your own conclusions. Kendra, come into my office. We need to have a chat."

"Yes, Bob. We do."

The staff of Let's Go Travel worked in one large room at individual stations separated by oak filing cabinets, wrought iron brochure racks and a small jungle of banana plants and ficus trees. Bob Warren indulged himself with a private office that could have belonged to a robber baron of the last century.

An antique Persian rug in shades of wine, gold, and black covered a significant portion of the parquet floor. Diamond-paned windows filled the wall behind the massive slab of Carrara marble that served as his desk. When he swiveled around in his Italian leather chair, his gaze contemplated a private courtyard patio with a fountain, a sundial, and a couple of Greek statues.

Floor-to-ceiling, glass-fronted display cabinets lined two walls and housed a collection of pricey art objects and conversation pieces accumulated on his trips around the world. The entire effect was intended to impress clients with Bob Warren's good taste, sophistication, and travel experience.

Kendra considered his office a shrine to the gods of plunder, blandishment, and conspicuous consumption. She disapproved of the pre-Columbian jade carvings she felt belonged in a Mexican museum. And she particularly hated the caribou head mounted on a wall plaque. Bob claimed to have "bagged" the trophy in the wilds of Quebec Province years earlier. Frankly, she had a hard time imagining Bob "bagging" anything more challenging than a spider in his linen closet, but she'd never called him on the matter. Yet.

"Sit down, Kendra." Bob settled himself behind his marble desk, and folded his hands over a pile of unopened mail.

Kendra met his gaze with one of her own, struggling for a control she was a long way from feeling.

"First, I want you to know that I've spoken extensively with my daughter, Lily, about the trip. She had nothing but rave reviews for your performance. Those kids had the time of their lives. For that, I commend you as an employer, and I thank you as a parent."

Kendra nodded, knowing there was more.

"However, I was quite disturbed to learn about the events in that hamburger place." He stabbed one thick finger in her direction, and his tone turned accusatory. "While I can only be glad that you managed to save that little boy's life, I am appalled at your lack of judgment in attempting to do so."

"I beg your pardon?" Her temper started to simmer. How could he describe saving a child's life as *appalling* in any sense?

"The publicity would have been disastrous, a nightmare, if things had turned out differently. There may be some derivative benefit for Let's Go Travel from the fact that the kid is Jean-Michel Bourquel's grandson, but what if he'd turned out to be a nobody? Or worse, what if you'd bungled your attempt at saving his life?"

"Gee, Bob, I guess I just didn't think enough about the 'kid's' pedigree when I jumped up to keep him from choking to death in front of your daughter and her friends."

"You're paid to think about how your actions affect my business when you're on my time," continued Bob, oblivious to her sarcasm. "That fact aside, I have decided *not* to put in a claim for my rightful portion of the reward you received."

"Excuse me?" Kendra's stomach clenched painfully with the effort of will required to keep her temper from boiling over. She hadn't wanted the reward. She hadn't even fully assimilated the knowledge that by most standards, she was now a wealthy woman. But one thing she knew for sure. She would fry in hell before she let Bob Warren have one penny of that money.

"You were on company time, Kendra. I believe a good argument can be made that the company should share in any reward one of its employees receives while in the course and scope of employment. Nevertheless, I've decided to let you keep the entire amount."

She gripped the twisted chrome armrest of her chair so tightly her knuckles turned white. "Let's talk about my employment for a moment, Bob."

"I'm not finished discussing the tour—"

"Yes, you are." Kendra felt a surge of power as she noted his surprise at having the reins of conversational control wrested from his grasp. She discovered she liked the feeling.

He blinked rapidly several times, then looked down at the pile of mail before him and began shuffling envelopes nervously. "I suppose you could make a written report."

"No." Kendra took a slow, deep breath, enjoying his discomfiture. "We're going to talk about my promotion."

"Ah, yes, your . . . that is . . . the promotion." He ran two fingers around the inside of his shirt collar. "The fact is, Kendra, the events of this tour have convinced me that you need a little more . . . seasoning."

"Seasoning?" She raised one eyebrow, trying desperately not to laugh at the gallows humor that made visions of salt and pepper shakers dance through her head.

"Seasoning," repeated Bob firmly, obviously believing himself to have taken charge of the situation once more. "In a year, maybe two, we'll see what's available and discuss again the possibility of a managership for you."

"Let me be sure I understand your point here correctly, Bob. You think I have sufficient seasoning to be entrusted with sole responsibility for your thirteen-year-old *daughter* in a foreign country for ten days, but you think I lack the seasoning to be entrusted with managing one of your *offices* at this time?"

"Exactly." He smiled the way a teacher smiles at a clever answer given by a particularly bright pupil.

"And you came to this realization after I completed the tour in France?"

"I may have had some doubts before you left," he admitted. "But I didn't actually finalize my decision until afterward."

Kendra's temper rose and spilled. "And was that *as* the plane was taking off, or just *after* the last girl had checked her luggage?"

"Huh?"

"Save the innocent act, Bob. I already know you gave the promotion to Theo Canlis." She didn't even try to hide her disdain.

"Theo's the perfect man for the job."

"Man being the operative word."

"That's not fair. Theo's done a great job in the Salinas office this past year."

"I've done a great job here for the past *five* years."

"Theo also has experience running his own business, and he has a certain . . . maturity that only age can bestow."

"Theo owned a used-car lot! How exactly does that experience relate to the travel industry?"

"I don't need to justify my decision to you," he said coolly.

"You played me for a fool, Bob. You intended to promote Theo all along. But because you needed me to escort your daughter's tour, you strung me along and held off announcing your decision until the day I left."

Kendra leaned back in her chair and stared at her boss, amazed at the sense of calm suddenly pervading her body. A number of things slid into perspective for her. No matter how much experience or "seasoning" she acquired, Bob was never going to let her manage one of his offices. A quick mental inventory reminded her of one salient fact.

All of Bob's managers were men.

She had been both naive and gullible to believe that her business degree, coupled with her hard work, would make the least bit of difference in her advancement opportunities. Bob was never going to promote a woman to a managerial position in one of his branches, she realized, least of all, her.

Why should he when she made his life so much easier as the assistant manager right here in the main office?

Bob went out to lunch and dinner and golf with clients. Kendra spent hours on the phone trying to confirm their reservations. Bob proposed travel destinations. Kendra did all the research and follow-up necessary to ensure fabulous trips with no glitches. Bob hustled new business during office hours, secure in the knowledge that in his absence "my girl is holding down the fort." Kendra spent evenings and weekends soliciting new clients to prove her worth.

For five years, she'd taken care of the million and one routine administrative details that made the Carmel office run smoothly, efficiently, and profitably, thinking she was acquiring the experience, paying the dues, that would lead to a position as manager.

For a smart woman with a good education, she'd been remarkably stupid and blind.

"If you have no other questions, I think that pretty much settles things, Kendra. We should be leaving for the Convention Center. The place was jumping when I checked our booths earlier." Bob rose, sliding a sheaf of brochures for a new Brazilian resort into his ostrich skin briefcase. "And I'm sure that being the good sport you are, you'll congratulate Theo on his promotion while you're there."

Kendra took one look at the smug, self-satisfied expression on Bob's face and began to tremble with a strong desire to wring his neck. Something snapped inside, and she found herself shaking her head, incapable of uttering anything except a choked "No."

"No? What do you mean, no?" Bob closed his briefcase and looked up. "Lindy can handle the phones and any walk-ins until you get back."

"I mean no more, Bob. I quit."

"Very funny, Kendra. Get your purse, and let's go."

"You know, Bob, that's the trouble with business*men*. They don't listen." She placed her palms on the obscene hunk of marble he called a desk, and leaned forward until her face was mere inches from his. "I am not going to the Convention Center with you. I'm quitting. On the spot. No notice."

Bob Warren's face suffused a mottled shade of red and purple. "You can't do that."

"Watch me."

Kendra spun on her heel and walked toward the door.

"Wait."

She kept walking.

"Wait . . . *please*."

She looked back over her shoulder. "Yes?"

"Maybe we can work out a . . . compromise over the promotion."

"What did you have in mind?"

Bob waved her forward, a crafty glint in his eyes. "Theo walked away from the sale of his used-car lot last year with a hundred grand burning a hole in his pocket. He invested that money in the Monterey branch of Let's Go Travel. Now, I'm not guaranteeing that I'd turn over a forty percent share of another branch to a young girl, uh, young *woman* without Theo's same qualifications. But if you'd like to use some of your reward money to make me an offer on, say, the Pacific Grove branch, I'd be interested in hearing what you had to say."

"Gee, Bob, I don't know that I want to buy a used-car lot and have a sex change operation in order to duplicate Theo's *qualifications*."

"I meant," he asked with a touch of impatience, "what do you have to say about investing some of that reward money in a Let's Go Travel branch?"

Kendra smiled serenely. "I'd rather burn every last dollar of that reward than invest one dime to buy a promotion we both know I've earned."

"Then I guess you're going to be an *assistant* manager for a while longer."

"You just don't get it, do you, Bob?" She shook her head in disbelief. "I am out of here. Now. Permanently."

Chapter Ten

Kendra closed Bob's office door soundlessly behind her, went directly to the phone on her desk, and punched in a familiar number.

"Mom, how about some unexpected company for an early lunch?"

"I'd love it, darling. How does chicken salad sound?"

"Chicken salad sounds great. Just don't go to a lot of trouble, okay?"

"I know, I know, you get exactly one hour for lunch, and Bob has a fit if you're two minutes late getting back."

"Uh, Mom, that's not going to be a problem anymore."

"Does this mean you got the promotion?" her mother asked excitedly.

"I'd rather wait and tell you everything in person."

"I'm looking forward to seeing you, darling."

Kendra replaced the receiver and turned to face

Lindy, who was watching with an anxious expression on her face.

"How awful was your meeting with Bob?" asked Lindy.

"Not awful at all. In fact, it was kind of fun . . . I quit."

"You *quit?*" Though hushed, Lindy's words were anguished. She glanced nervously at the closed door leading to Bob's office.

"Don't worry. That coward won't show his face out here until he's sure I'm gone. Come on. I'll tell you everything while I clear out my desk."

It took Kendra less than five minutes to gather up her few personal possessions and place them in the cardboard box Lindy scavenged from the supply room. Kendra contemplated her "Life's a Beach" coffee mug, a large group photograph of her family, the laser-etched wooden desk set her brothers had given her for Christmas, a blown-glass paperweight a grateful client had brought her from Venice, and the pathetic African violet she never could get to bloom.

"Not much to show for five years, is it?" commented Kendra, waving her hand over the contents of the box.

She glanced around the office to make sure she wasn't forgetting anything. Her gaze turned speculative when it came to rest on a fat, battered three-ring notebook shelved among a collection of similar notebooks. Her personal "book," a compilation of notes containing the names, telephone numbers and trip histories of nearly two hundred satisfied clients. Clients who made a point of working only with Kendra when they booked travel with the agency.

A determined gleam lit her eyes. There was no way Bob could claim the client list as proprietary information of the agency. In every instance Kendra had been the one to generate the business during off hours and pursuing leads that came from her personal contacts in the community.

Surely she owed each and every one of those people the courtesy of a phone call to let them know she would no longer be working for Let's Go Travel? She plucked the notebook from the shelf and added it to the box of her personal possessions.

"God, Kendra, I'm going to miss working with you."

Kendra noted the suspicious brightening in her friend's eyes. "Don't start crying, Lin. I refuse to slink out of here bawling like a whipped puppy. I want to sail out in . . . in—"

"High dudgeon?" offered Lindy, with a telltale sniff.

"I'd prefer righteous rage, but high dudgeon is good." Kendra hugged Lindy once quickly, tucked her new black handbag under one arm, the cardboard box under the other, and flashed her friend a swift grin. "Don't bother getting the door for me, Lin. I want to kick it open on my way out. And don't forget, I'm expecting you after work."

"I'll be there."

One of the things Kendra liked most about her hometown was the diminutive size that made Carmel a pedestrian's paradise. She walked back and forth to work except in the worst weather. She walked to the beach, to the bank, to the library, to the movies, and unless she needed to stock up on staples and cleaning supplies, she even walked to the grocery store.

The six short blocks between the tiny stone cottage she rented and the Let's Go Travel office on Ocean Avenue made it possible for her to eat lunch at home when she wasn't picnicking in the small grassy park set like a jewel in the center of the village. The pleasant stroll between the house she'd grown up in and the cottage she rented made visits with her family frequent and easy.

The Pacific Ocean was just a few blocks down the street, and the Del Monte Forest curled around Carmel's northern boundary. Kendra took a deep breath, enjoying the faint salt tang and the scent of pine resin perfuming the air. The morning fog had burned off, and the sun was warm on her face. Ancient gnarled oak trees shaded the profusion of flowers blooming in flagstone planters along the meridian on Ocean Avenue. Pansies in a dozen shades of purple and yellow, as well as violet blue lobelia, sweet alyssum and pink and red impatiens created an impressive photo opportunity for sauntering tourists.

She stopped at her cottage just long enough to deposit the ungainly cardboard box on her back porch. Then, she continued on her way. She was surprised to see both of her parents waiting for her in their front yard.

"Dad, what are you doing home at this time of day?"

"Your mother called and said she was making chicken salad. Naturally, I hurried right home for lunch." Kirk Martin kissed his daughter on the cheek and winked at his wife.

Kristen Martin gave her husband a playful swat. "Don't keep us in suspense, Kendra. Make the announcement official, so we can start celebrating your promotion. That's why your father is here."

Kendra followed her parents into the house, leaving her purse on the old upright piano in the living room before settling back against the cushioned banquette built into a sunny nook in the kitchen. The room was a pretty blue and white haven of serenity. Now.

Chaos had reigned the previous summer when her father had insisted on remodeling the kitchen himself as an anniversary present for her mother. Kristen Martin had threatened divorce more than once during the dusty, aggravating, seemingly endless task. Her father had simply growled, cranking up the juice on his power tools and continuing to saw and drill with a vengeance.

"Actually, Mom, Dad, what we'll be celebrating is my unemployment."

Kristen gasped. "Bob Warren *fired* you?"

Kendra watched the expression on her mother's face go from aghast to furious in ten seconds flat.

"How dare he!"

"You haul his girl and her friends all over France for ten days, and he cans you on your first day back at work?"

"He didn't exactly fire me. I quit."

"You quit?" Kendra's mother sat down heavily

beside her. "Did he do something, say something he shouldn't have? You've complained before about some of his comments, but did he . . ."

"He'll be eating knuckle sandwich if he did," vowed Kendra's father darkly.

"The man is an unrepentant sexist, but I'd have flattened him, myself, if he . . . uh, if he . . ." Kendra searched for a euphemism that wouldn't offend her ladylike mother as much as the act she was clearly afraid had occurred. "If he stepped over the line."

"Thank goodness." Kristen rose to her feet and began bustling around the kitchen, preparing lunch. "Set the table, Kendra, and start explaining what you mean by this 'quitting' nonsense."

"It's not nonsense, Mother. Bob Warren gave my promotion to someone else. So I quit." Kendra set three places with the serviceable everyday china, thick glasses, and stainless steel flatware that had been a fixture in the Martin kitchen since her childhood, last summer's remodeling project notwithstanding.

"Now, darling, to be fair, your boss never *promised* you that promotion, did he?" Kristen looked up, spoon in hand, from a heavy ceramic serving bowl filled to the brim with succulent chunks of chicken, bits of celery, minced onion, chopped pecans, and her own special dressing.

"No, Bob never promised me the promotion, but he promised to give my application due consideration. I felt like such a patsy when I realized that he'd just been stringing me along until after I returned from the tour with his daughter and her friends."

"Who got the job?" Kirk Martin snuck a piece of chicken out of the bowl.

"Theo Canlis," answered Kendra, sneaking a piece for herself when her mother turned to pull a tray of sourdough rolls from the oven.

Kirk wrinkled his forehead. "Isn't he the guy who used to make those goofy television commercials for his used-car lot? When did he become a travel agent?"

"Last year, when he sold his car business," said Kendra grimly. "He had some kind of mid-life crisis when he turned forty and decided to become a flight attendant or a travel agent so he could see the world. Bob hired him for the Salinas office."

"Don't eat out of the common bowl." Kristen smacked the back of her daughter's hand with the serving spoon. "A good job isn't easy to come by, Kendra. I hope you didn't say anything you'll regret later."

"I don't regret a single word I said to Bob Warren, Mom. Especially the part about quitting."

"Let's all sit down," suggested her father. "We'll eat, talk calmly and after lunch, Kendra, you can go back and have another conversation with Bob. Explain that you were disappointed, apologize for any hasty words and I bet the man would be willing to ignore your decision to quit. In time, I'm sure you'll earn that promotion you want so badly."

"Five minutes ago you were ready to feed him a knuckle sandwich, Dad. What's going on?"

He sighed. "Kendra, you're only twenty-seven years old. True, you have a business degree and five years of work experience. But Bob has been in the travel industry here for longer than you've been alive. I have to believe that he had sound business reasons for promoting someone else."

"The only reason I didn't get that promotion is because I lack an appendage Bob Warren considers essential to managerial responsibility," Kendra stated evenly.

Kristen winced at her daughter's words. "Darling, your father is right, you'll have other opportunities for promotion. But how many times does a plum job like the one you have—"

"Had," corrected Kendra.

"I don't like to hear you sound so hard," reproved Kristen. "Even if you *never* get promoted to manager, the job at Let's Go Travel is secure, well-paying, and loaded with nice benefits like free travel and good health insurance. It's a wonderful job that affords you a very respectable position in the community. Reconsider, Kendra. Please."

"Mother, I doubt I have a chance in hell of ever managing one of the branches."

"Is that really so important?"

Kendra set her jaw at an uncompromising angle.

"Yes." She gave a sharp, bitter laugh. "Of course, Bob made it very clear that I could 'buy' myself a promotion by investing my reward money in his business."

Her parents exchanged a troubled look. Kirk cleared his throat and opened his mouth to speak, but his wife placed a restraining hand on his arm. "Maybe this isn't the right time to get into that other matter."

"What other matter?" asked Kendra.

"It's nothing. We'll discuss it later, when you're not quite so . . . agitated."

"Mother, I am not agitated. I'm *furious*. I was denied a promotion I happen to believe emphatically that I deserve—"

"Don't take that tone with your mother, young woman."

"Kirk, please, she's not thinking clearly. She's upset."

Kendra felt like screaming. Instead, she lowered her voice and spoke very slowly.

"I am not *upset,* and my thinking is perfectly clear."

Kristen shook her head sadly. "This is not like you, Kendra."

"Maybe not," she acknowledged. "But nothing has felt so right, so necessary, so damn *good* in ages as quitting my job. In fact, what I mostly feel right now is ecstatic."

"And just why is that?" A truculent expression spread over her father's weathered features.

"I mean to make a number of changes in my life, Dad," she began.

"And we want to hear every one of them, darling," interrupted Kristen in a conciliatory tone. "But your father has to get back to his office, and before he leaves, we have something we want to discuss with you."

Kendra rested her fork on her plate and reclined

against the banquette. "I'm listening."

"Daddy and I have been talking. We think you should let him handle your reward money for a while."

"If the two of you need money, you can have as much as you want," said Kendra, surprised at this first inkling of financial difficulties. "Take it all."

Her father drew back, clearly affronted. "Your mother and I don't need or want your money, Kendra."

"Then I don't understand."

"We want to safeguard the money for you," explained her father. "Not permanently. Just until you learn how to manage such an enormous sum and get it all invested wisely."

"We're afraid the temptation to fritter away that money will be too great." She exchanged another look with her husband. "Especially now that you've quit your job."

"You're serious." Kendra stared at her parents, incredulous. "I can't believe this. You two are acting like I'm a ditzy fifteen-year-old girl about to squander her allowance on makeup. I've managed my own bank account since I was old enough to baby-sit for fifty cents an hour."

"We're talking about considerably more money than you ever earned baby-sitting, Kendra."

"I had the presence of mind to save a child's *life*, and you're worried about my ability to manage the *reward?*"

"Three hundred and fifty thousand dollars is a lot of money."

"So what, Dad?"

"That's exactly the attitude your mother and I are concerned about."

Kendra could feel herself shaking with anger, and even worse, with hurt and disappointment. How could her parents think so little of her? Didn't they respect her, didn't they know her at all?

"You know, maybe Bob isn't the problem," she mused aloud.

"Bob?" Kristen's perplexed expression gave way to a worried frown. "Oh, Kendra, you're not seriously thinking of buying that promotion, are you?"

Kendra shook her head in exasperation, searching her mother's face for an understanding she didn't really expect to find. "Maybe the problem isn't even you and Dad. Maybe *I'm* the problem. How I present myself. How I let others treat me. I don't know."

She rose from the table and carried her dish and utensils to the sink. "I can't talk about this anymore right now. I need to think about some things."

"What are you going to do?" asked her mother.

For just an instant, Kendra wasn't quite sure how to respond. Then, she was hit with a wonderful, liberating sense of purpose. There was one thing she wanted to do very much. She squared her shoulders and faced her parents with a burgeoning confidence.

"I'm going back to France. I believe I'll take the Bourquels up on their offer to visit them in Normandy."

"France? Kendra are you out of your mind? You can't go to *France.* You'll never get your job back that way."

"I don't want my job back, Mother."

"Kendra, you're being completely irresponsible. I cannot agree to this plan. You scarcely know these people. Have you lost all sense of—"

Kendra forestalled the rest of her father's lecture with an upraised hand.

"Please, don't make me say things we'll both regret, Dad. I'll be glad to have your advice and suggestions about my reward money. I've always respected your experience in financial matters, but understand this: I intend to manage that money myself. And I am going to France." She gave her mother a peck on the cheek. "Thanks for lunch, Mom."

Kendra let herself out, an overwhelming sadness washing over her as she closed the front door on the house that for the first time in her life no longer felt like home.

She covered the few short blocks to her cottage in a virtual daze. Too much strong emotion and too many drastic changes in the past few days had left her feeling buffeted off-balance, and at the same time, strangely exhilarated.

By nature, Kendra wasn't tempestuous or belligerent. Yet, in the space of hours, she'd fought with her boss and her parents. She was a responsible woman who thought long and hard before making decisions. Yet she'd quit her job on the spot and decided to return to France with scarcely a minute's consideration. She'd always been careful and controlled where men were concerned. Certainly, she'd never had a one-night stand. Yet it had taken every ounce of willpower she possessed not to throw herself into Jackson Randall's arms and beg him to take her to bed.

What was wrong with her?

Nothing. Everything. Kendra realized with surprise that she didn't really care. For once, she wasn't going to analyze everything to death. She wasn't going to worry about her underlying motivations, or weigh every possible consequence of her actions. She was going to pack her bags, fly to France, and unless she was the unluckiest woman on the face of the earth, she was going to have the time of her life.

Back at her cottage, she hefted the box of office possessions and carried it inside to the kitchen table. Then she went into her bedroom, hauled out her garment bag and a suitcase and began rifling through the clothes in her closet.

The wardrobe she examined was depressingly modest. Two suits, three silk blouses, a couple of tailored dresses, and some coordinated skirts and sweaters for work, plus casual outfits and some exercise gear for her own time. She owned a couple of circumspect bathing suits, a dark raincoat, and shoes suitable for work and play.

She suddenly hated all of it.

The clothes in her closet were perfectly nice, perfectly appropriate for a young career woman, but there was nothing suitably dazzling for a visit to the Bourquels' villa in Deauville. No exotic bikinis, no dashing playclothes, no colorful resort wear. Kendra pushed the clothes to one side and went through them again, refusing to acknowledge the underlying cause of her dissatisfaction.

Five days ago, she wouldn't have cared that her wardrobe didn't contain a single item she could honestly describe as even remotely alluring. No sexy cocktail dresses, no slinky little tops, no form-fitting slacks. Nothing designed to catch a special man's attention or put a gleam of appreciation in his eyes. Five days ago, it wouldn't have mattered that her lingerie was made to last, not to indulge a man's fantasies.

Five days ago, she hadn't known Jackson Randall.

Her lips twisted in a wry little grimace. Involvements had been few and far between since she'd become Bob's assistant manager. There'd been no man in her life at all the past couple of years, let alone a man she wanted to entice and please. She wouldn't have walked away from a relationship if the prospect for happiness had presented itself, but she hadn't been eagerly seeking "Mr. Right," either.

Kendra continued to flick hangers along the bar in her closet. A new and tempting idea began forming in her mind as each item of clothing passed under her hand. She had a check for two million francs in her purse. She could easily buy a new wardrobe if she wanted to. A smile spread over her face, and a sense of excitement burst into life. She could buy a new *Parisian* wardrobe if she wanted to.

For the first time since accepting Jean-Michel's

reward, Kendra was conscious of *feeling* rich.

An image of Jack's face flashed through her mind. She remembered his eyes, their unique shade of misty green, the way they blazed with heat and desire when she looked at him a certain way. Oh, yes, she decided, she very definitely wanted a new wardrobe. Composed entirely of the kind of clothes capable of making a man like Jack Randall drool. Starting with some glamorous underwear.

She ran into the kitchen, pulled her "book" from the box on the kitchen table and flipped pages until she came to the listings under S. She reached for the phone and dialed. Vivian Solis would know exactly where to go shopping in Paris.

The transplanted New Yorker was the wife of a retired garment district jobber who'd made a second fortune when he sold his building to some Japanese investors. Vivian had fabulous taste, she loved good clothes, and her favorite boast was that though her husband could well afford the cost, she hadn't paid retail in the thirty years they'd been married.

"Vivian? Kendra Martin here. May I ask you a small favor?"

"Name it, doll. That bungalow in Tahiti was everything you promised and more. My husband hasn't been so inspired since our honeymoon."

"I'm glad the trip turned out well. Um, Vivian, I'm planning to do a little shopping in Paris, and I need a list of resources. Can you help me out? I don't mean the couture houses, but the places you go on your annual jaunt with your sisters."

"Get yourself a pen and a *big* piece of paper. I rate a good bargain right up there with great sex. If you know where to look, and I do, doll, Paris can be one endless climax."

Kendra grinned at the woman's bawdy humor and spent the next twenty minutes writing. After concluding her conversation with Vivian, she settled down to a stint of even more serious telephone work, utilizing every bit of the experience she'd gained as a travel agent.

Two hours later, she'd booked a flight for early the next week and reserved a room at a charming but little-known hotel near the Place des Vosges. Since she liked the idea of having some flexibility and independence during her visit to the Bourquels, she'd also ordered a French rail pass and arranged to have a rental car available. All of the paperwork confirming her reservations would be arriving by express mail within 48 hours.

The vice-president of her bank had agreed to meet with her at ten the next morning to accept deposit of her two million francs, convert them into dollars, and issue enough traveler's checks to last a month. There would be plenty of time to get serious about managing her new fortune when she returned from France. In the interim, she wanted her money absolutely safe and completely liquid. The vice-president had promised to outline her options at their meeting.

By mid-afternoon, she'd worked up the nerve to call the Bourquels. The first number on Laurent's white card had been busy, but Nadine herself had answered the second number listed. She'd assured Kendra that they would still be delighted to have her visit their villa in Deauville, and she'd offered once again to have their driver meet her at de Gaulle airport. Kendra had demurred, explaining that she intended to spend a few days shopping in Paris, but promising to call Nadine when she was ready to leave so they could arrange the details of her arrival at the villa.

Lindy Hughes stopped by after work to pick up the additions to her trousseau. Kendra invited her friend to stay for dinner, preparing a meal of broiled Monterey Bay salmon filets, vine-ripened tomatoes in a light vinaigrette, and steamed artichokes from nearby Castroville. Lindy's lively conversation and hilarious account of Bob Warren's perturbed and agitated state following Kendra's departure occupied the evening hours until well after ten p.m. Eventually, however, Lindy thanked her for the meal, wished her a good time in France, and departed.

And Kendra was left alone with the essential question she had avoided all day.

What was she going to do about Jack? Call him . . . or not? See him . . . or not? Forget him . . . or not?

It was fine to make a rash of glorious plans and declare a bold, daring stance about the future course of her life. Visiting the Bourquels promised to be a once-in-a-lifetime kind of adventure. Shopping in Paris and seeing at her leisure all the sights she'd missed while on tour with the girls, even revisiting some of the same sights, sounded like a dream come true.

But how much of her decision to return to France was simply an excuse, a means of creating an opportunity to see Jack?

Could she trust that sense of connection he'd talked about? Was she reaching for her destiny . . . or was she just chasing rainbows?

Chapter Eleven

Kendra gave her old lawnmower a final push and cut the last swathe of overgrown grass in her backyard. She wiped the perspiration from her brow with the back of her hand and gave a sigh of relief. Done at last. She'd put off mowing the lawn since before leaving on tour with the girls, and she'd been paying the price for the last hour. The grass had grown tall and thick in her absence, and her upper arms and calves ached with the exertion of pushing the old-fashioned mower back and forth across the steep incline of her backyard.

She seated herself on the back porch steps and wished for the energy to walk to the kitchen for the large pitcher of iced tea she'd had the foresight to brew before starting her yard work. It was then that her brother appeared.

"Jerk. I would have mowed your lawn for you. Ask next time."

"Don't yell at me while I'm dying, Kent."

"If you'd mow your lawn every two weeks instead of every two months . . ."

"I'd suffer four times as much." She smiled at her brother. "Want some iced tea?"

"Sure."

"It's in a glass pitcher in the fridge. Bring me some, too."

Kent gave a disgusted snort, then went into the house. He returned with the iced tea and a bag of potato chips.

"You're not drinking that tea straight out of the pitcher, Kent."

"You sound more like Mom every day, sis." Kent winked, took a long swig from the pitcher, then reached into the bag for a handful of chips.

"What the hell. We've been sharing germs since we were little. Give it here." Kendra took the pitcher and drank deeply. "Have you come to wish me a *bon voyage?*"

"Actually, I came to talk about your car."

"What about my car?" she asked warily, sinking back down onto the porch steps.

He grinned. "Well, now that you're rich you'll probably be wanting new wheels. I wondered if I could take the old Volkswagen off your hands."

"You want me to *give* you my car?"

A bewildered expression crossed his face. "No, I want to *buy* your car."

"Sure . . . I'll sell it to you for cheap," she said with a wry, knowing smile.

"You'll sell it to me at blue book," he retorted. "What's the matter with you?"

Kendra didn't answer, ashamed to have jumped to such suspicious conclusions about her brother's intentions. But before she could explain herself, he rose to his feet shaking his head.

"Keep your damn car. You've changed since you got all that money. I thought buying your car would be a good deal for both of us, but if you're so paranoid about your own brother ripping you off or cheating you, just forget it. I'll buy another one." He flipped her a handful of change. "That's for the tea."

"Kent, don't be that way. I didn't mean—"

"Save it, Kendra. Have a real great time in France with your important new friends." He walked away without looking back.

Kendra banged the back of her head against the porch railing twice, swearing silently. Then she began swearing aloud.

Oh, yeah. Having money was all kinds of fun.

An empty suitcase lay open across Kendra's bed, a garment bag collapsed next to it. Freshly laundered clothing basics made neat piles across the pillows—a few changes of underwear, a sleepshirt, the slate-blue washed silk outfit, a bathing suit, a couple of casual outfits, and her favorite leather flats.

The nearly empty suitcases would arrive in France containing the barest essentials. Kendra grinned. But those bags were going to return home bulging with her fabulous new Parisian wardrobe. She stuffed the last of her toiletries into a battered carry-on, then drew a firm line through several more items on the list of trip preparations tucked beneath the lamp on her nightstand.

Nearly done. Her French rail pass had arrived that morning. She'd picked up her laundry, canceled her newspaper, and arranged for the post office to hold her mail. She'd prepaid her rent and her other monthly bills, and the bank card company had been most accommodating about increasing her credit limits once they'd verified her new account balance.

She'd even said a strained goodbye to her family, leaving her parents a copy of her itinerary and promising to call at least once while she was away.

Now, all she had left to do was pack, get a good night's sleep so she'd be ready for her flight tomorrow at noon . . . and decide whether or not she was going to call Jack.

The debate had been raging in her head for nearly ten days. Nadine Bourquel had insisted that Kendra stay a minimum of two weeks at the villa. Kendra had tacked another two weeks onto her trip 'just in case.' She'd researched the D-day beaches and other sights she thought a marine might find interesting 'just in case.'

In fact, all of her trip preparations had been made 'just in case' she decided to call Jack, see him, spend time with him. She wanted to . . . but she was afraid. What if she'd been mistaken about the intensity of feeling between them? What if he'd changed his mind about her?

The telephone shrilled. Kendra raced for the kitchen, cursing the thrift that had prevented her from adding an extension in her bedroom.

"Hello?" She heard a series of clicks and some static and then a faint echo of her breathless greeting.

"Hello!" she repeated loudly.

"Why . . . shouting?"

The words faded in and out over the line, but she recognized Jack's deep voice instantly. She felt a thrill of excitement. He'd called her. He'd called her from Paris.

"Jack, the connection is awful on my end. Hang up and try again."

". . . kidding me? Now that I finally . . . me to hang up? I'm able . . . perfectly."

Kendra gritted her teeth in frustration. "I only understand about every fourth word you say, and everything *I* say echoes back over the line. Give me your number, and I'll try calling you."

The line suddenly went dead. And Kendra's decision about Jack was made.

How could she go to Paris and *not* see him? She was going to call him right back and . . . damn! She didn't even have his telephone number. The irony amused her. She'd planned half her trip around the possibility that she and Jack would meet. Now that she'd finally made up her mind, she didn't have the least notion . . . Of course, the embassy. She could get in touch with him through the embassy.

The phone rang again.

"Any better?" Jack's voice was warm, husky, and completely audible.

"Much better."

"I haven't been able to stop thinking about you."

"I've thought about you a little, too."

"Only a little? I guess I need to practice my goodbye kiss."

"Your technique was perfect," she murmured. The bold comment seemed to spring from her mouth of its own volition, surprising her. She wasn't a flirt by nature, but Jack's elemental masculinity had a way of making her want to flex her femininity.

"Nope," he said firmly. "I better practice. How about at Thanksgiving? I just learned that I have a chance to take ten days' leave the end of November. Can I come and see you."

"Thanksgiving is a long way off." Kendra took a deep breath and let 'just in case' become a reality. "How about if I come to Paris a little sooner?"

"You're escorting another tour here? That's fantastic! How did you manage to get another tour so soon after getting back? Especially now that you're a manager?"

Pleasure and satisfaction filled her. His confident assumption that she'd been promoted nearly wiped away the bitterness of her confrontation with Bob Warren. "I'm not going to be escorting any more tours, Jack. Listen, it's a long story. I'll tell you when I see you."

"I can't wait. How long can you stay this time?"

"The Bourquels invited me to spend a couple of weeks at their villa in Deauville. I thought . . . if you still wanted to see me . . . that I'd spend another couple of weeks in Paris."

"Kendra, I'd burn up the phone lines if I told you just how much I want to see you again. When do you arrive?"

She did a quick calculation of the time difference. "About eight in the morning Paris time, the day after tomorrow."

"Damn! I want to meet your plane, but I don't think I can arrange a replacement to cover my duty on such short notice."

"We can always wait until Thanksgiving to see each other again," she teased.

"Cute, Kendra. I loved your sense of humor right off the bat. Let me think about this for a minute."

"Think fast. This phone call must be costing you a bundle."

"You're worth it."

"Jack?"

"Yeah?"

"Don't worry about meeting my plane. After ten days on tour with the girls, getting a cab to the hotel by myself will be a breeze."

He chuckled. "Okay. Get a pen, and I'll give you a couple of numbers where you can reach me. And then I need the name, address, and phone number of your hotel."

A long silence followed their exchange of information. There was so much Kendra wanted to say, but she felt tongue-tied and awkward doing so over the telephone. She was aware of the seconds ticking expensively by.

"Are you still there?" asked Jack.

"Yes."

"You're not having second thoughts about seeing me, are you?"

"Only about a million of them," she answered honestly. "Are you?"

"Hell, no. I think meeting you might be the luckiest thing that ever happened to me. And I'm going to do my damndest to make sure you feel the same way about me once you get to Paris."

"Jack?"

"Yeah?"

"I lied. I've been thinking about you a lot."

"Thinking, or *worrying?*"

"You're very perceptive."

"Kendra, don't worry. We're not going to rush anything. We'll take it slow and easy and just . . . get to know each other. Okay?"

"Okay."

"I don't want to hang up."

"Me, either, but it's late, and we've been talking a long time."

"I'd kiss you good night if I was there."

"I'd . . . let you."

The timbre of his voice roughened. "I'll remember you said that."

"Good night, Jack."

"See you soon, Kendra."

Kendra sat on a park bench in the Place des Vosges, watching a group of toddlers splash their hands in the stone fountain, oblivious to their mothers' admonitions about not getting their clothes wet. Neat rows of huge leafy trees cast long shadows in the late afternoon sun, providing shade to one or two old men smoking and reading *Le Figaro*. A trio of teenage boys kicked a soccer ball up and down the wide, packed earth walkways, respectfully skirting a statue of Louis XIII astride a horse.

Patches of perfect emerald lawn grew here and there around the park set squarely in the center of the Place. Beyond the wrought iron park railing, a narrow street encircled the park. Beyond the street, the Place was completely enclosed by the mellow rosy glow of seventeenth century townhouses. The three-story *pavillions* were built of red brick and pale golden stone, surmounted by mansard roofs with dormer windows. Roman arches pierced the cool shadows of the long arcades running beneath.

Kendra thought the Place des Vosges was both elegant and charming, and she was glad her hotel was less than a block away. She could picture herself and Jack strolling in the park, exploring the tiny shops and art galleries, the restaurants housed the length of the arcade on the ground floor of the *pavillions*. She imagined walking with him along the winding streets and visiting the small museums of the surrounding Marais.

Any moment now, she would see Jack. She scanned the small park, eager for her first sight of him.

After a quiet cab ride from de Gaulle airport, Kendra had checked into her hotel and called Jack at the embassy. The hotel was small and quaint with a small, quaint lobby to match. She had wanted a little more space and privacy the first time she saw Jack alone. He knew how to get to the Place des Vosges, so they had arranged to meet by the equestrian statue of Louis XIII when Jack went off duty at five p.m. She'd requested a three-thirty wake-up call. Then, exhausted from her flight, she had crawled between the thick sheets of what surely was the most comfortable bed in Paris for a long nap.

At precisely three-thirty, the owner, a fiftyish woman with shrewd eyes and a kind smile, had tapped on Kendra's door, bringing her a complimentary "breakfast." On a tray had been a tall glass of cold orange juice, a small ceramic pot of strong coffee, some steamed milk, and a piece of *pain au chocolat,* a long strip of bittersweet chocolate baked in a square of *croissant* dough.

Kendra had thanked the woman for her thoughtfulness, devoured the snack, and stepped into a hot shower. She'd dressed in the slate-blue washed silk pants and top, and she'd left her hair loose. After dabbing on a few drops of her new perfume, she'd turned in her key at the front desk, and walked the few short steps to the Place des Vosges.

The equestrian statue was easy to find and visible from almost any angle. Kendra looked up and all of a sudden Jack was walking toward her, his wide shoulders and brisk stride immediately recognizable. She waved, and even from twenty feet away his smile began to melt her heart. He broke into a quick jog and closed the remaining distance between them. She caught a faint whiff of his citrusy after-shave when he came to a halt beside her.

"I can't believe you're really here," he said.

"Me, either."

He reached out and twined a strand of her hair around his index finger. "You wore your hair down."

"You said you liked it down, so . . ."

"You look . . . beautiful."

"I'm . . . so glad to see you, again."

Jack didn't answer. He simply pulled her into his arms, hugging her tightly. "All day long, all I could think about was meeting you after work, seeing you again. I came straight here after I got off duty. Sorry about the uniform."

"I don't mind your uniform." She should step away, she really should. But Jack felt so strong, so solid, and he smelled so damn *good*, she was content to let him hold her.

"I promised myself that I'd go slow, that I wouldn't rush you. But all I can think about is how sweet you feel in my arms. I want to kiss you so badly, I'm shaking like a boy," he murmured close to her ear.

The whisper, the feel of his breath stirring against her ear caused a shiver of awareness to race over her skin. Her body, her senses were attuned to his in a way she'd never before experienced. Just knowing that he wanted to kiss her created a reciprocal need in her.

She shifted position in his arms and pressed her lips to his. A shudder rippled over his body, and she deepened the kiss. His lips were as firm and warm as she remembered, the corner of his mouth as intriguing to the tip of her tongue. She ran the flat of her hands over the hard muscles of his back, liking his breadth, his strength.

Liking the way he kissed her back.

He rubbed his mouth back and forth across hers in a gentle motion that was as arousing as it was restrained. He angled his head, softening his mouth in silent invitation. She wanted to open her mouth, feel again the riot of sensation she'd felt when he kissed her goodbye at the airport. She wanted to give him the same intense pleasure.

Instead, she drew back reluctantly, letting a few inches of space separate them without breaking his embrace. There was still so much they didn't know about each other.

"I feel like my body is getting way ahead of

my judgment right now, Jack. I'm not sure kissing is such a hot idea."

"Honey, kissing is an idea that's only going to get hotter the more time we spend together. There's no ticking clock this time and no teenage girls observing our every move."

He pulled her back against his chest, rubbing his chin over the top of her head. The gesture was tender, affectionate and that moved her as much as his passion.

"But we can slow down a little," he said.

"Thanks."

"So. If we're not going to kiss each other anymore right now, what would you like to do?"

She knew immediately. "I'd like to take a cab up to Montmartre and watch the sun set over Paris from the steps of Sacré Coeur."

Jack laughed, a full-throated sound of pure joy.

"Does that mean yes, or no?"

"Kendra, the way I'm feeling right now, you could ask for the Eiffel Tower, and I'd find a way to get it for you. Hell, yes, let's go find a cab and watch the sunset."

The wide steps of Sacré Coeur were crammed with students, lovers, tourists, clerics, and even some gypsies, all watching the sky turn pink and gold as the sun began its descent over Paris.

Protesting loudly and swearing creatively, the cab driver had taken Kendra and Jack all the way to the top of *la butte,* as Parisians referred to Montmartre. He'd let them out at the basilica, and Jack had added a healthy tip to the fare.

"Tomorrow night we take the stair paths," said Kendra, wedging into a small space beneath one of the basilica's arched white portals.

"Tomorrow night we take the *funicular railway*," retorted Jack, squeezing in next to her.

"Where's your sense of adventure? All those adorable twisty little side streets—"

"All those hundreds of steep little stairs," he mimicked. "I might be persuaded to walk *down* this mountain, though. That narrow-gauge railway is going to be hard-pressed to disperse all these people, and good luck finding a taxi."

Jack scanned the crowd growing larger and noisier by the minute. The throng had spilled over into the narrow one-way street running in front of the white-domed basilica. Directly in front of them, some German students were passing a bottle of wine among themselves with rowdy abandon. A large young man lurched backward into Kendra. Jack caught him under the shoulders and gave him a good-natured heave forward into a knot of his friends.

"Okay?" He wrapped one arm protectively around Kendra's shoulders.

"Fine." Nestled against his side, what could be wrong?

"Somehow, I pictured this moment as being a lot more romantic," said Jack dryly. "I think we were doing better before, when we only had twelve teenagers watching, instead of four hundred strangers."

"True, but you can't beat the view."

"No . . . you can't beat the view." Jack looked down at her, shielding her with his shoulder as he absorbed another jolt from the crowd. He cupped the side of her face with his free hand, brushing his thumb over her cheek.

"You're flirting with me."

"Yes, I am. Do you like it?"

She reached up, covering his hand with hers. "Very much."

"Ready to walk down some of those adorable twisty streets? I understand the nightlife can get pretty rowdy on Montmartre once the sun goes down."

"Transvestite hookers and raunchy burlesque don't appeal to you?"

"Oh, I like raunchy burlesque as much as the next red-blooded American male . . . I just prefer it in the privacy of my own bedroom." His slow, seductive smile carried an element of challenge.

Kendra smiled back, a full, womanly smile that held a challenge of its own. "You're male, all right."

"You're flirting with me." His voice was lower with a husky note that hadn't been there a moment before.

"Yes, I am. Do you like it?"

He chuckled softly. "Very much. Come on. I'll buy you dinner."

207

Chapter Twelve

Kendra and Jack wound their way down the narrow cobblestoned streets, descending a series of stair paths until they ended up in the Place du Tertre. There were still a number of sketch artists plying their trade in the famous square in spite of the encroaching dusk. Jack waved off a couple of the more importunate artists as he and Kendra ducked into a rustic *bistro*.

The proprietor acknowledged them with a nod, shouted an order into the kitchen and seated them at a table along a whitewashed wall. The ceiling was low with rough-hewn timbers showing through the plaster. An accordion player sat on a high stool near the bar, playing folk songs. The savory smells of traditional French cuisine filled the air, and incredibly, only a few of the patrons were smoking.

The proprietor handed them hand-written menus covered in clear plastic and asked in broken English what they wanted to drink.

Jack ordered a bottle of still mineral water and a carafe of *vin ordinaire*.

He picked up his menu, a slight frown furrowing his brow. "I can't believe it. Now, that I'm finally learning to recognize some of the words for food, I end up in a restaurant where I can't read the writing. You've just got to love this town." He pointed to a line on the menu. "Can you make this out?"

"Oysters. Six kinds."

"Great." He grimaced, pointing to another line. "And this?"

"Snails."

He shuddered. "God, no. How about this?"

"I think that might be dinner," said Kendra, her mouth watering. "How do you feel about beef burgundy?"

His eyes lit up. "Stew? With meat? And carrots? Fantastic. Order it."

"For me, too, I think." Kendra gave their order to the proprietor when he returned with their drinks. She tasted the dark red wine. "Good. A little rough, but good."

Jack took a sip, nodded, then leaned forward resting his elbows on the table. "When I called you the other night, you mentioned something about not escorting any more tours. Feel like telling me the rest of the story?"

"It's pretty simple. I quit my job."

Jack looked shocked. "I thought you got promoted?"

"A promotion is what I expected. Instead, my first day back at work I learned that my boss had promoted a man from another branch. Promoted him the same day I left on tour with his daughter and her friends."

"Ouch."

"Not only that, but my boss made it pretty clear that the only way I was going to get a promotion was if I invested some money in his business."

"He sounds like a helluva guy."

Kendra giggled. "My dad was ready to feed him a knuckle sandwich."

"Your dad sounds like my kind of guy. Have you got something else lined up?"

"No, I'm taking a little time off first."

"What about when you go home, will you be able to find another job with a travel agency, or will you look for a different type of work?"

"I haven't decided. I have money . . . saved up, so I don't have to make a decision right away."

"This trip is a complete vacation? You don't have to do *any* work?"

"Only if you consider a heavy-duty shopping assault on the *dégriffe* boutiques to be work."

"What's a *dégriffe?*"

"A discount boutique. One of my clients told me about them. *Dégriffes* stock big-name designer ready-to-wear from previous seasons. The shops have to remove the designer labels in order to sell the clothes off price. But if you don't care about the missing labels, you can get some fabulous bargains."

"Do you?"

"I've never worn a designer *anything* in my whole life. I couldn't care less about the labels, but I can't *wait* to go to work bargain-hunting."

He rolled his eyes. "I've got two sisters, remember? I know exactly how much work shopping can be. I've carried their bags around a mall more times than I care to remember."

"Does that mean I shouldn't invite you along on my shopping spree?"

"That depends . . . are you going to try on any low-cut dresses or short skirts?"

Her face assumed a prim expression. "My style tends to run to the businesslike and practical."

"Kendra?"

"Yes?"

"Change your style."

"Oh, right away, Jack. And just because you *asked* so nicely."

He gave her a lazy grin. "What else have you got planned while you're in France?"

"A trip to Deauville. The Bourquels invited me to spend a couple of weeks with them at their villa."

"I meant to ask you about that the night I

called, but I got sidetracked thinking about kissing you goodnight."

Kendra felt the heat of a quick blush rise up her neck to color her cheeks. "I thought we decided kissing was a dangerous topic for the next little while?"

"Uh-uh, we decided kissing was a hot topic. So hot, I think we should consider the whole issue again."

Even thinking about kissing Jack made her mouth tingle with remembered sensations of pleasure. "Do you want to hear about my plans to visit the Bourquels, or do you just want to torment me?"

"I want to hear about the Bourquels . . . and I want to *kiss* you."

"Originally, I declined the Bourquels' offer," she continued, deliberately ignoring his last comment. "After I quit my job, I called back and asked if their invitation was still open. They said yes, so here I am."

Jack sat silently for a moment, running the tip of his index finger around the rim of his wineglass. "If I hadn't called you, would you have gotten in touch with me?"

There was so much feeling in his question, so much need stamped on every sharp plane and hard angle of his face that Kendra didn't even think of hedging.

"Yes," she said softly. "I questioned a hundred times whether seeing you again was really a good idea, but in the end, I would have called you at the embassy. "

"I'm glad."

A waiter arrived at their table with an oval copper pot, two crockery bowls and some silverware. He lifted the pot lid and began ladling large portions into each bowl. Thick steam curled up, scenting the air with the rich aroma of *boeuf Bourguignon*.

"I had a snack this afternoon after my nap, but suddenly, I'm starving." Kendra dipped her spoon into the rich gravy.

Jack speared a bite-sized morsel of tender meat and chewed with obvious relish. "God, the French can cook."

For a few minutes, they ate in companionable silence, listening to accordion music and French conversation, watching the lone waiter bustle around among the tables.

Jack wiped his mouth with the red and white checkered napkin, and leaned back in his chair. "When do you go to Deauville?"

"On Monday."

"Perfect. That means we can spend some time together this weekend. How are you getting to Deauville?"

"I'm not sure. I reserved a rental car, but I'm supposed to call Nadine Bourquel to finalize the details of my arrival at the villa."

He grinned. "You're living pretty ritzy for a woman with no job."

"Ludicrous, isn't it? I can hardly believe it, myself. My parents think I'm crazy. They want me to crawl back to my boss and beg for my old job. They didn't want me to visit the Bourquels, or even take this trip."

"Because of me?"

"They . . . don't know about you."

"Were you afraid they would disapprove?"

Kendra met his gaze squarely. "I didn't think it was any of their business. I wanted some emotional privacy while we figured things out."

"Do you have any answers yet?"

"No."

"Me, either. You took me by surprise, Kendra. So did the feelings that exploded between us when we met." He leaned forward, taking her left hand in both of his. "I broke my cardinal rule for you."

"Which rule is that?"

"The one that says 'Don't get involved in a long-distance relationship.' Military life is hell on the best marriages, let alone any lesser commitment at long distance. I've never loved a woman enough to risk that kind of pain. I didn't want to cause it, I didn't want to feel it."

"Jack, the defining fact of our situation is that we live five thousand miles apart. Maybe seeing each other again, trying to pursue the feelings we have was a mistake," said Kendra, suddenly afraid that there was no way to bridge the disparate circumstances of their lives.

He dismissed her argument with a wave of his hand. "Once we'd met, seeing each other again was inevitable, it was just a matter of where and when. We can't go back. The feelings are there. We can only go forward and see where they lead."

"Meeting you has been like stepping into a whirlwind, Jack. I don't regret the experience, but I wish everything didn't feel so . . . rushed." She gave him a quirky grin. "Hell, I don't even know if I *like* you!"

"Oh, you like me, all right. The same way I like you. We just haven't had enough time together to learn all the reasons *why*."

"I'd still like to follow a more conventional course."

"I know. I *know*." He let go of Kendra's hand, raking his hair impatiently. "That's the trouble with long-distance relationships. Everything is so . . . compressed. There's no opportunity to go slow, and there's no such thing as "normal." The whole relationship has to happen in sporadic, intense increments."

"What if I can't handle that kind of emotional turbulence in a relationship?"

"What if *I* can't?" Jack drained the last swallow of wine from his glass. "That's why we need more time. I talked to my commanding officer about taking my leave *now*, while you're in France, instead of at Thanksgiving. If my leave comes through, then we'll spend a couple of weeks finding out exactly what each of us can handle in this relationship when you return from Deauville."

"Won't your family be disappointed when you don't go home for Thanksgiving?" asked Kendra, a touch of uncertainty in her voice. She was thrilled at the prospect of spending whole days with Jack, apprehensive about the spiraling pace that would set for their relationship.

"I wasn't going home, anyway. I was coming to visit you," he reminded her. "Besides, after seventeen years in the Marine Corps, my family doesn't expect to see me every holiday."

"They must miss you."

"I miss them, too, but I go home when I can. Things work out."

"I can't believe I don't know this about you yet, but . . . where's home?"

"Grady, Oklahoma."

"What's it like?"

"About what you'd expect from a rural midwestern community. Ranches and some farming, small local businesses, like that. My dad's a mechanic at the garage in town. My mom does a little part-time bookkeeping now that my sisters and I are grown."

"What are your sisters like?"

He grinned suddenly. "Married. Sometimes

when I go home and listen to them yelling at their kids, I have a hard time believing they're the same girls I grew up with."

There was an ease, an affection about the way he spoke of his family that told Kendra he had no hang-ups about what sounded like a modest background. She wanted to know more about his family, about his childhood, about his experiences in the Marine Corps.

She wanted to know him. Really know him. Not just the superficial things, like what his favorite foods were, or what kind of books he read. She wanted to know the important things about him, the forces that had shaped the man he was. She wanted to know what he thought, what he felt, what he dreamed. She wanted to know his heart, his mind.

No, not wanted, she realized. She *needed* to know him that intimately. Needed it way down deep in some essential part of her soul. Because she was growing more certain by the hour that she and Jack would be lovers. And when that happened, it wouldn't be enough simply to acknowledge the passion between them.

She would need to know why.

Kendra set out early the next morning with Vivian's list in her hand and a burning desire in her heart to purchase at least one low-cut dress with a short skirt. She descended the steps to the Métro stop a block from her hotel and exited at the church, Saint-Germain-des-Prés.

Nearby was the colorful crowded market she'd visited with the girls a few weeks earlier. Though some of the shops and offices were closed for the annual August holidays, the street was alive with the sights and sounds of Parisians going to work. Shopkeepers were busy rolling up the grilles covering their storefronts and sweeping the sidewalk from their doors to the street. Office workers walked briskly, swinging thin leather briefcases, or scanning a folded copy of *Le Monde*.

Kendra glanced at her map once more to get her bearings and turned down a side street that led to the first boutique on Vivian's list. The narrow paving-stone sidewalk was charming, but treacherous to heels, and she was glad she'd worn her leather flats. Two blocks further on, she found *Carina*.

"Walk in like you're ready to buy the place, doll, you'll want to within ten minutes. Try and sweet-talk the dragon lady who owns the boutique," she'd counseled. "She can be a real bitch, but she's got the best inventory and the best bargains on the street. She's got great fashion sense, so trust what she tells you. You'll walk out looking like a million."

Kendra had been terrified by the description

and even considered skipping the boutique entirely, but Vivian's promise of beautiful clothes at wonderful prices was too enticing to ignore. Vivian had gone on to add a whole slew of instructions, information, and advice.

"Don't touch the clothes. Wait for a *vendeuse* to help you. Parisians are very touchy about respectful manners, so be sure to greet the proprietor and the salespeople as soon as you walk in the door. Say something nice about the shop right away, too. Don't say, don't even think, the word 'browsing.' The *vendeuse* would rather haul out every dress on the rack and have you say you don't like *anything* than have you spend ten minutes on your own 'looking.'"

"You can't be serious," Kendra had protested.

"Trust me, doll, shopping for clothes is serious business over there. Frenchwomen don't buy a lot of clothes, so they make the ones they buy count. The *vendeuses* in these boutiques expect to serve the customer. If you don't let them do their job, you're not only being disrespectful, but you're cutting off even the chance for them to make a sale."

"Sounds like a whole different system."

"Sure is, but once you understand it, you can get downright spoiled. Once you start trying on clothes, maybe choosing one or two outfits, they'll warm right up. They'll bring you coffee, a snack, the whole nine yards. But be real sure when you buy something. French shops don't have the same kind of flexible exchange and return policies we do. And don't turn down a great buy on an item you like that's even close to fitting. They'll usually do alterations for free. Ask to have everything delivered to your hotel, most boutiques do that for free, too. I hate schlepping a bunch of bags around with me, don't you?"

"What about prices?" Kendra had asked.

"Fabulous. Especially when you see the clothes. To die for, I'm telling you. You'll find marvelous shops filled with clothes by designers you've never heard of. Don't forget to wear nice underwear and a decent outfit if *you* want a little respect. You know about *détaxe,* the export discount, don't you?"

"Yes."

"Then you're all set. Have a great time!"

Kendra walked slowly back and forth in front of *Carina,* pretending a keen interest in the window display while working up the nerve to go inside. She clutched her new black handbag from the Bourquels like a talisman, took a deep breath, and walked in.

Used to the enormous size, bright lights, linoleum floors, and crowded clothing racks of American outlet shops, Kendra was almost disappointed by the subdued lighting and tiny floor space of the French *dégriffe* boutique. The clothes, however, were spectacular.

And the dragon lady was as formidable as Vivian had promised. Petite, rail-thin, and dressed severely in black, the boutique owner evaluated Kendra with a practiced eye. Her expression softened immediately upon noting the black handbag.

"Bonjour, madame." Kendra hid her diffidence behind a wide smile.

"Bonjour, mademoiselle."

"I'm Kendra Martin. My friend, Vivian Solis, told me I absolutely could not leave Paris without visiting your boutique. I can see now why she said so, your shop is lovely. I want a few things for a trip to Deauville. Can you give me some guidance about what sort of clothing I'll need? I place myself entirely in your hands."

The woman's chilly demeanor warmed up a few degrees, and she answered Kendra in English, which Vivian had told her was a mark of acceptance.

"Madame Solis has been a client for many years. I will do what I can for you. I am Madame Olivier." The woman examined Kendra from head to toe, then pronounced, "You are a size eight. We will start with clothes for daytime."

She moved to the double-tiered racks along one wall and began pulling out armfuls of slacks and blouses, walking shorts, tops, jackets, and even a few one-piece, knee-length rompers. Kendra stood humbly by her side feeling like an acolyte at a church service. Madame Olivier was quick and decisive, her hand sweeping over the hangers like a predatory bird deciding between field mice.

The fabrics were gorgeous. Crisp cotton, Irish linen, every weave and weight of silk Kendra knew and some she'd never seen spilled over Madame Olivier's arm. The design details on each item were intricate but not fussy, and the workmanship was superb. Jackets, slacks, even the walking shorts were lined, but so cleverly that Kendra knew they wouldn't add an ounce to a woman's figure.

"Oh, wait," said Kendra, spying a pair of raw silk slacks in a shade of shell pink she'd always admired. "I'd like to try those slacks, too."

"Non," said Madame Olivier curtly.

"But I love the color." Kendra began reaching for the hanger, then remembered Vivian's stricture and pulled back her hand.

"For lingerie, or a blouse, yes, you can have this color. But slacks? No, your *hanches* are *un peu trop fortes.*"

Fat hips? Kendra swallowed a quick retort. Vivian had told her to trust this woman's fashion instinct, but she wasn't sure she was going to enjoy the experience very much. She'd never been told she had fat hips in her life. Of course, compared to this . . . this *twig,* she probably seemed like an elephant. In fact, the longer Madame Olivier looked at her with those thin, pursed lips, the fatter her hips felt.

Madame Olivier turned back and pulled another pair of slacks from the rack. *"Voilà!"*

"Oh, how pretty." The woman knew her colors, acknowledged Kendra. The slacks Madame Olivier had chosen for her were made of a soft dupionni silk with small slubs running through the fabric. And the only word to describe the deep camellia color was luscious.

Madame Olivier added a long-sleeved handkerchief linen blouse in a slightly lighter shade of pink, a short-sleeved white cotton shirt with a delicate lace edging around the neck and a sleeveless silk shell in exactly the same camellia shade. Kendra noted the shell's deep V-neck and knew the entire outfit was going home with her.

"So . . . with the slacks you wear the shell for evening, the T-shirt for play and the blouse anytime," explained Madame Olivier. "The coordinating jacket I have only in size ten, but I can make it fit you. There is also a skirt. Very short, but I think you have the legs to wear such a skirt."

She led Kendra to a dressing room that was surprisingly spacious compared to the rest of the shop. "I will return with some dresses. Do you plan to visit the casino in Deauville?"

"I don't know," said Kendra. "Why?"

"Formal attire is required, of course."

"I see." She glanced at all the clothes spread out around her and began to worry about the cost. Still, how many times did a woman have a shopping spree in Paris? Surely there was no harm in simply trying on Madame's idea of suitable evening dresses, was there? "Bring me one or two. I may need something very dressy, I'm just not sure."

"Certainly."

Once Madame Olivier left, Kendra took a quick look at some of the price tags discreetly attached either to an inside seam or in the neckline where the label had been removed. She breathed a sigh of relief. The prices were not exactly cheap according to her standards, but they weren't outrageous, either. She would expect to pay about the same amount if she was buying clothes at full retail in a moderately priced department store back home.

Of course, the last time she'd bought a dress that wasn't on sale, she'd been graduating from college. But, she couldn't go to Deauville with the pathetically few clothes she'd brought with her, she *had* promised herself a new wardrobe and even more amazingly, she could afford the clothes. She could buy every single outfit in the dressing room, and she would still have money left over, she realized. An indecent amount of money.

Kendra began to undress, anticipating the fun of trying on such beautiful garments. Madame

Olivier returned, her arms bulging with dresses, just as she finished fastening the camellia pink slacks.

"Very nice. We need a small tuck in the waist, but otherwise a good fit." The boutique owner twitched a front pleat into place and favored Kendra with a frosty smile. "Would you like a coffee, mademoiselle? Or perhaps a small sandwich while we work?"

Kendra felt a rumble of laughter build in her throat, along with a modest pride. She'd just surmounted the highest peak of shopping endeavor . . . she'd won over a Parisian saleswoman.

Five hours later, Kendra surveyed with a sense of dismay the collection of glossy shopping bags from numerous boutiques decorating every nook and cranny of her room. She'd completely lost her mind. Scattered around her were more clothes, shoes, and accessories than she had in her closet back home. And the lingerie. She closed her eyes and shook her head. Every bra, every panty, every slip, camisole, teddy, and nightgown was skimpy, ultra-feminine, and dripping with lace.

And what in the world had possessed her to buy garter belts and filmy stockings in pastel shades? She'd never worn any of those items in her life. Of course, she'd never been daydreaming about Jack Randall when she bought lingerie before, either. But what kind of an excuse was that? She would never have the nerve to wear any of the sexy garments for him. *Looking* at them embarrassed her.

And she couldn't take a single thing back.

She got out her calculator and tallied up the receipts in her wallet. She blanched at the figure appearing on the liquid crystal display. Eight thousand dollars. She'd spent eight thousand dollars. On clothes. She hadn't spent eight thousand dollars on her college education.

Another brusque knock sounded at the door. Kendra opened it to find the grinning hotel owner bearing yet another delivery of merchandise.

"Do you think this is the last one, mademoiselle?"

"I fervently hope so, madame."

The woman laughed, waving her arm over the bed piled high with boxes and shopping bags. "I am quite anxious to see the man responsible for all this, mademoiselle."

"He'll be picking me up at seven p.m.," said Kendra.

"It's almost six. You had better choose something to wear . . . though with such a selection *I* would have difficulty." Silvery peals of friendly laughter spilled from the woman's throat.

Kendra laughed, too. What else could she

do? The damage was done. "Really, madame. This sort of extravagance is not at all like me. I'm usually a very sensible, practical woman."

"Ooh, là . . . now, I *shall* be waiting eagerly behind the front desk for my first glimpse of your man."

The woman closed the door behind her, still laughing.

Kendra pawed through the mound of packages. The few items that had needed alterations would be delivered before she left for Deauville. The dress she was looking for had been a perfect fit, so she knew it had to be . . . there. She closed her fingers around the satin rope handle of a shiny red *Carina* shopping bag and pulled.

Inside the bag, wrapped in white tissue paper, was the dress she intended to be wearing when Jack picked her up that night. A self-satisfied smile curved her lips.

She'd lost her mind this afternoon.

Tonight was his turn.

Chapter Thirteen

Kendra waited for Jack in the lobby. Her room was still a confusion of boxes, bags, and tissue paper. And the double bed was way too prominent in the small room to ignore. That kind of goad could be plain dangerous given the amount of sexual magnetism between them.

For that matter, so could the dress she was wearing.

"Wear something dressy," Jack had told her when he'd dropped her off at the hotel last night. "I want to take you out for the kind of special evening most couples starting a relationship take for granted. We'll go to a club, hear some music, dance. Later, we'll have a late supper in some swank restaurant. We'll walk along the Seine, and we won't come home until dawn. And by the time we do, we'll have answered all the important questions for each other but one."

Kendra had known she shouldn't ask. There'd been something in his voice, some quality of intensity in his eyes, that told her his response would take them across a significant demarcation line in their romance.

"What question is that?"

"When?' "

Kendra had a sneaking suspicion that when Jack saw her in the dress the answer to the question might very well be "soon." She had chosen to wear the dress for exactly that reason. To let him know that she wanted him . . . soon. To tell him that even though she wasn't quite ready for him yet, she hoped to be . . . soon.

The bias-cut slip dress had a deep V-neck and a flirty skirt that ended well above her knees. The midnight blue fabric was a slippery silk charmeuse that flowed over her body in a way that was provocative without being vulgar. Because of the neckline and the thin straps, a bra was out of the question. Every time Kendra moved, the soft cool silk caressed her breasts, teasing her nipples erect.

At another of the boutiques on Vivian's list, she'd found a pair of black patent leather high heels with a thin gold chain running diagonally across the instep. The chain bounced lightly when she walked, flashing glints of light.

The sheer smoky stockings she wore were stamped at the backs of her ankles with tiny sparkling rhinestones in the shape of a bow. The garter belt that held them up was nothing but a piece of spidery black lace, some black silk ribbons, and a couple of fine metal clasps.

The matching black silk panties were cut high on her leg, leaving a shocking amount of skin exposed above the tops of her stockings.

Kendra had never worn such a glamorous, provocative set of underwear in her life. She'd had no idea lingerie could feel so sensuous against her skin . . . or keep her mind fixed so firmly on the prospect of sharing intimate pleasures with Jack in the near future.

A swift intake of breath and the hotel owner's sharply whispered *"Mademoiselle!"* alerted Kendra to Jack's arrival. He stepped across the threshold, and Kendra drew a swift, sharp breath of her own.

Jack looked magnificent. He wore a black tuxedo that seemed to stretch forever across his wide shoulders. A wine satin cummerbund encircled his taut waist. Mother-of-pearl studs gleamed down the front of his pin-tucked dress shirt. The shirt's stark white color set off his deep tan handsomely. The black bow tie and tuxedo slippers that had always looked ridiculous to her when she'd spied them in magazines, only emphasized Jack's hard masculinity.

He came toward her, radiating strength and virility. A shiver raced down her spine, part awareness, part fear, part desire. No man had ever made her feel so female. She was vulnerable to him, only to him. The realization excited her.

"Too much?" She ran the backs of her fingers lightly over her dress.

"Not enough." His voice was low and husky. "There's not *nearly* enough to that dress."

She watched his pupils dilate, his hands clenching and unclenching reflexively at his sides. A feeling of purely feminine power surged through her at the knowledge that she could affect him as strongly as he affected her.

"You look wonderful in a tuxedo," she complimented softly.

"You look like an incitement to riot in that dress." He swallowed, reaching out one hand, then letting it fall back at his side. "I'm afraid to touch you, afraid I wouldn't be able to stop touching you."

"That should make dancing interesting." She arched one brow. "Or are we going to one of those hot music places where they never play a slow song?"

"Wherever I'm with you tonight is going to be hot. And you can bet your . . . life that there are going to be a lot of slow songs playing."

The waiting cab took them to a crowded jazz club with a minuscule dance floor. The moment Jack took her in his arms, the size of the dance floor ceased to matter. He held her so close to his body that the width of his shoulders was all the space they needed.

Expertly, he moved her around the floor, swaying, turning, guiding her steps with a light, sure hand at the base of her spine. He rubbed his thumb gently in the small of her back, and she quivered. The husky notes of a wailing sax rose above the pounding riffs of a piano accompaniment. Jack insinuated his knee between her thighs, the swirling silk skirt rippling around them as he spun her in a slow, sexy rhythm.

She clung to his shoulders as they danced, liking his hard strength and sure steps. He slid one hand over her bare arm from her wrist to her shoulder, then down the side of her body to her waist. She raised her arms higher, tall enough in her heels to clasp her fingers behind his neck, wanting to be even closer to him.

He took advantage of the greater access afforded by her action, smoothing his palms up and down her sides, the silk dress slipping sensually between his hands and her naked skin. She felt him brush the plump underside of her breasts once, unobtrusively, and a soft sigh escaped her lips. He did it again, and she felt a tiny tremor ripple over his body.

"This dance is getting way out of control, Kendra."

"Do you want to sit down?"

"No," he murmured. "I love the way you feel too much to stop dancing just yet."

"I like the way you dance," she admitted, stroking the nape of his neck. Her fingertips dipped inside the collar of his jacket and found the muscles at the base of his neck. The muscles were hard, tight, and his skin was hot beneath the cotton shirt.

"I like the feel of your hands on me," he whispered.

"You feel so strong," she marveled, smoothing her hands over his powerful shoulders.

Jack eased his hands slowly down her body. He gripped her hips, his fingers biting into her flesh as he moved her back and forth against his lower body in time to the music. He was fully aroused. She could feel him, hot, heavy, and straining against the fabric of his tuxedo slacks. His touch burned through the silk of her dress, burned her skin all the way to the bone.

Burned until there wasn't a single nerve ending that wasn't wildly aroused and screamingly aware of the man holding her.

They danced for hours, their dinner plans forgotten as they fed their hunger for each other. Jack ordered a bottle of cognac, and they sipped the fiery alcohol from thin crystal snifters. They talked, laughed, flirted and by the time they left the club well after midnight, they knew not only an astounding number of facts about each other, but they'd become emotionally intimate, as well.

Kendra learned that Jack had entered the Marine Corps at eighteen because he wanted to make something of himself beyond the limited opportunities he perceived in his hometown. He told her about growing up in the midwest as the son of a solidly blue-collar family. She learned that he didn't have a favorite color, and that he liked to read techno-thrillers.

But more importantly, he'd revealed the determination he'd brought to the difficulty of earning a college degree while in the service and the pride of being chosen for officer candidate school.

He recounted countless stories about some of his tours of duty, about the gypsy existence of moving from place to place, about having many acquaintances, but only a few close, treasured friends.

Jack learned about Kendra's family, about the teasing, the closeness, the love she hoped would transcend the current strains among them. She told him about working her way through a state university, about her childhood, about some of her wackier clients. She shared her dreams about one day owning her own travel agency and the wanderlust that had guided her career choice after college.

He learned that she loved to walk on the beach early in the morning, and that she hated techno-thrillers only marginally less than she hated horror films. But more importantly, he learned that she valued a sense of personal honor as much as a sense of humor, fidelity, and commitment as much as passion, and children probably more than any other group of people she could name.

"How about that walk? I need to cool down," said Jack bluntly, guiding her back to the table after another dance.

"I could probably use a walk to clear my head after all that cognac and all this cigarette smoke," acknowledged Kendra. "But it's so late, and Paris is a big city . . . do you think it's safe?"

"Don't worry. You're with me. No one's going to bother you." There was no arrogance, no bravado in his comment. Just the calm statement of a man who knew his strength and took his fighting skills for granted.

Kendra picked up the tiny black patent evening bag that matched her shoes and took Jack's hand. Once outside, he hailed a cab and instructed Kendra to have the driver let them off at the Pont Neuf.

"Are you sure you can walk all the way back to your hotel in those shoes?" he asked her, reading the digital display on the meter and handing the driver a folded bill.

"I think I can manage a nice slow amble along the *quai*."

"You can lean on me if your feet start to hurt." He put his arm around her waist and hugged her to his side. "You can lean on me, anyway."

"Actually, these shoes are extremely comfortable."

"Those shoes are extremely *sexy*. I haven't been able to take my eyes off that little gold chain and those damn glittery bows all evening!"

"How . . . gratifying."

"You don't know the meaning of the word. Yet."

A balmy breeze blew off the river, even this late at night. There was no moon, but just ahead of them on the Île de la Cité, the towers of Notre Dame were lit by orange floodlights. The *quai* along the left bank of the river was nearly deserted, only an occasional taxi or police car passing them on the street. They walked in silence, content merely to be together.

"Feel any cooler?" she teased, as they crossed the small bridge behind Notre Dame.

"No."

Jack stopped halfway across the bridge and shrugged off his jacket, draping it over the heavy decorative iron railing. Reaching again for Kendra, he shifted her in his arms so that she stood in front of him, giving them both a perfect view of the awesome Gothic cathedral straight ahead. He wrapped his arms around her waist and tenderly nuzzled her temple with his chin.

The flying buttresses and the tall spire of the cathedral were lit by floodlights. Water lapped beneath the bridge. The scene was serene and beautiful. Kendra scarcely noticed. She was conscious only of Jack's solid chest pressed against her shoulderblades, her derrière cuddled into his groin, the backs of her legs touching the front of his muscular thighs. Heat and desire poured off of him, and she shivered in his arms, knowing she was the cause.

"Cold?" he murmured against her ear.

"Are you kidding me? You feel like a blast furnace." She gripped the top of the railing, tightly.

"Your doing." He dropped butterfly kisses across her cheek and along her ear.

She turned her head, searching for his mouth and finding it. He tasted of cognac and passion, a hot, sweet flavor she wanted to savor forever. Through the haze of cigarette smoke clinging to his clothes, she could smell his faint citrusy after-shave mixed with the natural fragrance of his skin. The warm, musky scent made her want to rip open his shirt, bury her nose in his chest, and breathe her fill.

"God, you taste good," he muttered, his hands stroking over the flat plane of her stomach to her hips.

"Then, kiss me some more."

One large hand tangled in her hair, pushing the heavy blond mass to one side. He kissed her neck, his mouth warm and moist against her skin.

Kendra gave a little groan. "No ... my mouth. Kiss my *mouth*."

"I plan to ... in a while," he said, continuing to caress her hip with one hand, stroking her in circular fashion.

She reached one arm up behind her, lacing her fingers through the hand tangled in her hair. "Please, Jack."

He covered her lips with his, and she began to soften and melt beneath his kiss. Her lips parted, and she felt his tongue glide inside her mouth. The taste of cognac was stronger. And the taste of his passion. His breath came in labored pants. She wasn't sure she was breathing at all.

"Is this the kind of kiss you want?" He kissed her long and deeply, his tongue sweeping her mouth, plunging in and out in a blatantly seductive rhythm.

"Yes," she answered. "Kiss me exactly like that."

Pleasure shimmered in her veins, intense, sweet pleasure made all the more erotic by the echoing pleasure she felt shaking his big body. She kissed him back as passionately as she knew how, opening her mouth wide, teasing his tongue with her own, sucking his lower lip between her teeth.

His free hand slid down the front of her thigh, coming to an abrupt halt, then rubbing over the clasp of her garter twice. "Is this ...

tell me you're wearing panty hose, honey."

"No."

He crushed a handful of midnight blue silk in his fist, inching her dress up with his fingers. When he found the creamy skin above the top of her stocking he groaned, rubbing her thigh beneath the ribbon garter. She trembled from the force of arousal he stimulated with his gentle stroking touch. Slowly, his hand moved under her dress, moved up her thigh beneath the black silk ribbon.

"I'd better find a pair of panties in the next three seconds, or we're in big trouble, honey." His voice was thick as he pressed his hips forward.

Kendra felt his hard erection, felt the heavy, pulsing beat of engorgement pounding against her derrière.

"You will . . . but feeling you against me like this almost makes me wish that you . . . wouldn't." She felt his fingers slide under the narrow lace edging of the tiny panties, and she moaned softly.

In one smooth motion, he turned her around, holding her tightly around the waist with one arm. He slid his hand beneath her knee and pulled her leg up on his hip, stroking the sleek expanse of thigh above her stockings. His hand cupped the cheek of one buttock, sweetly kneading the tender flesh.

A deep shuddering breath escaped his lips as

he held her tightly against him, letting her feel his hard arousal against her mound. Then he eased his hold so that her leg slid slowly down his. He held her in a loose, careful embrace.

"I'm sorry." His voice was strained, ragged.

"I wasn't exactly fighting you off," she murmured, resting her head against his chest. His heart pounded beneath her cheek.

"You get to me like no woman ever has. This may not be the place, but it sure as hell feels like the time." His arms tightened around her. "Come on. I'd better get you back to your hotel before we get arrested."

She stayed his movement with one slim hand. "Thank you."

"For what?"

"Five minutes ago, I didn't even *care* that we were in public . . . I wanted you that much. It would have been easy for you to take advantage, but you didn't."

"Kendra, I don't want to *take* advantage. Sure, I've got enough male ego to *love* the idea that I arouse you so much you'd give yourself to me on a public bridge, but what I feel for you is deeper and more intense than hot sex. You don't just get to me sexually, you get to me everyway."

"I know. I feel the same way."

"Then, tell me that you're going to put us both out of our misery soon."

"I want to. Believe me, I've never felt the

kind of sexual hunger you make me feel."

"But?"

She shrugged. "I've witnessed the dynamics of long-distance relationships before. They're passionate and exciting, but unless the couple involved can find a way to bridge the distance, can manage somehow to stay in close proximity, the relationship simply dies out."

"And you're afraid of that happening with us?"

She nodded.

"I can't give you any guarantees. Military life is hard on women, the separations, the moving, the loneliness. It's one of the reasons I've never married."

"I'm not asking for guarantees. I could become deeply involved with you, emotionally, sexually . . . every way. But I'm not sure about the endless round of separations. I don't know if I can handle the pain that I know would be an inevitable part of . . . loving you. I'm just not sure."

"Then, we're nowhere *near* ready to go to bed together. No matter how much either of us wants to."

Kendra nodded. "I know. I just wanted to tell you that I appreciate your . . . control."

He chuckled, a low, sexy shiver of sound. "Oh, honey, not half as much as you're going to."

"You're right," she agreed, smiling. "You

have lots of male ego."

The rest of the weekend passed in a blur.

They spent Saturday in the Louvre, enjoying the luxury of moving slowly among the fabulous art treasures. There was no schedule to meet, no quota of sights to see by the end of the day. They wandered the long halls, hand in hand, looking and talking. They ate *baguette* sandwiches filled with thin slices of cucumber, tomato, and egg in the museum's tiny basement cafeteria. They bought postcards and art posters in the bookstore.

Jack pored over the antiquities from Mesopotamia, Iran, and Assyria, and Kendra learned that he was passionately interested and impressively knowledgeable as a result of his previous tour of duty in that region of the world.

He approached a carved black stele with something like awe on his face. "Kendra, come here. Do you know what this is?"

"An ancient fertility symbol?" she asked, casting a skeptical glance at the unmistakably shaped stone.

"*This* is the Code of Hammurabi. The triumph of the rule of law over the affairs of men."

"I suppose *women* are mentioned in their customary position . . . right down there at the bottom with the slaves, children, and chattel?"

"Bear in mind that this was carved in Babylonia eighteen centuries before Christ."

"Women are valued *less* than chattel?"

"Women can divorce their husbands and take their dowries back. Slaves are permitted to own property in their own names. The strong can't simply ride roughshod over the weak. Examples of royal judgments are engraved here. This is an important historic artifact." His eyes were shining as he glanced around for an attendant, then reached out his hand and reverently touched the basalt stele.

Kendra picked up an English translation of the cuneiform writing from a box on the wall and tucked it in her purse, inspired by Jack's enthusiasm.

"Come on, I'll buy you an ice-cream cone, and you can tell me more about crime, punishment, and alimony in ancient Mesopotamia."

They bought cones from the vendor near Notre Dame and Kendra learned that Jack didn't simply like ice cream, he loved ice cream. A long line wound around the square in front of Notre Dame.

"Translate some of the flavors on the list for me while we wait."

"Do you like ice cream or sherbet?"

"Both."

"Okay, for ice cream you have the usual vanilla, chocolate, and strawberry—"

"Wait. Is it vanilla, or vanilla bean, or French vanilla?"

"It just says vanilla, Jack."

"What about the chocolate? Is it milk chocolate, or bittersweet, or . . . I don't suppose they have white chocolate?" He noted her astonished expression. "Never mind. Go on."

"Mocha, hazelnut, pistachio, coffee, honey, mint—"

"Spearmint, peppermint, or wintergreen?"

"Jack, it says mint, okay?"

"Well, no. Peppermint is great with chocolate and spearmint is nice with vanilla, but—"

"Listen, Jack, we're almost to the front of the line, and this guy gets a little testy if you don't know what you want. He almost made Lily cry the last time I was here."

"Kendra, I promise you, nobody is going to make me cry . . . and nobody is going to rush me over something as important as ice cream. I sweltered in a desert for a year dreaming of ice cream. I've been eating it steadily since I got to Paris three months ago, and I haven't even begun to take the edge off my appetite."

A small, dangerously erotic thought brushed the corners of her consciousness. There hadn't been any women in the desert, either. He'd told her so himself. She wondered if his "appetite" was still intact, or if he'd "taken the edge off" since he'd arrived in Paris? A part of her liked the idea of being the woman to slake the full intensity of his passion. A part of her was afraid.

Especially when she remembered the rest of

his comment that night in her suite. "It's been a long time since I've been with a woman, period," he'd said.

Kendra pushed the errant thought from her mind and continued reading aloud. "Do you like exotic flavors?"

"I like exotic *anything*."

She ignored his meaningful grin. "Okay, there's guava, kiwi, mango, coconut, kumquat, banana, and passion fruit."

"Go on."

"Jack, I must have read off twenty flavors so far."

"And I'll probably taste most of them. I just want to make sure I don't miss any."

She shook her head, rolling her eyes heavenward. "For sherbet you can have apricot, cherry, lime, pear, plum, rhubarb, pink grapefruit, fig, tangerine, blackberry, blueberry, cantaloupe, black currant . . . shall I go on?"

"How much money do you have in your purse?"

She glanced over at him. He was serious. "Enough for gallons of ice cream. Go ahead, Jack. Knock yourself out."

"I'll start with tangerine and coconut. What's the largest size cone he makes."

"Two balls worth," said Kendra, translating the vendor's reply literally.

"Excuse me?"

"I mean scoops," she said, blushing. "Two

scoops. Of each flavor."

They sampled so many of the flavors that neither of them was hungry for dinner.

Later, they walked in the Latin Quarter, enjoying the raucous carnival atmosphere of the Boulevard Saint-Michel on a Saturday night. Hours slipped away as they sipped tiny cups of espresso at a sidewalk cafe and watched the endless parade of people and fashion pass before them.

"This sure beats food in a pouch in the desert," commented Jack, stretching his long legs out in front of him as he perused the menu. "A steak and some of those skinny french fries sound good. How about you?"

Kendra shook her head emphatically. "After all that ice cream? Not a chance. I don't want to outgrow my brand-new wardrobe before I have a chance to wear it."

"Are the rest of your new clothes as fetching as that little blue number you wore last night?"

"I'll wear them for you, and you can decide for yourself," she teased.

"Too bad you're going to Deauville soon. You could spend the rest of the week giving me a fashion show."

"I'll be back in two weeks."

"After this weekend with you, I have a feeling those two weeks are going to seem like two years."

Kendra sipped her coffee, growing serious. "I

don't know how people in the military stand the separations."

"Depends on the people. Some aren't very good at them."

"Are you?"

"I've never really had to find out . . . until now." He reached across the table and held her hand.

"And now?"

"I think I could handle separations for the right woman. In fact, I've started to think that a lot of things about military life would be easier with the right woman."

"You mean being a marine isn't all flashing swords, dress uniforms on parade and embassy duty in Paris?" Kendra gave him a smile filled with the understanding she was beginning to have about what his life as a marine entailed.

"Don't get me wrong. I've enjoyed being a marine, the vigorous lifestyle, the sense of doing right in the world. I owe the corps a lot, not least for the engineering degree I hope to use once I retire. But it hasn't been an easy life, and I doubt I'll put in more than my twenty-five years."

Kendra tilted her head sideways, studying Jack. "Yeah, I can see you in a hard hat inspecting some bridge or highrise you built."

"Gee, thanks. I'm relieved to know I fit your image of an engineer."

"There's just one thing . . ."

"Yeah?"

She nodded, a naughty twinkle in her eye. "You're going to have to quit using words like 'fetching.' You need a rough, tough, manly vocabulary to work in the construction field."

"Thanks for the tip. I'll be sure and practice my grunts and swearing."

Once again, it was well past midnight before she returned to her hotel.

"I'd love to kiss you good night," said Jack, standing with her in the tiny lobby under the watchful, interested eyes of the hotel owner.

She stood on her toes and brushed the corner of his mouth with her lips.

"I want the kind of kiss we had last night," he said in a low, husky voice. "I want you in my arms, shaking with need, and kissing me back with everything you have. I want my tongue in your mouth, and I want to hear those sweet sounds you make when I touch you. I want to feel your hands on my chest, at my waist, on my—"

"You don't want much," she interrupted nervously, her mouth going dry at the word pictures he painted.

"Honey, with you, I want it all." He glanced over at the hotel owner who was pretending to read a copy of *Paris Match*. "Only not with an audience."

Jack showed up at the hotel again before dawn on Sunday.

"Dress warmly, and fast, and come right down," he said. "I'm in the lobby, and I have a surprise for you."

"I'm always surprised to be rousted out of bed this early," she responded tartly.

"That's right," he said. "You wake up cranky. I'd be glad to come up and put a smile on your face with my surefire cure—"

"I'll be down in five minutes," she said quickly. The tension between them had been simmering all weekend. The least additional provocation would bring that tension to a full rolling boil. The invitation offered by a cozy bed and a light quilt while Paris woke up around them would just about do it, she was sure.

"Okay. In that case, I'll wait down here with the *brioches*."

"Brioches?"

"Yeah, it worked like a charm last time. Why? What did you think I meant?"

She could just imagine the naughty grin accompanying his oh-so-innocent tone. But why should she, when in five minutes she could see it for herself?

Jack's surprise turned out to be a boat ride on the Seine. He put his arm around her shoulders, and she snuggled against him, ignoring the disgruntled mutterings of the boatman he'd persuaded to accommodate them. They drank hot chocolate from a thermos Jack brought and shared the *brioches* with the boatman.

Kendra watched the sun rise slowly over the water, sure that she'd never seen a more beautiful, a more romantic sight than daybreak lighting the lean planes and handsome angles of Jack's face.

He was a man filled with passion. The deep, abiding, intimate kind of passion only a man who is capable of commitment is capable of feeling. She'd always hoped to find that kind of man, that kind of passion.

And yet, she was terrified.

Not of Jack. Not even of the way he made her feel. What scared Kendra was the knowledge that no matter where the passion led, no matter the eventual outcome, she had no choice but to open herself fully, unreservedly to a relationship with Jack. The feelings between them demanded no less.

The unknown yawned before her with all its myriad undiscovered problems . . . and all its glorious promise of fulfillment.

A full, womanly smile spread slowly across her face, softening every contour of cheeks and lips and forehead.

She could hardly wait.

Chapter Fourteen

Kendra had seen smaller, less imposing châteaux in the Loire Valley than the villa that met her eyes when the car finally emerged from the thicket of trees two miles from the guarded gatehouse where she turned off the main road. Easily ten acres of luxuriant lawn led up to the entrance. The lush green expanse was broken only by the crushed sandstone drive that swept a circle in front of the entrance and a few ancient yew trees that had probably been growing since William the Conqueror set out to visit England.

A copse of trees grew on either side of the villa, and she could see the slate roofs of auxiliary buildings peeking through the thick foliage. Kendra knew from her experience with Rémy that there was a stable somewhere on the grounds. She'd bet her new wardrobe that there was probably a pool and tennis courts, too. All the simple comforts of home, she thought wryly, slowing the car to a halt to take in the view.

The villa itself was three stories of stone mellowed by age to a warm ivory color. The slate tiles of the mansard roof gleamed a dull charcoal in the mid-afternoon sun. Over the central portion of the enormous villa rose a cupola. The blue, white, and red Tricolore flew from the cupola, fluttering languidly in a gentle breeze. Twin round towers with conical roofs and matching second-floor balconies graced the front corners of the villa with a pleasing symmetry.

Tall paned windows pierced the facade every few feet, promising a light, airy interior. Decorative capitals and cornices enhanced the elegant exterior. Broad horseshoe shaped entrance stairs with stone balustrades met in a large bow front landing before a set of massive wooden doors. Vermilion geraniums growing in stone planters between the balustrades provided a splash of color.

Kendra tried to imagine Nadine and Rémy waving Laurent off to work from the impressive landing and chuckled. It was easier to picture the family in period costume accepting a humble salute from an assemblage of serfs. Off in the distance, behind the villa, sunlight glinted off the deep blue water of the English Channel. She eased her foot off the brake, a sense of exhilaration sweeping through her.

This was going to be fun.

She slowed the car to a stop at the foot of the horseshoe-shaped stairs and noticed Rémy, sitting on the top step. His head barely cleared the fat stone planter beside him. He was spinning a black and white soccer ball between his hands, oblivious to her arrival. A thickset unsmiling man stood nearby, noticing everything.

Kendra honked the horn twice and waved. Rémy rose to his feet and slowly descended the stairs, a welcoming smile on his thin little face.

"Bienvenue, Mademoiselle Martin!"

Kendra slammed her door shut and enveloped the boy in a tight hug. "Thanks, Rémy. I'm so glad to be here, I can hardly stand still!"

He looked up at her, nodding, a solemn expression on his face. "Me, too. I have that problem of standing still. But I am working on it very much."

"Don't try too hard, squirt. Little boys aren't supposed to stand still for more than a few minutes at a time."

"Squirt?" Rémy wrinkled his nose, obviously perplexed.

"Squirt means 'little guy,' kind of like *'minou.'* It's something a grown-up who likes you might call you for fun." She gave his shoulders a fond squeeze, walked around to the trunk and began unloading her luggage.

"Squirt," repeated Rémy, as though savoring the term. He followed Kendra, laying a restraining hand on her arm. "Leave your *valises* for Luc, mademoiselle."

Kendra glanced up at the guard.

"No, mademoiselle, that's Jean, my bodyguard."

The man grunted once grimly by way of acknowledgment. He made no attempt to hide the gun he wore holstered under his left arm. Given his hard face, hard hands, and hard, muscular body, Kendra suspected he practiced a martial art or two. She gave him an awkward smile. She was relieved to find Rémy so obviously well-protected . . . and disconcerted by the boy's calm, almost offhand acceptance of such a terrible intrusion into his childhood.

"*That's* Luc," said Rémy.

A deeply tanned, sturdily built man of about sixty wearing a blue smock and a beret came around the side of the building. All he needed was a dark kerchief around his neck and a smoldering Gauloise cigarette dangling from his mouth, thought Kendra, wishing she dared to grab her camera and snap his photograph. He nodded respectfully at Kendra, then began unloading the car.

Jean moved to a position at the bottom of the stairs.

Rémy's hand slid into Kendra's as they climbed the wide stone steps. "Did you have a pleasant journey, Mademoiselle Martin?"

Kendra was struck once again by the little boy's serious demeanor and formal manners. Listening to him, she had a hard time remembering he was only five years old . . . and that English was his second language. "Listen, squirt, you have to stop calling me Mademoiselle Martin. Call me Kendra, like my friends do, okay?"

He nodded shyly. "Will you explain to Nanny, please?"

Kendra's lips tightened. 'Nanny' was undoubtedly the martinet she'd glimpsed in the ambassador's office. "Sure."

"Good. Nanny says Americans are often too familiar, but since we are friends, and I have your permission, I think it will be . . . okay, to call you Kendra. I like 'okay,' " he confided.

"I'll make a deal with you, squirt. I'll teach you some great American slang, and you can help me with my French accent." Kendra stood for a moment on the landing, enjoying the view across the lawn and out beyond the perimeter of trees.

The estate was surrounded by farmland, well-tended fields of grain, pear orchards, and neat rows of sugar beets. Normandy cows, their hides distinctively marked in white, brown, and cream, grazed in lush pastures. Some of the farmers had started to bring in their hay, the bales rolled into huge cylinders instead of formed into rectangles like at home. Sheafs of ripe golden wheat were bundled upright and left standing in partially harvested fields. Slender wooden poles supported tree limbs heavily laden with dark red apples almost ready to be picked. The air was rich with the scent of dark earth and sweet grasses and spiked with a faint salt tang.

"Mademoiselle Martin?"

Kendra turned to face the stern woman she remembered from the ambassador's office. She was accompanied by a slightly older woman in a neat gray dress.

"I am Madame Allard, Rémy's nanny. Perhaps you remember me?" She shook Kendra's hand in a cool, formal manner.

"Of course, I remember you, Madame Allard," acknowledged Kendra.

Madame Allard gestured toward the woman next to her. "This is Madame Duchêne, the housekeeper. You will meet mademoiselle Léon, the other nanny, when she relieves me tomorrow morning."

"Très heureuse, Madame Duchêne." Kendra shook hands with the housekeeper, stupefied. *Two* nannies? For one little boy?

"I am happy to meet you, also, but unless you wish to practice your French, feel free to speak English. Most of the staff is bilingual," answered the housekeeper with a sweet smile.

Given the heavy traffic back and forth across the Channel, it was only natural that many people in this part of France would speak English, Kendra realized. But what a relief to learn that she wouldn't have to depend solely on her less than perfect French to communicate during her visit. She felt Rémy squeeze her hand as they followed the housekeeper and Madame Allard through the massive carved doors into the villa. Jean, the bodyguard, slid in behind them, a constant, silent presence.

Kendra stepped into the entry and was filled with a sense of awe.

The room was an enormous rotunda soaring three stories high beneath the cupola. The ceiling of the rotunda was painted the robin's egg blue of a perfect summer sky with clouds so white and fluffy they seemed real. The walls and floor were brilliantly polished porphyry in variegated shades of plum and wine, lightened by chips of pink and white feldspar. A triple-tiered chandelier at least six feet wide dripped hundreds of crystal teardrops from an intricate profusion of gilt branches. Kendra imagined the light was probably blinding when the chandelier was turned on.

Twelve scallop-shaped art niches held a collection of porcelain vases in cobalt blue, deep rose, bright turquoise, lemon yellow, and jade green. Medallions painted on the front of each vase depicted a series of eighteenth century beauties frolicking in bucolic settings with well-dressed courtiers. A closer look revealed an exact rendering of the Bourquel villa in the distant background of each painting. Kendra inhaled sharply, recognizing the vases as museum-quality antique Sevres. But even in the Louvre, she'd never seen an even dozen of them, not three feet high, perfectly matched and clearly designed specifically for display in the rotunda.

Interspersed between the art niches were daintily carved chests, wall tables decorated with mother-of-pearl inlay and six, Louis XV armchairs that Kendra knew instinctively were not reproductions.

At the far end of the rotunda, a free-standing white marble staircase with a heavy bronze banister and railings led to the upper floors. A wall of windows twenty feet high rose behind the staircase, bathing the room in brilliant sunlight. Paneled doors painted white and gold opened onto numerous other rooms. Kendra suppressed a tremendous urge to go exploring, scarcely able to imagine what the rest of the villa must be like.

Madame Duchêne began speaking. Reluctantly, Kendra turned her attention away from the splendors displayed in the rotunda and listened.

"Monsieur and Madame Bourquel have asked me to assure you of their warm welcome. They invite you to consider the villa your home for the course of your stay. You may use the pool, the tennis courts, the boat, the bicycles, and of course, the private beach."

"Thank you, everything sounds wonderful."

"Monsieur Laurent has instructed the stableman to choose a suitable mount if you ride. If there is anything else you desire, you have only to ask." Madame Duchêne reached into the pocket of her dress and withdrew an envelope. "From Madame Nadine."

"The Bourquels aren't here yet?" asked Kendra in surprise as she took the envelope.

A perplexed look etched the housekeeper's face. "No. Monsieur Jean-Michel, he never comes since the death of his wife, Madame Liliane. Monsieur Laurent, he passes an occasional weekend. Only Madame Nadine visits regularly. And Rémy, of course." She ruffled the boy's hair. "We have our Rémy two months every summer."

"Maman comes on the weekend," offered Rémy.

"I see," said Kendra with some relief. Nadine had undoubtedly explained the change of plans in her note.

"Dinner is normally served at eight o'clock in the formal dining room," continued the housekeeper. "But since you are our only guest, you may wish to take your meal in the small dining room. Or, if you prefer, you may dine with Rémy in the family dining room at seven."

Formal dining room? Small dining room? Family dining room? Just how many dining rooms did the villa possess, she wondered incredulously?

"Now, if you come this way, I will show you to your *appartement*." Madame Duchêne gestured toward the marble staircase. "When you have had a chance to get settled I will explain the . . . security measures."

Kendra managed a weak smile. *Appartement?* Based on what she'd seen so far she'd braced herself to expect a spacious, even luxurious room with a private bath. But an *appartement*, a whole suite of rooms, was really straining her ability to cope with any degree of equanimity. She was beginning to feel less and less like herself, and more and more like Cinderella at the ball. No, she corrected herself silently, smothering a panicky giggle, Cinderella at Versailles.

"I hope you enjoy your stay, Mademoiselle Martin." Madame Allard gave Rémy a short command in French, then disappeared through a door on the left.

"I take my swimming lesson now," explained Rémy, fixing a hopeful look on Kendra. "But I will see you for dinner, yes?"

"Yes," agreed Kendra. Even in the family dining room, the meal would probably be served on gold plates by liveried servants.

Kendra read Nadine's note a third time, shaking her head. The family had never planned on coming to Deauville. The knowledge rattled her composure.

Her assumption that she would be joining the Bourquel family on their vacation couldn't have been more wrong. True, she would get to spend some time with Rémy, and that would be fun. But apparently, even Rémy wasn't spending his summer vacation with his family. Her brows knit together in a pensive frown.

Maybe she'd been right to refuse the Bourquel's invitation that day in Ambassador Whittington's office. Maybe the invitation had simply been one of those social niceties, not an offer she was actually meant to accept. Maybe she'd committed a horrible gaffe by calling Nadine back and accepting the invitation to visit

Deauville.

Kendra reread the note. No. Nadine couldn't sound nicer, or more welcoming. And the staff, from the guards behind the electrified gate who'd known her name and obviously been expecting her, to the housekeeper who'd made it clear that the villa was hers to enjoy, had plainly been instructed to treat her well.

No, she decided finally. She hadn't imposed on the Bourquels so much as misunderstood the invitation. She'd been invited to visit the *villa,* not the Bourquels. And their offer, while sincere, was not an extension of personal friendship, but their idea of the correct, slightly more personal thanks required by her actions in saving their son's life. A sort of obligatory, but neutral hospitality.

Had she realized that fact at the outset, she would never have come to Normandy. She could hear her mother's voice in her head, urging her to come home. But leaving at this point wouldn't rectify the situation. In fact, it would be rude beyond belief considering the preparations made for her arrival.

Kendra tapped against her chin the sheet of thick vellum embossed at the top with Nadine's initials. She might be excruciatingly uncomfortable about continuing her visit. She might feel foolish, naive, and embarrassed. But there was nothing she could do now, except stay and make the best of things.

The next two weeks loomed ahead, seemingly

endless. Even so, there were a number of bright spots to look forward to. She honestly liked Rémy and was delighted at the prospect of spending some time with him. He was bright, charming, and sweet, a wonderful little boy, despite the reserve she still found unnatural in a five-year-old.

There was Deauville and all of Normandy to explore. Since the adult Bourquels weren't around, surely no one could object if she did some sight-seeing away from the villa. Maybe she could take Rémy with her. The poor kid might enjoy an outing with his parents away. But who would she ask for permission? The housekeeper? The bodyguard? The nannies? She had no idea who had ultimate charge of Rémy when his parents were absent. She determined to ask Nadine when she saw her this weekend.

And there was Jack. The prospect of spending more time with Jack filled her with a deep satisfaction and a thrilling sense of anticipation. She couldn't ask him to stay with her at the villa, though she would love for him to see the place. She would ask Nadine about that, as well. But she and Jack would have two whole weeks together when she returned to Paris. And he could certainly come to Deauville on a weekend. There were any number of inns, hotels, guest houses, and farms where he could get a room.

Kendra grinned suddenly. She was a travel agent, and she knew these things. Even during the August high season, she could probably find him an affordable place to stay. Her grin disappeared. She *used* to be a travel agent.

Quitting her job had been the most personally liberating act of her life. Not for a moment had she ever doubted her decision to do so. But, every now and then, when she remembered how much she had loved her job, how good she had been at her work, she was overwhelmed with a sense of loss and a feeling of anger. Though the choice had ultimately been hers, the circumstances forcing her decision had been beyond her control.

She didn't like that one bit. For now, she simply had to accept the fact of unemployment. But as soon as she returned to Carmel, she was going to do some serious thinking about her future. And she hoped desperately that after the time they spent together in France, Jack would figure largely in her plans.

Kendra rose from the chaise longue upholstered in celadon satin damask and placed Nadine's note on the bedside table with her purse.

The *appartement* she'd been given was larger than her cottage in Carmel. There was a small, pretty entry that opened onto a large *salon* with tall casement windows over-looking a formal garden laid out with terraces, fountains, statuary, and a maze. An enormous mirror with a heavy gilt frame carved with cupids and birds hung over a white marble fireplace. The oak parquet floors throughout the suite were covered with Savonnerie carpets in shades of moss green, rose, and cream.

The bedroom contained a huge four-poster bed hung with embroidered tapestry fabric in the same soft green, pink, and cream color scheme. There were a number of massive oak wardrobes burnished by time to a warm golden amber and carved with scallop shells, wheat sheaves, and flowering vines. A pink and white marble fireplace was flanked by wingback armchairs upholstered in rose velvet. A misty Renoir of a mother and child hung above.

The bathroom could have been carved from one solid block of pink marble, and the fittings were crystal and gold. Kendra had a hard time imagining herself shaving her legs in the marble tub or spitting into the gold sink. For sure, she didn't plan on using the bidet, enclosed within its own marble compartment complete with skylight.

But beyond any doubt, the *appartement*'s most spectacular aspect was the view from the bedroom balcony. Through French doors hung with rose velvet curtains, Kendra could see the English Channel breaking in sea-green waves upon the Bourquels' wide sandy beach. Other villas dotted the steep cliffs and dark green forests rising above the water in the distance.

Kendra stepped out onto the balcony and drew the salty-sweet sea air deeply into her lungs. Gulls split the stillness with their cries. The visit to Deauville wasn't working out quite the way she'd expected . . . but maybe that wasn't such a bad thing.

She went back inside, leaving the French doors open to let the sea breeze fill her suite with fresh air. Her luggage stood in a neat row next to the padded bench at the foot of the bed. There was a brisk tap at the door, and a young woman wearing a gray and white maid's uniform entered.

"May I unpack your *valises* now, Mademoiselle Martin, or shall I return later?"

"How nice of you to offer," said Kendra. "But I'll unpack them myself, later. I'd be grateful if you could bring me an iron and an ironing board, though, to press out the wrinkles."

The woman looked aghast, then drew herself up proudly. "That is *my* job, Mademoiselle. I attend to Madame Nadine's wardrobe when she is in residence. I assure you, I have yet to ruin a single garment! And every item is from the finest couturiers in France!"

Kendra winced at her unintentional slight, grateful that her own wardrobe was now suitably improved as she hurried to make amends. "Please forgive me. I meant no insult. Of course, unpack my suitcases. Feel free to press whatever needs pressing and attend to . . . whatever needs attending to."

She felt like an idiot. She sounded like an idiot. How did one talk to a maid, anyway? The only other person besides herself to iron her clothes had been her mother, and that had been a long time ago. The idea was tempting in theory, but face-to-face with a real live maid, Kendra found herself tremendously uncomfortable.

"Of course, mademoiselle," said the young woman, only slightly mollified. "Would you care for a coffee, or some tea?"

"No, thanks. I'd like to take a walk outside, maybe go down to the beach, but I have to make a telephone call first. Is there anything special I need to know?"

"You are making a local call?"

"No. I'll be calling the United States, and maybe later, Paris. I'll charge any calls to my telephone credit card, of course," she hurriedly assured the woman.

"As you wish, mademoiselle, but it is not necessary, you know. Simply dial direct, using these prefixes." The woman crossed to a marquetry escritoire placed between the pink marble fireplace and the balcony, scribbling a few numbers on a pad.

"Thank you," said Kendra.

"I shall return later, after your telephone call."

Kendra brooded over the sheet of paper the maid handed her. She'd put off calling her parents since her arrival, not wanting to wrangle with them, especially at such long distance. But she'd promised to call, and she wouldn't renege. She glanced at her wristwatch. Good. Not quite eight a.m. in Carmel. Maybe she could catch both of her parents at home. Her mother answered on the second ring.

"Hi, Mom."

"Kendra! What's wrong?"

"Nothing is wrong, Mom. I just wanted to let you and dad know that I'm in Deauville, now, at the Bourquels' villa."

"That's . . . nice, darling." Kristen's voice was strained. "How are they?"

Great, thought Kendra, just what she wanted most to do. Make more explanations. "Uh, Nadine's not here, yet."

"You're there all by yourself? How in the world did you get in? Kirk, don't leave yet. Get on the extension. It's Kendra. She's at the villa by herself."

"Hello, Kendra." Kirk sounded severe.

"Hi, Dad. I was just telling Mom about the villa."

"What's this about you being there all alone?"

"I'm not alone. Rémy is here with me, along with a staff of about twenty. In fact, my maid is coming up later to unpack and iron my clothes. Can you believe it?"

"A maid? You've hired a *maid?*"

"Oh, for heaven's sake, Mom. I didn't hire the maid, she works here."

"I see. Well, don't get used to that kind of lifestyle, darling. You'll be home in two weeks, and back to doing your own ironing."

Kendra could picture her mother's lips pursed tightly, a disapproving expression on her face.

"Nothing wrong with doing her own ironing. You've done it for years," added Kirk.

"You both know I'm planning to stay in France a month," said Kendra, refusing to be drawn into yet another discussion about her reward "changing" her "values."

"I still don't understand why two more weeks of vacation isn't enough," said Kristen. "We all had that nice two-week trip to Lake Shasta earlier in the summer, then you had the trip with the girls, and now two *more* weeks in a chateau. I just don't understand why you need a whole month in France."

Kendra bit her tongue, tempted by pique to tell her mother about Jack, explain exactly why she wasn't coming home yet. Common sense prevailed, and she said patiently, "I've always loved France, Mom. I'm going to do some sight-seeing after I leave Deauville. I'll be back as planned and not before."

"Why isn't the rest of the family there?" asked Kirk.

"Nadine is coming up this weekend," she hedged. "Old Mr. Bourquel doesn't come up since his wife died. I get the feeling Laurent comes up when business permits. This isn't where they live, anyway. It's just a summer place."

"Are you sure you're safe? Your mother and I . . . worry about you, honey, that's all."

"I know, Dad. I'm perfectly safe. There's all kinds of security measures in place here, and Rémy has a bodyguard, now." Kendra could have bitten her tongue as dual gasps came through the receiver.

"Bodyguard!"

"Bodyguard?"

"Kirk, talk to her, I simply don't like this."

"Now, Kendra—"

"Please, Dad," forestalled Kendra. "Don't worry. I'll be fine." No, she decided. She most definitely would *not* enlighten them about Jack just yet.

"Uh, before we hang up, Kendra. I want to tell you that I ran into Bob Warren at the bank yesterday."

"That's nice. I'll be—"

"He was very interested in what you were doing." Kirk interrupted in a torrent of words. "Now, he didn't come right out and say so, but I really think you could get your job back if you come home in two weeks and go talk to the man."

"He's already got an advertisement in the paper for a new agent," added Kristen. "I'd hate for you to lose out on the chance to get your job back if a suitable candidate walks in. Good jobs aren't easy to find, Kendra."

"So you've told me, Mother." At least a hundred times.

"Bob made a point of telling me that he hadn't filled your old position yet, and that it would be hard to replace you," added Kirk. "I think he wants you back, Kendra. I really do."

"Good."

"Then, you'll cut your trip short and come

home?"

"Not a chance in hell, Dad." A full, womanly smile spread over her face. "The best part of my trip is coming up. I wouldn't miss it for the world. But I love knowing that worm, Bob Warren, is squirming and having a hard time replacing me."

"Kendra, I don't know what is wrong with you right now, but you've got to get your head out of the clouds," said Kristen.

"Come home, Kendra," said Kirk. "Get your job back, or find a new one. Get your windfall invested sensibly. Get your life back to normal."

She sighed. Same arguments, different day. She despaired of making her parents understand. She resented their constant allegations that she'd changed . . . and not for the better. Her circumstances had changed because of the reward, but *she* hadn't changed. At least, *she* didn't think so.

"I don't want to argue with you, Mom and Dad. I love you both—"

"We love you, too, darling," said Kristen. "Come home. We'll talk things over—"

Kendra's tone hardened. "In a month, Mother. I'll be home in a month. We can talk then."

Chapter Fifteen

"What a wonderful potpourri," said Kendra, inhaling appreciatively as she stepped into the library. She'd spent the last few days acquainting herself with the routine of life at the villa. Today, the entire morning had been dedicated to a tour of the interior with Madame Duchêne.

"What you smell is sandalwood." Madame Duchêne waved her hands over the intricately carved panelling interspersed among the deep floor-to-ceiling bookshelves. "A Bourquel ancestor sent home the wood for the 'new' library from his estate in Indochina."

Kendra noticed several illuminated medieval manuscripts resting open on lecterns situated away from the windows and began to wonder just how long the Bourquels had been rich.

The music room contained not only a concert grand piano, but a harpsichord, a cello, a flute, and, enclosed in a glass cabinet, a beautiful Stradivarius violin.

"Does the family collect musical instruments?" asked Kendra.

"*Non*. The violin belonged to Lucien Bourquel. He dabbled in music."

"He must have been more than a dabbler if he played on a Stradivarius," commented Kendra. "I love classical violin, but I don't recognize the name Lucien Bourquel."

Madame Duchêne laughed, a warm, easy ripple of sound that contained not the slightest hint of malice. "Jean-Louis died in 1740, mademoiselle. The Stradivarius was made for him, and at the time did not carry nearly the value it does today."

Kendra smiled sheepishly. "I see."

"Come. I will show you the trophy room."

Kendra followed, expecting to find sports memorabilia, perhaps even Olympic medals, given the Bourquels' phenomenal success at whatever activity they pursued.

Madame Duchêne pushed open a set of double doors. "Voilà!"

The trophy room contained enormous elephant tusks, zebra skins, tribal masks, beaten bronze plates, as well as stuffed lions, cheetahs, gazelles and even an enormous giraffe, all mute testimony to the Bourquel presence in French Colonial Africa.

"Uh, very nice," said Kendra glancing quickly around. The room gave her the creeps.

"When Monsieur Laurent was a child, he used to climb up on the lion and pretend to ride him. Ooh-là, the spankings he received."

"What a . . . spirited boy," said Kendra, edging toward the door.

"Oui. Like his mother. Madame Liliane shot the lion on her honeymoon with Monsieur Jean-Michel."

"How . . . romantic."

Madame Duchêne showed her the wine cellar, the chapel, and a kitchen that could easily have prepared food for a hundred. Considering the size of the formal dining room, Kendra was sure that it had. The cherry wood dining table was twenty feet long.

"For large dinners, there are three identical tables that can be added end to end," explained Madame Duchêne. "For *really* large parties, twelve round Empire tables of ten are set with the Sevres porcelain service ordered by Christiane Bourquel."

"How convenient," murmured Kendra. Christiane was undoubtedly another Bourquel ancestor who'd recognized early the potential value of items that would later become a synonym for costly luxury.

"Such violent times." Madame Duchêne made the sign of the cross. "Such a sad ending, *la pauvre.*"

"The French Revolution?" asked Kendra, beginning to get an inkling of Christiane's time period.

"No, Algeria. A car bomb. Christiane and her husband both were killed. She was Monsieur Jean-Michel's only daughter. She had been married but six months. The porcelain service was ordered for her engagement party."

Kendra swallowed. They had not been without their tragedies, the Bourquel family.

"Now, in here, you will be interested to know . . . Madame Duchêne slid back the heavy ivory and gilt doors leading to an immense ballroom with four crystal chandeliers hanging from the decorative plaster ceiling. "Thomas Jefferson danced a minuet. Such a cultured man, Monsieur Jefferson. And such an appreciation of our French burgundy."

They passed into a dark study with a stone fireplace blackened by years of use. Madame Duchêne continued her lecture. "This is the *cabinet de travail*, the study where the men of the family have always retired to discuss serious business. Portions of the Louisiana Purchase were negotiated in the *cabinet*. A very good deal for your country, *non?*"

The nursery suite contained twelve rooms, including two classrooms.

"Though with Rémy spending only two months in the summer," Madame Duchêne noted with regret, "the rooms are mostly unused these days."

Besides Kendra's *appartement*, there were six other, similar guest suites.

"The family has always preferred intimate visits with friends, rather than the unwieldy country house parties more generally popular among their set," explained Madame Duchêne with a note of pride in her voice.

Kendra found the notion of "modest billionaires" hilarious. She didn't view the servants wing or the private quarters belonging to Nadine and

Laurent, but Madame Duchêne was thrilled to show off the villa's latest innovation, Laurent's gym.

Besides weight training equipment, a rowing machine, two stationary bicycles, a stair-stepper, a skiing machine, and a ballet bar across a mirrored wall for Madame Nadine, there were two saunas, wet and dry, and a tiled spa set into a windowed nook overlooking the Channel.

She didn't know about the Bourquels, but Kendra was certain that the splendid surroundings would stimulate *her* motivation to exercise regularly. After promising herself several vigorous work-outs during her stay, she retired to her room, dazed by all the stories, all the history attached to the villa.

The opulence alone was staggering, but the *implications* of that opulence added a whole new dimension to her thoughts about money on such a grand scale. And about the family that had possessed such wealth for so many generations.

The Bourquels were players on the world stage. It wasn't a position Kendra wished for herself, but she was beginning to think she might like the self-determination that wealth provided. She didn't admire all the choices the Bourquels had made over the generations, but she envied their ability to decide the course of their lives without interference, and then live those lives in comfort and freedom.

Kendra's whole life had been determined by the fact of growing up in a family that knew the value of money in a middle-class way. She'd always had everything she truly needed, a little of what she wanted and a taste of what she dreamed of. But never in her life had she been free to make a choice without considering the financial cost that might be involved. And the financial cost had always determined the extent and variety of the choices available to her.

Until now.

The Bourquels' reward, while not making her wealthy within their understanding of the word, certainly made her wealthy by comparison to her life before meeting them. The money didn't just mean she could stop buying her clothes on sale, stop turning off the lights when she left a room. The money didn't even give her license endlessly to re-enact her shopping spree in Paris last week.

What the money did, Kendra realized, was to give her, within the boundaries of her own life, exactly the kind of freedom that the Bourquel family had taken for granted for God alone knew how many generations.

The new knowledge was dizzying, her choices suddenly endless.

She could change her whole life if she wanted to. She could go back to college for an advanced degree. She could invest her money safely in stocks, bonds, and certificates of deposit and live off the income without ever working again. She could invest her money with a lot more risk in the hopes of obtaining even more wealth. She could give every dime away to the charities she'd supported for years on a much smaller scale and continue her life as before.

She could start her own travel agency.

Restlessly, Kendra prowled the pretty *salon*, her head spinning with new ideas. She wanted to talk to Jack, she realized with surprise, wanted to hear his calm, steady voice. With any luck, she could catch him in his office before he went to lunch.

"Randall here."

Jack's tough, no-nonsense telephone voice made Kendra smile and remember the softer, huskier tone he used in private with her.

"Martin here," she mimicked.

"Kendra! How's life among the rich and famous?"

"Do you remember Versailles, Jack?"

"Vividly."

"The Bourquels would feel right at home."

He gave a low whistle. "That rich, huh?"

"Jack, my bathroom has a *gold* sink! And the villa has *three* dining rooms. I've seen art treasures I had no idea were in private hands, and the private beach is about two miles long. There are acres and acres of grounds I still haven't seen yet. I'm going to tour them after lunch. The villa itself, the size, the luxury, the sheer amount of incredible *stuff*, well, you just wouldn't believe it."

"But are you having any fun?" he teased.

"Not nearly enough without you, Jack."

"You'll have all the fun you can handle in a about a week," he promised. "My leave came through. Starting at twelve-oh-one a.m. a week from Saturday, I'll be a free man for fourteen days . . . and nights."

"I thought you only had ten days' leave

coming?"

"Somehow my boss wangled me an extra four days."

"Jack, that's fantastic. I could hug the man."

"You're pretty free with those hugs, Kendra. Why don't you just save them all for me?"

"Jealous?"

"No. Just . . . anxious."

"I . . . know the feeling."

"When, Kendra?"

"Pretty soon, Jack."

"I wish I could see you before my leave starts. How about coming back to Paris a few days early?"

She was tempted. Strongly. "I feel bad leaving Rémy."

"He has parents."

"They're not here."

Kendra explained the situation, surprised to find that she didn't feel at all foolish, gauche, or unsophisticated sharing her mistaken assumptions about the visit to Deauville with Jack. He was so matter-of-fact that talking things over with him seemed natural, not awkward, and he was a wonderful listener. She felt torn, wanting to be with Jack, but unable to disappoint Rémy by going back early.

"I don't suppose there's any chance I could come and visit you in Deauville this weekend?" asked Jack.

"Let me call and ask Nadine first. She's supposed to be coming to the villa this weekend, too. I don't know what she has planned, if anything."

"Kendra, I don't give a damn about seeing the villa. I want to see *you*. You don't need Nadine's permission to meet me in town. Will you?"

"Yes," she answered without hesitation.

"I could get a room and stay the weekend. You could show me around Deauville."

"I'd love to."

There was a long pause, then he said softly. "You could stay with me . . . at night."

"I could. I . . . might."

"Give me your number so I can let you know my plans. In the meantime," he gave a low, sexy chuckle. "I have a feeling this is going to be the longest, *hardest* couple of days I ever spent."

Kendra was silent for a moment, a sudden insight stilling the quick retort she'd been about to make. "The separations of military life are hell, aren't they?"

"Yes."

"Missing someone you care about, wanting to be together and knowing you can't must be rough to take over a long period of time. Especially when you know that the separations will continue to occur at regular intervals."

"Yes."

"Spending a weekend together is going to involve a lot more planning and organization than I thought, and we're not that far away from each other. Can you imagine trying to plan times together with thousands of miles between you? Or worse yet, waiting out the times without seeing each other at all?"

"Kendra honey, don't start throwing up roadblocks. Don't start pulling away. Give us an honest chance. Please."

"I'm not pulling away. I'm just beginning to understand more fully, more . . . personally, the difficulties of a long-distance relationship."

"And I'm beginning to believe there are relationships that are worth the effort and the sacrifice," he countered. "We'll talk more this weekend. Until then, concentrate on the reunions, not the separations, okay?"

"Okay. Bye, Jack."

"Bye."

Of all the rooms in the villa, the family dining room had the most "normal" scale. Kendra wasn't sure whether it was the room's smaller size, the comparatively modest oak dining table with a mere six chairs, or the French doors leading to an informal flagstone patio. Whatever the reason, she was able to relax there in a way she wasn't able to relax anywhere else in the villa.

Or maybe, she mused, it was simply Rémy's presence at meals that lightened her mood and eased the careful etiquette she observed the rest of the time.

She'd fallen into the pattern of eating meals with Rémy, and despite the presence of Jean and whichever nanny was on duty, they always managed to laugh and have fun. Every day after his swimming lesson, they played together in the pool. In the morning, after his breakfast but before his lessons, they went for a walk along the beach under Jean's watchful eye. Before dinner she visited the stables with him and fed each of the sixteen horses an apple. And every night before he went to sleep, she dropped by his room to say good night.

Despite the enormous wealth and privilege of his existence, Kendra felt sorry for the boy. She'd been shocked to find him alone at the villa except for the company of paid caregivers. Particularly considering his recent kidnapping. She couldn't understand how Nadine and Laurent could bear to let him out of their sight. She'd spent a lot of time with Rémy in the last few days, and she didn't know how they could stand to be apart from him, period.

In spite of his serious demeanor, Rémy had a charming sense of humor, he was bright and fun to be with—the kind of child any parent would enjoy.

She knew that the Bourquels loved Rémy from seeing them together in the ambassador's office. True, their affection had been reservedly expressed, but they were obviously grateful for his return given the enormous reward they'd pressed on her. Even so, in the time she'd spent at the villa, Kendra had come to realize that neither the Bourquels' love nor their gratitude had changed the way they were raising the little boy.

Their methods were completely outside the realm of her experience.

Rémy lived a life essentially apart from his parents, and his relations with them seemed incredibly formal. He accepted as normal the fact that he was spending the summer alone, except for weekend visits from his mother and even more occasional visits from his father. He accepted as normal the ten-minute telephone "appointment" he had with his mother every Wednesday morning at ten, and with his father every Thursday evening just before dinner.

The housekeeper had shown more ease, more warmth toward the boy with her constant, casual gestures of affection than his own parents had displayed on seeing him for the first time after his kidnapping. Rémy couldn't walk past Madame Duchêne without the woman ruffling his hair, chucking him under the chin, handing him a cookie or a piece of hard candy from her pocket.

The nannies had been with him since his birth. *Both* of them. Which meant that even in Paris, neither of his parents had anything to do with his day-to-day care. The Bourquels' financial situation should have enabled them to spend more time with Rémy, playing with him, just being with him . . . yet they didn't. The thought made her sad.

She found herself wanting to make things better for Rémy, but she didn't know how. Even spending time with him required patience and diplomacy. Any activity she suggested had to be fit around the rigorous schedule adhered to by the nannies and fall within the strict behavioral standards they demanded. A staggering number of activities had been arranged to fill his days and groom him into a "proper Bourquel."

Rémy had explained his "responsibilities" to her

while they were in the stables, visiting his pony, Prix de Caen.

"Would you like to be a jockey when you grow up, Rémy?" she'd teased him.

"Oh, no, Kendra. I will work with my father," he'd explained, an earnest expression on his little face. "That is my duty. We have obligations, responsibilities, we Bourquels. People, even governments depend on us. Riding is for sport, it is not a job for a proper Bourquel."

Kendra had been so stunned by such a calm, clear statement of purpose coming from the mouth of a five-year-old child that she'd nearly lost a finger to the pony nibbling on the apple she held. He'd delivered another bombshell on the heels of the first.

"I shall miss my pony when summer is over," he'd sighed.

"Paris isn't such a long way from Deauville. I'm sure you parents will bring you back for visits."

He'd shaken his head. "No. I go to school in September."

"School will be fun. You'll meet lots of other kids and learn things together."

"Yes. I know. But I shall still miss my pony when I am in Switzerland."

"Switzerland?"

"My school is there. A very good one, my mother says. My father went, my grandfather went. We always go there."

Kendra nearly strangled trying to contain her outrage. A five-year-old boy in a boarding school? *In another country?* What were his parents thinking of . . . besides themselves? Surely there were schools in France that were exclusive enough, expensive enough to satisfy the Bourquels?

Maybe, she just didn't understand rich people.

Maybe, she didn't want to.

The next morning, Kendra decided to call Nadine right away instead of waiting for the weekend to ask her permission to take Rémy with her on some of her jaunts around the area. She also hoped to learn Nadine's plans for the weekend.

Nadine was a charming woman, and Kendra thought she would enjoy getting to know her. But she'd been wrong once before in her expectations of the Bourquels. The last thing she wanted was to be a burdensome guest, or intrude on Rémy's private time with his mother if Nadine's plans didn't already include her.

Especially if she had a chance to spend some time touring around Normandy with Jack. Besides the pleasure, the excitement of being with him, the awareness that they could become lovers, she wanted to talk over with him the idea of starting her own travel agency. An idea that had sprung fully grown to the forefront of her mind and was now clamoring for attention.

On the other hand, she could hardly skip out on her hostess if the woman was coming to Deauville with the intention of spending some time with her. Kendra grinned. The only way to find out was to pry, discreetly of course. She dialed the first number on Laurent's white card. This time the line wasn't busy.

And the woman who answered wasn't Nadine.

"Allo?"

The woman's voice was smooth, elegant and filled with sensual invitation. She was clearly no maid.

"Allo?"

Kendra heard a man's voice in the background. She heard the woman speak to him in the familiar tones only a lover would use. She heard the man invite her back to bed, and she heard the woman's sultry response.

"Allo?"

She heard Laurent Bourquel.

"Laurent? It's Kendra Martin calling."

"Ah, Kendra. How nice to hear your voice. I hope you are enjoying the villa?"

"Very much. Rémy and I have been having a wonderful time so far. Um, I was trying to reach . . . Nadine." Kendra winced, hardly able to believe she was having this conversation. She had zero experience discussing a man's wife while his mistress waited for him in bed a few feet away.

"Nadine? You can probably reach her at the house."

"I'm sorry, I thought that's where I was calling."

"Non. I keep a *pied-à-terre* near the office. My friends and associates know to call me here if they do not reach me at home or at work."

"I . . . see."

"Is there something I can do for you, Kendra?" he asked smoothly.

"Probably. I wanted permission to take Rémy into town. I thought he might enjoy an outing away from the villa."

"Take some sun, Kendra. Ride the horses. Have a swim. Don't worry about Rémy. His nannies make sure that he is well-occupied."

"I know, Laurent. But he seems kind of lonely. And I just thought —"

"He's a boy, Kendra. And you are our guest. Do not feel as though you must concern yourself with his moods."

"Actually, I'd enjoy taking him to town. He's wonderful company . . . as I'm sure you know," she said pointedly.

"Do as you wish, Kendra. I will inform Madame Allard, and Jean, of course. Naturally, I must insist that Jean accompany you whenever you leave the grounds."

"Of course, Laurent. I understand. And thank you."

"You're welcome. Try the second number on the card. Nadine should be at home."

"I'll do that."

No wonder Nadine came to Deauville alone, thought Kendra. No wonder Rémy was spending the summer by himself. No wonder Laurent came to the villa only occasionally.

The man was having an affair. And Nadine undoubtedly knew about his infidelity.

Kendra wondered if the reason they'd sent Rémy to Deauville for the summer was to hide the truth while they worked on a reconciliation, or to shield him from their arguments while they hammered out a divorce?

The woman who answered the telephone at Laurent's *pied-à-terre* hadn't sounded like a mistress who had any intention of losing her lover. And Laurent hadn't sounded like a man working on a reconciliation with his wife when he'd invited the other woman back to bed.

Kendra shook her head. Poor Rémy. She hoped his parents would work things out. Divorce was hard on children.

Even rich children.

It took Kendra all day to work up her nerve to call Nadine. She felt horribly uncomfortable knowing about Laurent's affair. She was going to feel worse talking to Nadine as if she didn't.

For the third time since speaking with Laurent, she sat down at the marquetry desk in her room and prepared to dial the second number on his card. The telephone buzzed as she was reaching for the receiver.

"Hello?"

"This is Nadine Bourquel, Kendra. I spoke to Laurent earlier. He told me about your call this morning. I think it's lovely of you to take Rémy on some of your outings around Normandy."

"He's a lovely boy, Nadine, but he seems a little bit lonely without you and Laurent."

"I'm sure you are mistaken. Madame Allard and Mademoiselle Léon keep him too busy to get lonely. He has his pony, and now he has your company."

"Even so, he's really looking forward to seeing you this weekend."

"I shall be sorry to disappoint him."

"You're not coming?"

"No. Next weekend, for sure."

Kendra worried her lower lip between her teeth. Had her call to Laurent precipitated a quarrel? Was that why Nadine had changed her mind? Because she was embarrassed to have Kendra know about Laurent's affair? Should she broach the subject, or continue to pretend ignorance? Should she simply leave the villa entirely?

"Was there anything else you wanted, Kendra?" Nadine sounded a trifle impatient.

She made an impulsive decision. "Actually, I wanted to invite you to a little family gathering. I intended to mention it to Laurent this morning, but I . . . forgot."

"Your family is in Deauville?"

"Not my family, Nadine. *Your* family. I thought we could have a little barbecue on the beach for Rémy. You, Laurent, his grandfather—"

"Jean-Michel never comes to Deauville anymore."

"So Madame Duchêne told me, but I thought for Rémy—"

"Kendra, I do not think you quite understand the situation. Jean-Michel is head of an enormously complicated business empire. He sees Rémy in Paris and on holidays. He does not come to Deauville for barbecues on the beach." Nadine started laughing, light silvery peals of well-bred laughter. "Laurent was afraid you might misunderstand."

"Misunderstand?"

"Kendra, you have a kind heart. But the sort of 'family gathering' you have planned is really not at all necessary. I know about Laurent's *poupée*. Set your mind at rest on Rémy's account. His family will remain intact . . . without beach barbecues."

"Poupée?"

"His mistress," said Nadine calmly.

Kendra was speechless.

"Listen to me, Kendra. Laurent and I have a marriage that is *convenable*. We have been married ten years. Certain things are understood between us."

She had to ask. Their marital arrangement sounded so bizarre, she couldn't help but ask. "You don't mind?"

"No. We have affection for each other, even passion. We have many common interests . . . and those that are not shared, are enjoyed in such a manner that they do not disrupt the fabric of our lives. Do you understand a little better now?"

"You're not planning a divorce?"

"Of course not! A divorce is unthinkable. I have given Laurent a son, an heir. I enjoy being his wife. He enjoys being my husband. We are quite happy together. We enjoy our marriage. Without being indelicate, we enjoy *all* aspects of our marriage. He simply enjoys an occasional outside interest, as well. And though I have yet to find one, I am free myself to have a . . . friend if and when I choose to do so."

"I still think Rémy would enjoy a barbecue, Nadine. And if you don't mind my saying so, I think he needs to spend more time with you. Please come this weekend."

"But I do mind you saying so, Kendra. Allow me to know what is best for my own child."

"Of course, you do, it's just that he spends so much time away from you—"

"Kendra, I do not care to discuss this matter further. Have a barbecue with Rémy if you wish, but I am unable to attend. Perhaps you should invite Madame Allard and Mademoiselle Léon. That sort of thing is what the nannies are for."

Kendra heard a dial tone before she could respond. No question about it, she told herself. She simply didn't understand rich people.

Chapter Sixteen

Jack arrived by train on Saturday morning. Kendra picked him up at the station in Deauville, filled with happiness, excitement, and the smallest bit of trepidation over the changes she expected the weekend to bring to their relationship.

"Welcome to Normandy!" she said, drinking in the sight of him with her eyes. He wore a billowy linen shirt in a soft shade of blue and a pair of lightweight gray slacks that hugged his lean hips.

"Come here and kiss me, and I'll believe it," said Jack, swinging her around in his arms.

His lips found hers. Warmly, sweetly, he kissed her as she slid the length of his hard body until her feet were touching the ground. She kissed him back, feeling the tenderness that infused his passion. Passion that simmered hotly just below the surface of his control.

"You look beautiful. I like this shirt." He traced with his fingers the deep V-neckline of her camellia-colored silk shell.

Her skin came alive where he touched her, and she put her arms around his neck and kissed him again. His breathing quickened, and his body seemed to shift and mold around hers. Once again, she had the sensation of being kissed by his whole self. The sensation was as much emotional as physical, and she felt a rush of desire in the pit of her stomach. A deep yearning ache spread slowly through her body. Skin hunger. Bone hunger. Heart hunger.

"I've missed you," he said, linking his fingers loosely at the base of her spine. "More than you could imagine."

"It's been a long week for me, too."

He pushed back and looked at her. Really looked at her. "What's wrong, Kendra?"

"Nothing."

"Kendra, every time one of my sisters says 'nothing' that way, a whole ration of grief is usually about to descend. Is it me? This weekend? Do you still feel rushed?" He brushed back a few curling strands of hair escaping from the headband she wore. "I can't deny how badly I want you, honey, but I can wait if you're not ready."

"Nothing about this weekend with you bothers me . . . except maybe the fear that I won't please you enough."

He chuckled. "Kendra, where you're concerned, I'm *real* easy to please. Even thinking about making love to you sends me right to the edge. Why don't we just see what happens, okay? We can do some sight-seeing, enjoy being together. No pressure, no expectations, just being together."

"I'd like that. I really would."

"Remember the bridge, Kendra?" he murmured, pulling her in close to his chest.

A quick, hot blush suffused her cheeks. "Yes."

"That's how I think it will be for us. Spontaneous combustion. Stop worrying about when or how or where. When it's time, if it's time, it'll happen. Now, where's your rental car? I want to stow my bag and start exploring Normandy."

She led him to the small parking lot and handed him the keys so he could put his suitcase in the trunk.

"Why don't you let me drive so you can enjoy the scenery. I got to see quite a bit on the train."

Kendra arched her brows and gave him a wide smile as she slid into the passenger's seat.

"What?" he asked with a defensive air, as he watched her fasten her seat belt.

Kendra beat her fists lightly against her chest without speaking, a parody of macho posturing.

"I'm hurt, Kendra."

"I don't notice you giving me back the keys."

"I didn't say you were wrong." Jack flashed her a quick grin as he got in on the driver's side. He started the engine and eased out of the parking lot. "I admit to a small streak of male chauvinism when it comes to who does the driving."

"Only a small streak?" teased Kendra.

"Okay, okay, it's a mile-wide streak, and I'm a big chauvinist jerk . . . but I'm still driving."

Kendra laughed, drunk on the pleasure of his

company and his wit. "Were you able to find a place to stay, or do you want to look for a hotel before we start exploring?"

Jack laughed, the sound easy and relaxed. "What an opening."

"Stop tormenting me."

He laughed some more. "Yes, Kendra. I found a place to stay. A nice little inn between the Bourquels' place and Deauville. They're holding my room. I thought we might have dinner there after we see the D-day beaches."

" 'Place' doesn't begin to describe the villa, Jack."

"I got that feeling from your description over the phone the other day. And I want to hear all about it, but first, tell me where we're going."

"I thought it might be fun to walk along the *Planches,* the boardwalk that runs across the sand along the beach. On one side we can see the Casino and on the other is the English Channel. There's a marina with all kinds of boats — yachts, sailboats, even a couple of fishing dinghies. It's nice. I've walked there with Rémy. She directed him through the streets of Deauville toward the water.

"Sounds good. Maybe we can have lunch in one of those ritzy bars where the celebrities are supposed to hang out."

"Bad news, Jack."

"What?"

"The Normandy coast is famous for its seafood."

"Good news, Kendra. They also do veal."

Jack found a parking space on a side street a short walk from the beach. They stepped onto the *Planches* and began walking hand in hand, the sun shining brightly, but not unpleasantly warm. The breeze off the Channel was cool, and the scent of saltwater and pine forest reminded Kendra of home. At one end of the beach stood a cluster of striped tents.

Jack pointed to some canvas beach chairs lined up in rows. "Want to sit down for a while?"

She shook her head. "I just can't make myself pay for the privilege of sitting on the beach."

"What?"

"Those chairs are a concession, Jack. This isn't a *California* beach where people can just plop down where they want for free."

"Do they charge for going in the water, too?"

"No. Only if you want to change in one of the cabanas." She indicated the striped tents. "But only tourists and children are crazy enough to swim in the Channel. Even in August the water is pretty chilly. Rémy dipped his toes in the other day, though."

"I can just see the two of you." Jack smiled as though the mental picture pleased him. "If you weren't wearing such a nice outfit, I'd suggest we sit on the sand as a matter of principle."

"I'd join you . . . as a matter of principle."

He squeezed her hand. "So, tell me, what's bugging you?"

"Money."

He was instantly serious. "I know this trip is expensive for you. Let me help you out—"

"No, that's not what I mean. I *have* plenty of money."

"Then I don't understand."

"Staying at the Bourquel villa has been an eye-opening experience."

"I imagine it would be—all those gold sinks, all those dining rooms," he teased.

"The Bourquels' lifestyle is opulent—their food, their clothes, their villa, their art. I don't deny that I've seen a few things I wouldn't mind having in my own home . . . on a much lesser scale, of course. But what I really mean by eye-opening is that being at the villa has made me think about money in a larger sense. I've been trying to figure out what my philosophy about money really is."

Jack looked perplexed. "Why?"

"Because I'm trying to figure out what to do with mine."

"Money isn't something you have a philosophy about, Kendra. Money is just something to spend, or not, as you have it."

"I used to think so, too. Now, I'm not so sure. Take Rémy, for example. All those billions of dollars didn't prevent him from being kidnaped, and only luck got him home. Now, that he *is* home, he still spends all his time with nannies and bodyguards, and in the fall the Bourquels are sending him to boarding school in Switzerland."

"It's a tough life for a kid, I agree, but a lot of

rich Europeans send their kids to boarding school."

"I know. That's one of the things I've been thinking about. Most people I know would kill to have the Bourquels' money because it would mean they could spend so much more time with their kids . . . and still be able to feed, clothe, and house them."

Jack nodded. "I'd feel that way."

"Me, too. The Bourquels should be able to spend all kinds of time with Rémy, yet they don't."

"You're worried that they don't really love him?"

"I *know* they love him, but the way they're raising him is so distant, so formal, so . . . odd. I tried to talk to Laurent and Nadine, but they think I'm an uninformed meddler." She jammed her hands in the pockets of her camellia silk slacks. "Maybe I am. But what I've been trying to figure out is if it's the Bourquels themselves, or the fact of having all those billions of dollars, that makes them act the way they do, with Rémy, with each other, with everyone."

"I thought you said they were nice to you."

"They've been very nice. But at the same time, I've come to realize that while they're grateful to me for saving their son, they see me, Kendra Martin, *personally,* as very insignificant. I've never been conscious of class distinctions before. It's a weird feeling to see yourself through the eyes of people who think of you as . . . well, inferior."

"Kendra, you can't possibly be that naive."

She made a dismissive gesture. "Of course, I've been aware that class distinctions *exist*. But they've never touched me personally. I've always felt that my worth as a person sprang from the way I treated others, from what I could make of myself through talent, hard work and a willingness to learn, not from the attributes of personal worth that I've come to understand *really matter* to people like the Bourquels."

"You mean having billions of dollars?"

"Yes, attributes like money, position, and an important family possessed of both for at least three hundred years are the qualities that count with them."

Jack's expression hardened. "I don't like that they hurt your feelings. I especially don't like that they made you feel inferior."

"That's just the point, Jack. They didn't make me feel differently about myself. But some of the things they've chosen to do with their money, some of the ways they behave because they *have* money has made me think a lot less of them."

"So has all this philosophizing helped you decide what to do with your money."

"Not completely. I do have one idea that really intrigues me, but I'm not quite sure. Things were a lot simpler before I cashed that reward check."

Jack gave her an indulgent smile. "You mean you haven't spent it all yet?"

Kendra thought of her eight thousand dollar shopping spree and grimaced. "Not for lack of trying, I assure you, but two million francs—"

"Two million francs? My God, that's over three hundred thousand dollars!"

"I know," she said drily. "My parents remind me of the amount every chance they get."

He shook his head in amazement. "I've been careful with my money and lucked out with a stock tip or two, and I have maybe a *quarter* of that amount in the bank. And it's taken me seventeen years to accumulate!"

"My parents have made similar comments. They're terrified I'm going to squander the money gallivanting around Europe."

"You still haven't told them about me, about us?"

"Jack, I honestly don't know what to tell them."

He stopped, turning to face her. "Tell them that I care very deeply about you. Tell them I hate the thought of you leaving so much I lie awake at night trying to figure out ways for you to stay."

"Jack, my parents, my family, are very conventional people. *I'm* a conventional person. I don't really understand why you make me feel the way you do, or even where the feelings are leading beyond the immediately obvious. How can I explain it to them?"

"We don't have to explain it."

"Maybe you're right. Relations with my family have been strained since I got that reward. At least, you'd be something different for them to worry about."

They walked in silence for a while, watching the

waves break on the sand, listening to the cries of shorebirds circling overhead.

"I can't wait to hear this 'intriguing idea,' " said Jack, capturing her hand in his and swinging their arms back and forth in a carefree manner. "Between your brains and your bankroll I'm sure it's something fantastic."

She was pleased and flattered by his interest in her plans and his assessment of her abilities. And she liked the fact that he didn't seem the least bit threatened or put off by the amount of her reward.

Jack didn't brag, and he wasn't self-aggrandizing, but he had a strong, honest sense of himself that had appealed to her from the first. He wore a solid, quiet self-confidence like a second skin, and he knew his worth as a man as surely as he knew his name.

"I want to start my own travel agency."

"You'll run your former boss right out of business. Why don't you tell me your battle strategy over lunch," he said, pointing to a restaurant with a terrace overlooking the water. "According to the guidebook I bought, that place is supposed to be a 'glamorous watering hole for the international set.' "

"Would you mind if we didn't eat there? After ten days at the villa, I'm pretty much maxed out on international glamour and ritzy surroundings."

"Like I said, Kendra, where you're concerned I'm easy to please. What do you suggest?"

"Do you know what I'd really like to do?" She

stopped, facing him with a growing enthusiasm. "I'd like to go on a picnic. We could buy some food at a *traiteur* in town and drive along the Normandy *corniche* all the way to Honfleur. The scenery is spectacular. There are hundreds of perfect picnic places along the route. And we'd still have plenty of time to see the D-day beaches later this afternoon. What do you think?"

"I think you're going to make a fortune selling travel," said Jack, laughter shaking his shoulders.

They found a *traiteur* near the tourist bureau in the center of town. They purchased a crusty *baguette* and a selection of mild Normandy cheeses as creamy and smooth as freshly churned butter. Kendra added some cold steamed shrimp, two smoked quail covered in aspic, and a slice of a three-layer vegetable terrine. Jack insisted on a whole roasted chicken and three different kinds of paté. A selection of French pastries, some mineral water, and a bottle of calvados completed their picnic.

"Think we got carried away?" asked Kendra, nodding her head toward the bags of food.

"Probably. But how many picnics do you think we'll have in Normandy?"

"Not enough."

Jack downshifted around a curve, then squeezed her knee. His hand remained, a warm, heavy weight that reminded her of other appetites. She watched him, her gaze caught and held by the play of his thigh muscles moving beneath the lightweight gray trousers as he drove, the fabric stretched taut across his groin. His handsome face bore a look of concentration as he negotiated the sharp curves on the narrow road.

They pulled off the road on a promontory overlooking the long sandy beach a hundred yards below. A sign indicated picnic facilities ahead, but when they reached a grassy area ringed by trees and rocks, the little park was deserted. A steep trail led down to the water.

"What'll it be, the sand or the grass?"

"The grass," said Kendra. The view and the seclusion of the little park appealed to her.

Jack dug a beach towel out of his suitcase and spread it out for them to sit on. "This is nice. It was a good idea."

"Thanks." She began unpacking the food, holding up the bottle of calvados. "I didn't know you drank this."

"I don't, but it's supposed to be a regional specialty, so I thought I'd try it. It's some kind of apple brandy, right?"

"So I understand, but I've never tried it either."

"Well, hell, let's crack that baby open." Jack pulled a multibladed utility knife from his pocket and released the opener blade. He pulled the cork and sniffed the contents of the bottle. "Smells pretty potent."

She had a sudden realization. "Jack, we forgot to buy glasses."

"Kendra, how very proper of you." He grinned, then tipped the bottle and drank straight from the narrow opening. He swallowed, sputtering.

"Strong?"

"But good. Want to taste?" He held out the bottle.

"Sure, why not." Kendra reached to take the bottle from his hand and found herself pulled into Jack's arms instead.

His mouth descended, and she tasted the calvados from his lips. Sweet, burning, even the fragrance was intoxicating, or maybe it was just the feel of Jack's mouth moving gently over hers.

She rose up on her knees, increasing their body contact. Her arms wound around his neck. He deepened the kiss, seducing her mouth open with the tip of his tongue, seeking her warmth, offering his.

His palms caressed the small of her back, making small circles over the cleft of her buttocks, kneading the pliant flesh below. He stroked the backs of her thighs, then pulled her up into his hips, thrusting gently.

A soft whimper of delight eased from her throat, and he gave a little push that toppled them both to the ground. He braced himself on his forearms, brushing her hair out of her face.

"You're so pretty, Kendra. So soft, so desirable." His fingers slid over her cheeks and down her neck, his thumb smoothing the pulse point in the hollow of her throat. He kissed her again, more forcefully this time, his tongue bold and seeking within her mouth.

The man knew everything about kissing. He knew the gentle beginning, the slow build-up and the fiery finish. And he knew all the shades and textures of kissing in between.

Her delight became arousal, and her arousal became need.

She swept her hands over his shoulders and down his arms, enjoying the feel of his muscles straining beneath her palms. She ran the flat of her hands up between their bodies, loving the way he shuddered when she touched him. The tiny buttons on his shirt slipped from their holes beneath her questing fingers.

She touched him, touched the warm bare skin stretched taut over layers of hard muscle. His chest hair was fine and silky. A faint citrusy scent mingled with the musky fragrance of his skin. She pressed her lips to his chest and breathed her fill. He let her kiss him, and she felt his body tremble with the force of his desire.

Her arms went around his waist, locking in the small of his back. She lifted her hips, wanting to feel him even closer, wanting to feel his heated, pulsing sex in the cradle of her thighs. A hoarse groan told her the effort it was costing him to leash his passion.

"Kendra, if you want to eat one bite of that food, then you'd better stop moving like that beneath me."

"I've been thinking about something, Jack," she murmured.

"What have you been thinking about?" The words seemed torn from his throat.

"About how much you'd mind missing the D-

day beaches this afternoon . . . about how long it would take to get to the inn you mentioned."
"Are you sure, Kendra?"
"Yes."

Chapter Seventeen

The inn Jack had chosen was situated on a bluff overlooking a spectacular stretch of rugged coastline. The geese and ducks running on the grass out front added a picturesque rural charm to the distinctive half-timbered walls and clay tile roof of the structure.

The proprietor came out to greet them, a large black Labrador padding quietly behind him.

"Don't mind the dog. He's gentle." The man picked up Jack's suitcase and led them into a tiny lobby with a low timbered ceiling. An ancient masonry fireplace filled one wall.

Jack took care of the check-in formalities, then they followed the proprietor up a narrow staircase. At the door to their room, Jack took his suitcase from the man and held out his hand for the key.

"I will just go in and make sure—"

"No . . . thank you." Jack stared at the man.

The man glanced at Kendra out of the corner of his eye, then gave Jack the room key on its heavy brass fob. "Certainly, monsieur. I understand completely."

"I don't know whether to be thrilled or mortified by how fast you accomplished that," said Kendra.

Jack closed the door to the room, and put his suitcase to one side. "There's no shame in what we're going to do, Kendra. But if you come over here, I'll do my best to thrill you."

The room had a window overlooking an herb garden. The window was open and the scent of thyme and rosemary drifted in with the sea breeze fluttering the ivory lace curtains. The bed was an old-fashioned sleigh bed, piled high with down pillows and covered with a lace-edged spread.

Kendra looked at Jack standing in a patch of sunlight. He was looking at her with a tender expression, but a small pulse beat furiously in the lean plane beneath his cheekbone, and his hands clenched and unclenched at his sides. He was as anxious, as nervous, as ready as she was.

They still lived entirely different lives on opposite sides of the world. They still hadn't known each other very long. But as she watched him, she felt for Jack a bonding, a closeness that transcended those obstacles. She felt the same way she had the moment they'd met in that fast-food restaurant on the Champs-Élysées.

At some bone-deep, soul-deep level they connected. And the connection was like a live wire joining their hearts. She knew what he was feeling, knew the intensity of his desire, felt the sense of impatience and the sense of restraint.

Without exchanging a word, she knew that he wanted her with every fiber of his being. And she wanted him exactly the same way.

"I had planned to be wearing a very lovely, very expensive negligee the first time we made love," she said softly, taking a step forward.

"You wouldn't have worn it for more than three seconds, anyway." He took a step forward and held out his arms.

"I have a bag packed, but it's back at the villa. I didn't think I'd need it until later." She moved into his embrace.

"You don't need it now. All we need right now is each other."

Jack bent his head and kissed her, his lips softer than they'd ever been. Ever so slowly, he increased the pressure of his mouth against hers, wooing her response by infinitesimal degrees. She breathed deeply, letting the pleasure build with each heartbeat.

"I've wanted to make love with you for days," she admitted quietly.

"I know. I can feel your response when I kiss you, when I touch you, and it excites the hell out of me." His low, husky voice was filled with masculine pride. He kissed her again, his mouth moving hungrily over hers. "The more you respond, the more I want to make you respond. Come to bed with me. Let me please you."

Her mouth went dry with excitement, with anticipation. She lay back on the bed, pulling him down on top of her, loving the weight of his body pressing her into the soft mattress. Loving everything about the man above her.

Her clothes seemed to dissolve in his hands. The silk shell came over her head, the camellia slacks slid down her legs. Her shoes dropped to the floor with a soft thump.

Jack drew back and looked at her, his gaze heated, admiring, desirous as he took in the lace bra and panties that were her only covering. He groaned. "This is going to be harder than I thought."

"No, Jack, it's going to be easy . . . very, very easy." She took his hand and slid his fingers beneath the tiny lace panties, parting her legs so he could touch her, feel the warmth, the wetness he had stimulated. "See how ready I am for you?"

He muttered a short, sharp expletive, his breathing harsh and labored. "Kendra, I spent a year in a desert without a woman. I've spent three months in Paris without a woman. I've spent every moment since I met you rock-hard and aching. I want to bury myself in your sweetness, and I want it hot and hard and fast. Trust me . . . making sure that you enjoy this at all is going to be agony!"

"I don't want you to be in agony," she murmured, reaching up to unbutton his shirt.

She smoothed her hands up over his chest and slid the blue linen fabric over his wide shoulders. He was built like the warrior he was, all hard muscle, lean sinew and dense bone. The freedom to touch him after wanting to so badly for such a long time was an additional stimulus. As her hands roamed his strong torso, she felt her own arousal grow with his.

Her fingers found the waistband of his slacks. She slipped the button and slowly undid the zipper. His hand came up to cover hers.

"Kendra, I want to make this so good, so exciting for you, but my control is about shot," he warned.

"Then, let me . . . please you first, Jack."

"Are you saying what I think you are?"

She pushed him down onto the bed on his back, pushed his slacks down his legs and reached into his briefs. He sprang into her hands, a thick, gratifying weight. She stroked him between her palms, rubbing up and down the solid length of warm flesh.

"Kiss me," he pleaded.

She bent her head and took him into her mouth, loving his taste, his urgency . . . just loving the entire man.

"That's good, so good, honey."

"I want all your passion, Jack. Give me everything," she whispered, swirling her tongue over him. She slid the briefs down around his ankles and felt him kick them off along with his shoes and slacks.

His arms gripped hers, and he hauled her bodily over him. He rolled her over onto her back and kissed her, his tongue sure and skillful in the warmth of her mouth, at the side of her neck, on her breasts. He sucked her nipples into his mouth until they hardened, unclasping her bra and tossing it aside.

She felt his mouth, moist and warm, glide down the center of her abdomen and then she felt his breath stirring the soft hair at the juncture of her thighs. With his teeth, he pulled at the narrow satin ribbons fastening her panties. Then he flung those aside as well.

"For a conventional woman you have scandalous underwear," he murmured against her flat belly.

"You don't like it?"

"I love it," he growled.

He kissed her belly and moved lower, probing gently, relentlessly with his tongue. He circled the hardening nub rising from the soft folds of skin, licking, kissing, until her whole body was on fire with need. Then he slowly worked his way back up her body. His hand parted her thighs, and she felt the blunt tip of his shaft rubbing against her.

"Feel me, Kendra. Feel how much I . . . love you."

He entered her, and she felt herself come apart in his arms . . . as much from his words as from the dizzying excitement of his hard shaft sinking into her. The pleasure was intense. His hands slid beneath her derrière, cupping the tender cheeks, pulling her into each slow, deliberate thrust. Endless waves of pleasure coursed through her body, completing her in a way she'd never before experienced. She caressed him with her internal muscles, loving the sudden moans he made, loving the way he began to come apart in her arms.

"All of it, Jack. I want all of your passion."

He thrust strongly a few more times and reached his own climax.

For long minutes, they lay quietly, hearts still beating furiously, skin moist and shining with their exertions. He nuzzled her face with his chin.

"Don't go back to the Bourquel villa, Kendra."

"Not immediately, anyway," she said.

"Not at all," he said. "Except for Rémy, I don't think you were having all that great a time. Stay with me this weekend, and then come back to Paris with me. We can have every night together, be together like this, until my leave starts, and then we can have the days, too."

She was so tempted. "What about Rémy? He expects me to stay another week."

"I know you've developed an affection for Rémy, and if you want to go back and spend another week with him, I'll understand. But do you really think you can change the family dynamics that bother you so greatly on his behalf?"

She thought for a minute, then admitted, "No. Nadine and Laurent don't have much respect for the things I've said."

"Do you think you'll see Rémy again after you leave at the end of next week? Will you write to each other, maintain contact over the course of his life?"

"No, I can't honestly say I believe any of that will happen."

"Then, give *me* the time, because as sure as we're lying here naked together, we will be part of each other's lives in the future. Stay with me, Kendra. Marry me," he said quietly.

She made a shocked sound. "What?"

"Marry me."

"You can't be serious."

"I've never been more serious." He thrust his hips forward, spent but still hard within her. "Things are so good between us."

"Jack, I like spectacular sex as much as the next woman, but I don't think it's any reason to get married."

"I don't just mean the sex. I mean everything between us is so good, so right. I love you, Kendra. I think you love me. The sex wouldn't have been spectacular if we didn't love each other."

Kendra smiled, running her fingers through the short hair at his temples. "You're a romantic, Jack."

"Are you saying you *don't* love me?"

"I'm saying I . . . love you very much, but marriage. I don't know. There's still so much we don't know about each other. Besides," she teased. "I don't think I have the nerve to go home and tell my parents that I'm marrying a man I've known for—"

"Don't," he covered her mouth with his fingers. "Don't joke. Don't add up the days. What matters is how we feel. What do you think more time will do for us?"

"Give us a better sense of whether or not we can make a marriage work."

"And if we spend the next year together, learning about each other, making love to each other, letting the feelings between us grow . . . would you walk away from a marriage at the end of the year because you found out I squeeze the toothpaste the wrong way, or have some other habits and hobbies that drive you crazy?"

"You make it sound so simple."

"Kendra, it *is* simple. When it's love, it's the simplest thing in the world. Do you honestly believe that with more time we're going to learn *anything* about each other that's stronger than the way we feel right this minute?"

"No."

"Do you think I'm a murderer, a thief, a child-abuser?"

"No."

"That I have a wife and ten kids stashed away in Grady, Oklahoma?"

"No."

"Then marry me, Kendra."

"But there are so many things to work out . . . your job, my family, the travel agency I want to start."

"Why do we have to be single to work on any of those things? Would you leave once we *were* married to work on a problem that might arise between us?"

"Jack, enough. You should have been a lawyer, not a marine."

He grinned, the mellow late-afternoon light softening the hard angles of his face. "Nah, lawyers don't go the distance with you the way a marine would."

"You're excellent at going the distance, Jack."

"Quit stalling, Kendra. I'm asking you again. Will you marry me?"

"Yes."

Jack kissed her. A kiss full of hunger, full of promise. "Don't worry about the details, Kendra. We'll do what married people do . . . we'll fight and compromise and take turns giving in until the problems go away."

"You said you didn't want a long-distance relationship. I can't wait to see how you think we're going to be able to manage a long-distance marriage," she said, kissing him back.

"I wasn't thinking of a long-distance marriage." He smoothed his hands over her naked back. "I could leave the corps. I have another eight years to go before I can retire as an officer. I'd forfeit my pension and my retirement benefits if I get out now, of course, but I'll probably make more as an engineer in civilian life anyway."

"But you love being a marine. You told me so yourself."

"I love you more, honey. I don't want to spend the next eight years facing a series of separations, or worse yet dragging you around the world with no chance to settle down, start your business, have kids."

She felt a swift, fierce thrill at the idea of having his child. "Lots of people raise kids in the military."

"Do you really want to do that?"

"No. But I think I could stand anything for eight years if it meant we could be together most of the time."

"What about your plans to start a travel agency? That means as much to you as the corps means to me."

"I don't have to start my travel agency right away. I could save the reward money and wait until you retire to open my business. We could live together right from the start. That's another way to compromise."

"What would you think of staying in Paris with me until the end of this tour?"

"I don't mind putting off a decision about the travel agency for a while," she acknowledged.

"Actually, I was thinking that you might explore the possibility of starting a small operation right here in Paris. You could run customized tours for 'people of privilege.'"

"Sort of like I did with the girls," added Kendra, excitement for his suggestion catching hold.

"Exactly. No bus tours, like we took to Versailles, but exclusive, luxurious tours. I could even come with you sometimes."

"Limousine tours of Paris. Private railway cars

through the French alps. Weekends in some of those chateaux in the Loire Valley. Intimate barge tours through Burgundy—"

"As long as I accompany you on any tour you bill as 'intimate!'"

"Deal." Her eyes shone as the idea took form in her mind. "Do you really think I could make a go of something like that?"

"Between the girls and your stay with the Bourquels, you certainly have the inside track on what the well-heeled traveler expects on a tour. Later, depending on where my next posting is, you could expand the range of tours you offer. And maybe, if you had work you really loved, the separations wouldn't be so hard."

"Being separated from you will always be hell."

"I know." He sighed. "So we're back to me leaving the corps."

"Not necessarily. What about when you become a successful engineer chasing all over the world to build things?"

"Then my beautiful, successful wife will just have to take advantage of the travel benefits she derives from owning a travel agency and plan a little private tour." He stroked her sides, then let the back of his hand rest against her belly. "And when we have kids, we'll both cut back on the traveling for a while. At least, as a civilian, I'd have the final say about where, when and if I travel away from my family."

"Jack?"

"Yeah?"

"I think we're going to be great at the compromising part."

"I think so, too . . . *hell!* I just thought of something."

"What?"

"We'll never be able to tell our children about the way I proposed."

"Jack, if that's the biggest problem we face in our marriage, we'll be getting off scot-free."

"What kind of ring do you want?"

"See? Just more problems to work out."

He laughed and kissed her again. She felt him hardening again inside her, and she writhed, a strong wave of longing sweeping her.

"We'll take a lot longer this time," he promised.

"But what about all the rest of the stuff we have to talk about?"

"That comes later. First, we're going to exhaust ourselves celebrating our future."

Kendra inhaled deeply, pleasure spiraling through her as Jack began to touch her.

Lucky, she was so lucky. The reward would make their lives easier, but the very best, the very luckiest aspect of her windfall had been finding Jack.

DISCOVER DEANA JAMES!

CAPTIVE ANGEL (2524, $4.50/$5.50)
Abandoned, penniless, and suddenly responsible for the biggest tobacco plantation in Colleton County, distraught Caroline Gillard had no time to dissolve into tears. By day the willowy redhead labored to exhaustion beside her slaves . . . but each night left her restless with longing for her wayward husband. She'd make the sea captain regret his betrayal until he begged her to take him back!

MASQUE OF SAPPHIRE (2885, $4.50/$5.50)
Judith Talbot-Harrow left England with a heavy heart. She was going to America to join a father she despised and a sister she distrusted. She was certainly in no mood to put up with the insulting actions of the arrogant Yankee privateer who boarded her ship, ransacked her things, then "apologized" with an indecent, brazen kiss! She vowed that someday he'd pay dearly for the liberties he had taken and the desires he had awakened.

SPEAK ONLY LOVE (3439, $4.95/$5.95)
Long ago, the shock of her mother's death had robbed Vivian Marleigh of the power of speech. Now she was being forced to marry a bitter man with brandy on his breath. But she could not say what was in her heart. It was up to the viscount to spark the fires that would melt her icy reserve.

WILD TEXAS HEART (3205, $4.95/$5.95)
Fan Breckenridge was terrified when the stranger found her near-naked and shivering beneath the Texas stars. Unable to remember who she was or what had happened, all she had in the world was the deed to a patch of land that might yield oil . . . and the fierce loving of this wildcatter who called himself Irons.

Available wherever paperbacks are sold, or order direct from the Publisher. Send cover price plus 50¢ per copy for mailing and handling to Zebra Books, Dept. 3865, 475 Park Avenue South, New York, N.Y. 10016. Residents of New York and Tennessee must include sales tax. DO NOT SEND CASH. For a free Zebra/Pinnacle catalog please write to the above address.

OFFICIAL ENTRY FORM
Please enter me in the

Lucky in Love

SWEEPSTAKES

Grand Prize choice: _____

Name: _____

Address: _____

City: _____ **State** _____ **Zip** _____

Store name: _____

Address: _____

City: _____ **State** _____ **Zip** _____

MAIL TO: LUCKY IN LOVE
P.O. Box 1022C
Grand Rapids, MN 55730-1022C

Sweepstakes ends: 4/30/93

OFFICIAL RULES
"LUCKY IN LOVE" SWEEPSTAKES

1. To enter complete the official entry form. No purchase necessary. You may enter by hand printing on a 3" x 5" piece of paper, your name, address and the words "Lucky In Love." Mail to: "Lucky In Love" Sweepstakes, P.O. Box 1022C, Grand Rapids, MN 55730-1022-C.

2. Enter as often as you like, but each entry must be mailed separately. Mechanically reproduced entries not accepted. Entries must be received by April 30, 1993.

3. Winners selected in a random drawing on or about May 14, 1993 from among all eligible entries received by Marden-Kane, Inc. an independent judging organization whose decisions are final and binding. Winner may be required to sign an affidavit of eligibility and release which must be returned within 14 days or alternate winner(s) will be selected. Winners permit the use of their name/photograph for publicity/advertising purposes without further compensation. No transfer of prizes permitted. Taxes are the sole responsibility of the prize winners. Only one prize per family or household.

4. Winners agree that the sponsor, its affiliate and their agencies and employees shall not be liable for injury, loss or damage of any kind resulting from participation in this promotion or from the acceptance or use of the prizes awarded.

5. Sweepstakes open to residents of the U.S. and Canada, except employees of Zebra Books, their affiliates, advertising and promotion agencies and Marden-Kane, Inc. Void in the Province of Quebec and wherever else void, taxed, prohibited or restricted by law. All Federal, State and Local laws and regulations apply. Canadian winners will be required to answer an arithmetical skill testing question administered by mail. Odds of winning depend upon the total number of eligible entries received. All prizes will be awarded. Not responsible for lost, misdirected mail or printing errors.

6. For the name of the Grand Prize Winner, send a self-addressed stamped envelope to: "Lucky In Love" Winners, P.O. Box 706-C, Sayreville, NJ 08871.

ISN'T IT TIME YOU GOT LUCKY?
LET ZEBRA SHOW YOU HOW... WITH THE
LUCKY IN LOVE ROMANCE SERIES!

BLACK-TIE AFFAIR (3834, $3.99)
by Jane Bierce

When Jeanellen Barbour discovers that her grandmother has left her a fortune in jewels, the young beauty learns that the value of love is more precious than all the gemstones in the world.

LOVE'S OWN REWARD (3836, $3.99)
by Dana Ransom

After saving a little boy's life and receiving a half-million dollar reward, Charley Carter's life is turned into a media frenzy. When she falls for a charming journalist, she learns that while luck can turn your life around, only love can make your dreams come true!

SUMMER HEAT (3838, $3.99)
by Patricia Pellicane

Cassandra Morrison is a penniless young widow who is yearning for financial security. But when she rents out her garage apartment to a wealthy man posing as a pauper, she learns that the riches of the heart are a far greater treasure than all the riches in the world.

SHINING TIDE (3839, $3.99)
by Karen Rhodes

Alyse Marlowe, a lovely art dealer, receives a generous reward for finding a stolen Japanese treasure, and must choose between enjoying the benefits of her wealth and enjoying the love of the man who has stolen her heart.

TIES THAT BIND (3840, $3.99)
by Nancy Berland

When Claire Linwood returns to her hometown to be the top-salaried doctor and part-owner of a new two-million-dollar medical clinic, she falls in love again with the man who broke her heart.

Available wherever paperbacks are sold, or order direct from the Publisher. Send cover price plus 50¢ per copy for mailing and handling to Zebra Books, Dept. 3865, 475 Park Avenue South, New York, N.Y. 10016. Residents of New York and Tennessee must include sales tax. DO NOT SEND CASH. For a free Zebra/Pinnacle catalog please write to the above address.

"SO, KENDRA... WHAT'S YOUR PLEASURE?"

Something in his voice, some brash, confident, unabashedly masculine quality challenged her femininity on a primal level. Challenged her in a way she'd never before experienced. A rising tension throbbed between them like an unspoken dare.

"What are you offering?"

"Champagne, vintage wine... something else?"

She settled back against the limousine's upholstery, trying to contain the reckless, provocative mood he evoked in her. "Any other options?"

"Scotch, vodka, mineral water. Shall I go on?"

"There's more?"

"There's probably more than you could handle."

"You'd be surprised at how much I can handle. To prove my capacity, I'll have... champagne."

He exhaled sharply. "You like taking risks." Gripping the bottle securely between his knees, Jack peeled the dark green foil off the top and removed the wire entwined beneath. Then he met Kendra's gaze, holding her attention captive by the sheer unyielding force of his will.

"Careful," he said softly. "Popping corks can be dangerous. The trick is to exert enough... control, at just the right... juncture." As he spoke, he twisted the cork smoothly out of the bottle in one easy motion. "Of course, experience helps."

Kendra found it entirely too easy to imagine the kind of control he possessed in bed. And the kind of experience.

WITHDRAWN
from
Funderburg Library

INDEX.

Spirit not less clearly known than matter, 38.

Spontaneous generation, 348.

Strauss, view as to the supernatural, 15; statement as to the importance of Christ's resurrection, 224; on the swoon - hypothesis, 242; testimony to the character of Christ, 368.

Supernatural Religion, its testimony to Paul's unquestioned Epistles, 112; Marcion's gospel admitted to be a mutilated Luke, 150; on the chracter of Christ, 380.

'Survival of the fittest,' 310.

Swoon - hypothesis as a means of explaining Christ's resurrection, 241.

Synoptics, their representation of Christ compared with that of John, 252.

Tait, Professor, his testimony as to scientific men, 12; as to age of the earth, 351.

Tatian's Diatessaron, proved to be a harmony of the four gospels, 146; Arabic translation discovered, 147.

Taylor, Isaac, on argument from congruity, 359.

Tertullian cited as witness, 87.

Tongues, gift of, 207.

Trench, miracles to be expected of Christ, 361.

Tübingen school, its origin, 110; falling away from its original position, 133, 153; no longer existing at Tübingen, 134, note.

Tyndall, Professor, on material Atheism, 13; on scientific specialists dealing with theology, 342; on spontaneous generation, 349.

Uhlhorn on the number of the early Christians, 314.

Unbelief, causes of modern, 3.

Unity of the Church, 70.

'Unknowable' of agnosticism not really unknown, 5.

Unseen Universe, mode of divine action in a miracle, 179, 358.

Vatican manuscript, 79.

Virchow on spontaneous generation, 348; on the descent of man from the ape, 349.

Wallace on descent of man from the ape, 350.

INDEX.

Peter's testimony to Christ's resurrection, 232.
'Physicus' on sadness of Atheism, 388.
Plato's picture of the truly just man, 366.
Polycarp cited as witness, 97.
Powell, Baden, on miracles, 167; on the proper sphere of science, 343.
Pressensé, evolution not necessarily inconsistent with Theism, 346.
Probabilities, Theory of, stated and applied to 'Converging Lines,' 301; and to the testimony for Christ's resurrection, 363.
Prophecy full of Christ, 286.

QUOTATIONS from the New Testament found in the Fathers, 353.

RELIGION, state of, in England last century, 2, 341; necessary to national welfare, 323.
Religious instincts point to a revelation, 53.
Renan, his view as to the supernatural, 16; testimony to Paul's unquestioned Epistles, 111; other Pauline Epistles accepted by him, 134; conditions of a satisfactory miracle, 192; New Testament books assigned to first century, 151; on the character of Christ, 373.
Resurrection of Christ, 223; what it implies, 245; its alleged unimportance, 362; testimony for, tested by the Theory of Probabilities, 363.
Revelation an acknowledged work of John, 110, 131; its testimony to Christ and Christian doctrine, 132.
Revelation needed, 167.
Richter on the character of Christ, 382.
Roman world, moral state of, 319.
Romans an unquestioned Epistle of Paul, 110.
Rousseau on the character of Christ, 371.

SACRED books, uniqueness of our, 281.
Schaff on the number of the early Christians, 315.
Science, physical, cannot reach religious truth, 17; its special instruments and field, 17; obligations of theology to, 29.
Scientific men not generally materialists, 11.
Scrivener, on patristic quotations of the New Testament, 355.
Sects in the Church do not imply uncertainty as to Christian truth, 70.
'Signs and wonders and mighty deeds,' meaning discussed, 212.
Sinaitic manuscript, 79.
Socrates of Xenophon and Plato, 253, 366; compared with Christ, 371.
Specialists of authority only in their special field, 13, 342.
Spectral illusions as a means of explaining Christ's resurrection, 243.
Spencer, Herbert, his agnosticism, 5; 'Creeds not priestly inventions,' 53.

Luthardt on the decline of morality in Germany, 323, 386.

M'Cosh, evolution not necessarily inconsistent with Theism, 344.

Man a religious being, 52.

Manuscripts of the New Testament, 78.

Marcion cited as witness, 101; his gospel a mutilated Luke, 148.

Martyrs for a *fact*, 120.

Materialism, the common form of modern unbelief, 6.

Materialists, many real, 8.

'Mighty deeds,' meaning of expression, 209.

Mill, J. S., evolution not inconsistent with creation, 25; on miracles as a 'violation of law,' 356; on the character of Christ, 376.

Milman on the number of the early Christians, 315.

Miracles, description of, 158, 175; not a 'violation of the laws of nature,' 160, 356; fall in with the highest order, 161; essential part of Christianity, 163; proper credentials of a revelation, 169; their object, 171; neither impossible, nor incredible, 168, 172; summary of evidence for, 185; 'signs,' 196; what they imply, 197; personal testimony to, 199; testimony of Paul to, 202; mode of divine intervention in, 357; naturally to be expected of Christ, 361.

Missions, their modern compared with their ancient progress, 314.

Mohammed did not claim to work miracles, 166.

Monotheism of the Jews, 280.

Montesquieu on state of religion in England last century, 341.

Moral nature, a guide to religious truth, 337.

Muratorian Canon cited, 85.

Mystery does not imply uncertainty, 45.

NAPOLEON on character of Christ, 381.

Natural Religion quoted, 223, 362, 388.

Nature not enough to meet man's religious wants, 55.

Negative criticism, recent reverses of, 137.

New Testament, authenticity of, 73; ground on which it is generally accepted at first, 74; according to Baur about one-fourth genuine, 137; about three-fourths according to present negative criticism, 154.

PAPIAS cited as witness, 97.

Parker, Theodore, on miracles, 167; on the character of Christ, 273.

Pasteur on spontaneous generation, 348.

Paul, his unquestioned Epistles, 110; character as a witness, 114; testimony to miracles, 121, 203; and to Christ's resurrection, 234.

Persecution by so-called Christians not an argument against Christianity, 324.

Personality of Christ, unique, 248.

Peshito cited as witness, 89.

INDEX.

GALATIANS an unquestioned Epistle of Paul, 110.
Genesis, first chapter of, 20.
Germany, apparent decline of morality in, 386.
Gibbon on the number of the early Christians, 315.
Godet on connection of the miracles with the gospel history, 194.
Gospels, table of dates assigned to, 153.
Greg, W. R., on character of Christ, 378.

HASE on the Socrates of Xenophon and Plato, 366.
Healings, gifts of, 207.
Heretics, their testimony to the New Testament, 100.
Hilgenfeld, New Testament books accepted by him, 134, 151.
Hippolytus cited as witness, 86; testimony of his 'Refutation of all Heresies' to John, 141.
Hodge on inspiration, 352.
Holtzmann, New Testament books assigned to first century, 152.
Hume's argument against the credibility of miracles discussed, 180; a perfect moral character contrary to 'experience,' 383.
Huxley on spontaneous generation, 349.
Hymnals of the Church prove its real unity, 71.

INCARNATION of God needed by man, 329.
India, progress of missions in, 316.
Inspiration, a theory of, not necessary at the outset, 58; three positions in regard to, 61; danger of pressing a rigid view at first too strongly, 67; quotation from Hodge, 352; from Baxter, 353.
Irenæus cited as witness, 83.

JANET, evolution not inconsistent with Theism, 345.
Jerusalem, its destruction prophesied, 295.
Jews, their monotheism, 280; wonderful preservation, 282; expectation of a Messiah, 288.
John's testimony to Christ's resurrection, 233.
Josephus on the Jewish expectation of a Messiah, 288, note.
Justin Martyr cited as witness, 96.

KEIM on the expectation of a Messiah, 289; on the character of Christ, 369.
Keshub Chunder Sen on the character of Christ, 374.
Kingdom of God, a new idea, 265.

LANGE on the number of the early Christians, 314.
Latin version, ancient, cited as witness, 85.
Lecky, W. E. H., on the state of religion in England last century, 341; character of Christ, 379.
Lord's day, a proof of Christ's resurrection, 240.
Lord's Supper, argument from, 296.
Lotze on the mode of divine action in a miracle, 178, 357; evolution not inconsistent with Theism, 347.

CHRISTIANITY, its relation and duty towards science, 29; adjusts itself to real discoveries, 31; only great religion authenticated by miracles, 165; victorious struggle with ancient heathenism, 312; modern progress compared with ancient progress, 314; its power unspent, 317; change produced by it in the ancient world, 320; sources and causes of its power, 326. Church, continuity of, 91; Paul's teaching in regard to, 127; its planting, 291; its universal destiny, 292; its corruption prophesied, 293.

Clement of Alexandria cited as witness, 88.

Clement of Rome cited as witness, 98.

Clementine Homilies, testimony to John's Gospel, 143.

Clifford, Professor, on loneliness of Atheism, 333.

Confucius did not claim to work miracles, 165.

Congruity, argument from, 359.

Convergence of Christian evidences, 384.

Corinthians, First and Second, unquestioned Epistles of Paul, 110.

Creation, Bible account of, 20; order of, 23.

Criticism, battle of, unavoidable, 155.

DARWIN, evolution not inconsistent with Theism, 347.

Davison on independence and convergence of the Christian evidences, 384.

Development hypothesis not necessarily inconsistent with Theism, 25, 344; only a *mode* of operation, 26; not yet an ascertained fact of science, 28, 348.

Difficulties in religion, whence they arise, 37; mode of treating, 42; no system without difficulties, 47; their uses, 48.

Doctrines of Christianity, taught in Paul's unquestioned Epistles, 126; run up into Christ, 249.

Du Bois-Reymond, thought a new beginning in nature, 351.

EARTH, age of, 351.

Ephraem's Commentary on Tatian's Diatessaron discovered, 146.

Evidence must correspond to subject, 4, 76, 225; what kind to be expected for the Christian miracles, 190.

Evolution not necessarily inconsistent with Theism, 25, 344; only an hypothesis, 348.

Ewald on the character of Christ, 370.

'Experience,' Hume's argument against miracles from, 180; has nothing to say against the Christian miracles, 187.

FATHERS, their mode of quoting the New Testament, 353.

Flint, Professor, on limits of physical science, 343.

Forgery of the New Testament in the second century impossible, 104.

Fulness of the times, 290.

INDEX.

—o—

ADDISON on religion in England last century, 2, 341.
Age of the earth, 351.
Agnosticism, 5.
Alexandrian manuscript, 78.
Aristotle, fate of his later works, 95.
Atheism often springs from moral causes, 9; its loneliness, 333, 388.
Atheists, many real, 8.
Authenticity of the New Testament, 73.

BARNABAS, testimony to Matthew, 139.
Basilides cited as witness, 102.
Baxter on inspiration, 353.
Baur, his view as to the supernatural, 15; testimony to Paul's unquestioned Epistles, 110; on the resurrection of Christ, 238.
Belief founded not upon comprehension, but evidence, 36.
Bible, special object for which given, 68.
Blackstone on religion in London churches, 2.
Bolingbroke on the death of Christ, 287, note.

'Book-revelation,' not impossible, 56.
Buddha did not claim to work miracles, 165.

CAIRNS, Principal, comparison of the Christ of the Synoptics with the Christ of John, 252.
Calderwood, Professor, evolution not inconsistent with Theism, 25; the Bible not a science-revelation, 343.
Carlyle on the power of faith, 325.
Certainty, reasonable, attainable without inspiration, 63, 65.
Christ, as set forth in Paul's unquestioned Epistles, 124; only founder of a world-religion who claimed to work miracles, 165; His resurrection, 223; the fountain of modern history, 248; peculiar relation to Christianity, 249; vain attempts to explain Him away, 251; His sinlessness, 255; power of His personality, 259; His teaching, 260; His kingdom, 265; universality of His purpose, 266; conquers by love, 268; His plan complete from the first, 269; His divinity, 275; testimonies to His character, 367.

cases of Jouffroy, as given by Naville, *The Christ*, p. 17; and of Renan, *Recollections*, pp. 293 f.

How very different the spirit inspired by the religion of the Bible, as we find it expressed by the ancient saints: 'Whom have I in heaven but Thee? and there is none upon earth that I desire beside Thee! My flesh and my heart faileth; but God is the strength of my heart, and my portion for ever.' 'Death is swallowed up in victory. O death, where is thy sting? O grave, where is thy victory? Thanks be to God, which giveth us the victory through our Lord Jesus Christ!'